Robert Rush is a po
non-fiction. He lives

Also by Robert Rush

THE BIRTHDAY TREAT

Robert Rush

The Birthday Girl

Futura
Macdonald & Co
London & Sydney

A Futura Book

First published in Great Britain in 1983
by Futura Publications, a Division of
Macdonald & Co (Publishers) Ltd
London & Sydney

ISBN 0 7088 2387 4

Filmset, printed and bound in Great Britain by
Hazell Watson & Viney Ltd, Aylesbury, Bucks

Futura Publications
A Division of
Macdonald & Co (Publishers) Ltd
Maxwell House
74 Worship Street
London EC2A 2EN

Prologue

'It won't be easy, Lois,' he said after the longest silence, during which the enthusiastic crackle of her words had become limp and wintry.

'I don't see why.'

'You're planning to go back, Lois, which is always a tough thing to do. Back to the place where terrible, damaging things happened to you . . .' He paused deliberately and waited, looking at the young woman who sat opposite him. Her body had slumped in the big, comfortable chair, lost its eagerness and confidence. Her chin was sunk on her chest so that her hair fell forward thickly, hiding her face. 'Aren't you, Lois?' he prompted gently.

'No. I'm going to London. Going to London to see a doctor, to stay with my friend . . . This . . .' She threw back her head so that the hair swung back, raised her left hand to point at or touch the puckered skin. Instead, she waved her hand impatiently, as though to eradicate the intended gesture, and said: 'We lived miles from London. It's not at all the same.'

'Near enough, as I recall, for your Daddy to commute . . .'

'I wouldn't go back there,' she said, her voice taking on the truculent edge of a stubborn, distrusted child. 'Why would I ever go back to Olton?' She raised her chin again, challenging him. Hair fell in a fringe over her good eye. She flicked it back and he stared at the unhappy patchwork of her face, the bright blue eye patch which today covered the seered cavity where her right eye should have been.

'I don't know, Lois. Why go back at all?'

'I've told you. Because Cassandra's asked me. Because

she recommends a doctor . . . Anyway, why shouldn't I take a vacation?'

'No reason. But let's look at this a minute . . .'

'I have looked at it. We've looked at it. Honestly, Mr Stryker, I sometimes wonder if you listen to a word I say.'

'You know I do, Lois. Every word. Now let's . . .'

'Then why do you have to bring me down like this? When I walked in here this afternoon, I felt great, excited even and now . . .' She shrugged and slid further down in the chair, crossed her booted ankles and began to twist a decorative string of gold-coloured cloth which hung from the bodice of her dress around her finger.

'I just want to make sure that you've got everything in proportion, Lois. Enthusiasm can be misleading. Take Cassandra, for instance. You really didn't know her very long or very well before your accident . . .'

'It wasn't an accident,' she said sullenly but without force, as though years of repeating it had dulled its cutting edge.

'So it isn't strictly speaking true to say that she is your friend . . .'

'We've been writing each other for years, almost ever since I got back here to the States. Don't you think friendship can grow through letters? Besides, there was always an affinity between us . . .'

He heard the note of pride in her voice, recognized the impulse he had seen so often in her to hold on to something, keep it entirely and pristinely hers, beyond reach of interference.

'Yes, I accept that friendship can grow in the way you describe, but I don't want you to expect too much. I don't think you can handle any more disappointments, Lois, and letters can also build up expectations, false expectations . . .'

'You think I didn't tell her about . . . about the way I look, don't you? And that proves you haven't been listening to me, because if I hadn't told her, why would she be recommending a doctor to me, a plastic surgeon?'

'That isn't exactly what I meant, Lois. You think about it. But, okay, let's look at this doctor thing. There are doctors in New York, Boston . . . Plenty here in LA if you . . .'

'You know about me and doctors,' she said, raising her voice. 'You know that I have tried and you also ought to know that the British pioneered skin-grafting and that Harley Street, London, England is where you find the best doctors . . .'

'Yes, Lois, I know all that and I am not opposed to your seeking a consultation with an English doctor. In fact, I think that's a very positive thing, a breakthrough. What concerns me, again, is the possibility that you will get your hopes way up too high . . .'

'That's not it at all,' she said and suddenly stood up. The long, pleated fall of her blue dress swung about her body as she walked rapidly and aimlessly across the room. Just expending energy, he thought, walking off her frustration. 'You think,' she said, her back to him, 'that I want to see them.'

He waited a beat, watching for a sign that by naming it the tension could flow out of her. Instead, her back shook a little, her whole body seemed to clench. Softly, he said:

'Them?'

She screwed up her face, closed her eye as if in an exaggerated effort of memory. He could not see this but sensed it and heard the effort it cost her in the soft, rushing sibilance of her voice.

'Amanda and Vanessa, Andy, the twins and William.' She turned quickly towards him, her face relaxing, her body easier.

'Why don't you sit down, Lois?'

'I'm okay.' She walked past him, round behind the big

chrome and glass desk to stand at the window, looking out and down.

'And do you want to see them?'

'No. Yes. Maybe. I don't know.'

He heard the muted rattle of the Venetian blind as she laid her forehead against it.

'Sometimes you do?' he suggested, turning slowly towards her.

'Yes.' The blind rattled again as she nodded her head.

'Why?'

'I don't know.'

'How do you imagine it?'

'Sometimes . . . you know . . . I want to kill them.' She drew a deep breath, held it, straightened and let it out in a long sigh. She turned towards him then, stood behind his desk, her hands resting on the glass, her head bent, her hair shading her face.

'And at other times?'

'I don't know. That's harder to answer.'

Good, he thought. She's working now, willing to think it through.

'You can do it, though.'

'I guess, maybe, I'm curious. I've been thinking a lot about it lately.' She turned and walked around the desk, trailing her hand along its smooth, cool surface. Stryker swivelled slowly in his chair, keeping her in view. She walked past him, her hands clasped in front of her and sat down again, leaning forward now as though anxious to talk. 'I've been thinking about them,' she said. 'How they must be. I mean, what are they like now? What are they doing?'

'Go on.'

'It's difficult. I . . . I guess what I mean is . . . Look, I've had to cope with what happened, right? And it's not been easy. In fact you could say it's screwed up my entire life. So what about them? I mean, they were involved . . .

Okay, they can look in a mirror without . . . you know . . . but they can't have forgotten. There's nothing to see, nothing to remind them when they look in the mirror, but they must know. There must be something in the eyes, something . . . Or maybe they have forgotten, just blotted it out. Maybe,' she said almost wistfully, 'they're having such a good time they never have to think . . .' Her voice tailed away. He waited patiently. 'So, anyway, sometimes I wonder. I think maybe I'd like to know how they dealt with it. Sometimes.' She pushed herself back in the chair, hands folded over her stomach.

'I think that's very important, what you've just said, Lois. So you see what's happening here?'

'I don't know. I guess I feel better about it . . .'

'What's happening is that you are beginning to think about them as people. Ever since you've been coming here, you've spoken of them as an entity, a group, your enemy. Today, you're beginning to question that feeling. You are becoming curious about a group of individuals and acknowledging that they have feelings, fears, responsibilities. Do you see?'

'Uh-huh. And that's good?'

'You said yourself it feels better.'

'Right.' She smiled. Her smile never quite worked. The burned and badly-patched skin on the right side of her face seemed stiff and intractable so that the smile bloomed incomplete and took on a sort of imbecilic twist. At least until you got used to it, he thought.

'Well, I think that's enough for today,' he said, glancing at his watch. 'I want you to think some more about this and next week . . .'

'No,' she said brusquely, reaching for her big, squashy purse that lay in a collapsed heap beside the chair. 'I can't come next week. I'll see you when I get back, tell you all about it.' She stood up, swung the bag onto her shoulder.

'You mean you've already made arrangements to go?'

'I'm on my way now to pick up my ticket from PanAm.'

'In that case . . .' He stood up slowly, playing for time.

'I know. I should have told you. But you'd only have tried to talk me out of it and I've decided. I'll be good. I promise. Don't be mad at me.'

'Lois . . .' He shook his head wearily. Sometimes, still, it seemed her only recourse was to withdraw back into childhood, to assume the accents and vocabulary of a wheedling adolescent confronting a feared parent. He found that tiring and worrying. 'I'm not mad at you. You're a grown person. You can do what you like . . .'

'But?' she challenged him, planting her feet apart as though squaring up to him or the blow she thought he planned to deliver.

'Since you've sprung this on me . . .'

'I have not. I told you two weeks ago . . .'

'You're definitely intending to go . . . I have to say this, Lois. I do not approve. I think you've reached a very important stage in your analysis. I think we are poised to make a big breakthrough here, but I do not think . . .' He walked behind the desk, placed it between them and, from this position of implied authority, said: 'I do not think you are ready to contact them and I am not convinced that that will ever be advisable.'

The mutilated side of her face twitched, the signals confused by severed nerves, impaired motor reactions, so that her expression was fragmented and impossible to read. The left side of her face was that of a child, confused, resentful and very, very frightened.

'Well, you'll see,' she said. 'I'll be sure to call you just as soon as I get back.'

'I'll be glad to see you, Lois.'

She turned and marched to the door. He waited for her to hesitate, as he knew she would.

'It's not fair,' she said, head bent and turned from him. 'You're always saying I should grow up, become an adult . . . Now I feel able to do something for myself, make my own decisions you . . . you ball me out.'

'I did not ball you out, Lois.'

'Okay. You disapprove.'

'Right.'

'You don't trust me.'

'I don't believe you're ready yet to take such a big step. I want you to be able to run before you jump.'

The buzzer on his desk sounded, reminding him that time was up, that Mrs Jameson was waiting.

'You won't even wish me luck,' she whined.

'Good luck, Lois.'

She went out then, snatching the door closed behind her to register her anger and disappointment. Stryker sat down behind his desk and put his head, momentarily, in his hands.

Later, when the parade of patients finally ended and his receptionist had gone home, Stryker fixed himself a highball and took Lois Carradine's file from the cabinet. It was fat with notes, records, transcriptions of their twice-weekly meetings over a three-year period. It was all there, beginning with the move to England that she had so deeply resented and had perhaps contrived to bring to a precipitate end? In its pages he could meet again the children who, on her thirteenth birthday, had mounted a concerted attack upon her, leaving her half-dead, semi-blind and cruelly disfigured. Those children whom she wanted to face at last, about whom she had developed some human curiosity. The longed-for return to America was in there, too, spoiled now by her damaged face and psyche. The long months that totalled up into years spent in hospitals her father could not afford and where the original crime had been compounded by incompetent or careless doctors. The long and dramatically publicized lawsuit seeking compensation for the failed skin-grafts, the nerves inadvertently severed by a qualified butcher's knife. Her father's rapid descent into alcoholism and the fatal, drunken drive that had deprived her of both parents at a single stroke. It was after the accident that she had first come to him, armed now with her grandmother's money, left in trust for the benighted family of which she was the sole survivor. Money she could now administer herself, which would enable her to go to England, to go back, to go looking . . .

Stryker pushed the folder away impatiently. He did not need it to refresh his memory. It was all up there, in his head, every obscene twist and brutal turn. He finished his highball and rose to mix another. What was he afraid of? That in England she would meet another rejection, more pain no one could expect her to handle? Yes, but . . . That of course, but . . . There was something unresolved in her, something that they had not really begun to explore. Something Lois dismissed as childish and of no account but of which he was afraid. The attack on her had not come out of the blue, as Lois liked to present it, but had been the last – thank God, he thought – in an escalating series of 'games', acts of torture, mental and physical, which Lois had perpetrated on them, individually. Stryker had long entertained the idea that the attack on Lois had been a collective act of revenge. After all, they were only kids . . . For all his knowledge of the darkness of the human psyche, he could not accept that she had fallen among monsters, unmotivatedly cruel. Something had driven them to that final act of cruelty and horror, something intolerable which had made them desperate and bestial. That something was Lois herself, or a part of her, something she still carried with her, unresolved and, perhaps, because of that, stronger now than it had ever been.

It was a mutual danger, he thought. Like Lois, he had often been curious about them, had wondered how they had coped with the knowledge that they had disfigured, blinded and almost killed her. Lois was right: their scars must be as deep if less visible than hers. Their guilt might be as intolerable as her burden. What then if they met, face to damaged face? One of the ways people dealt with guilt they could not resolve was by destroying its cause. After all, they had been violent before. And Lois had made no secret of her longing for revenge. It had been one of his major objectives to make her think and talk her way through that. Revenge was a terrible, self-perpetuating chain in which the next wrong always promised to make everything right. And people, he knew from long experience, could get locked into suffering, begin to enjoy it, other people's as well as their own.

Sweating a little, Stryker pulled the telephone towards him and rapidly punched out Lois's number. He tried to think what he would say to her. There had to be the right formula, an opening . . . He listened to the tone, ringing, ringing and somehow knew that she was not there, or if there, was not going to answer . . .

'You're sure you won't change your mind?' Julian stood in the doorway, knotting a bright yellow tie over a dark shirt, looking at his brother who was bent over a disembowelled amplifier, screwdriver in hand.

They were no longer identical. In the years of their growing from boys to young men it seemed that they had grown apart in many respects. Their fair hair darkened while their eyes remained a clear blue, but those had become similarities, not traits which led people to mistake them one for another. Julian actually looked older than his twin, carried more flesh on his athletic frame. Jason, though just as tall, had a gangly, unformed look, as though he was still growing. His face was all bones and hollows and his habitual expression was that of a troubled adolescent: contemplative and withdrawn. But their differences went beyond the physical. They seldom experienced now that special closeness, that almost telepathic communication, that had marked their childhood and made them a self-contained, separate unit. Julian no longer thought of Jason as his twin but simply as his brother. And like many brothers before him, he was becoming increasingly irritated by Jason's manner and attitudes.

'No thanks,' Jason said, without looking up.

'You'll be very welcome, you know. And Marcie'd like it.' He tucked his shirt more securely into his freshly laundered jeans, pulled his tie flat against his chest.

'I don't understand how you can,' Jason burst out, flinging the screwdriver onto his bed and turning impatiently to a rectangle of newspaper on which the guts of the machine were spread. His hands trembled as he sorted among the bits, his mind not on his work. A dark blush of anger or frustration mounted to his cheeks. 'We've never . . .'

'Marcie's having a party, right? I like Marcie. I go out with Marcie. I may even marry Marcie, so . . .'

Jason swung round, straightened up, his fists clenched at his sides.

'A Hallowe'en party,' he said. 'How can you go to a Hallowe'en party?'

Julian took a breath to steady himself. He had known it would come to this. In a sense, he had provoked it, just to have it out in the open, out of the way. As reasonably as he could manage, he said:

'That was years ago . . .'

'Ten. Exactly.'

'All right. I haven't been counting . . .'

'And we have never gone to a Hallowe'en party.'

'Then it's time we did. Time *you* did.'

Something flickered over Jason's face, softening his set,

angry features. He turned away, went back to fiddling with the bits and pieces of the amplifier.

'I can't,' he said. 'And I don't think you should.'

'Why not?'

'Because it looks as though . . . as though you don't remember anything . . . don't care.'

'I remember all right. You've never let me forget. But no, I don't think I do care very much. Why should I?' Julian was shouting suddenly. He took a step towards his brother.

'We nearly killed her,' Jason said in a shocked whisper, as though he had only just realized it.

'Nonsense. Anyway, William did it. You don't know any more than I do about what William did after he sent us out of the room.'

'We were there. We took part. We allowed . . .' Jason rocked himself to the rhythm of his words.

'I don't want to talk about it,' Julian said. 'I don't even want to think about it. And if you'd got any sense . . .'

'Because you think it will go away. You think if you pretend . . . Well, it won't. And by going to this party tonight, you're tempting fate.'

'Oh for God's sake . . .' Julian stalked out of the room, slamming the door behind him.

Jason remained crouched on the floor, his arms folded around his thin torso. It was not true that he refused to let the past go. He knew that was what Julian believed. There were whole stretches of time when he never thought about it, when even the nightmares ceased or, at least, became buried so that he woke without memory of them. The endless variations on the theme of chains and falling, of swinging with a crippling pain in his legs, in darkness. The terrifying swoop into unfathomable blackness from which her imagined face, burnt and bloody, lopsided, rose to claim him . . .

He shook his head to clear it and stood up. He had lost

all will to work, sat instead on the edge of his bed, his hands pressed together between his knees. He heard the front door slam, Julian's footsteps fast and heavy on the uncarpeted stairs. He turned his head sharply, his mouth shaping his brother's name which he never spoke. He did not want to be alone. Nowadays, he was always alone. He could no longer reach Julian. They had become strangers and he found that harder to bear than anything. It was unnatural. Throughout that terrible year, the year they had known and grown to be so afraid of Lois Carradine, the fact that they were twins, were together, never alone, had enabled them to survive. He got up and began to pace the rather chilly room, his feet sounding hollow on the boards beneath the thin carpet. Perhaps their mother was right. Last time he had gone home – alone because Julian had a date with Marcie – she had suggested that perhaps it was time for them to live apart. They had become so different. They were growing up, needed lives of their own, separate . . . But he did not want to be separate. Without Julian, he was afraid. He blamed Marcie, hated her for forcing her way between them. This party was only the latest instance . . .

But he knew it wasn't Marcie. He could not sustain his anger against her for long. It was Lois who had driven them apart. She had hated their special closeness, had known that the only way to hurt them was to separate them. That was why they had been blindfolded and led apart. Why he had had to climb the ladder to the barn loft alone, while Julian was strapped into that horribly real-looking electric chair . . . Why he had fallen into darkness, screaming, to dangle alone, bereft, lost . . .

He wished now they had killed her. Then they would have been punished, badly punished and that would have brought them closer together, identical, inseparable . . .

Now, when he looked into the mirror he did not see

Julian's face, but his own, alien, haunted by loneliness and fear.

The doorbell shrilled, startling him. He thought at once, felt certain, that it was Julian. Julian had forgotten his keys or wanted to say he was sorry or . . . By the time he reached the stairs, running down them towards the front door, he knew that Julian had changed his mind, had returned to spend the evening with him, was ready to admit that they could not, ever, either of them, go to a Hallowe'en party.

He wrenched open the door, his eyes fixed at the expected level of Julian's eyes. And saw nothing. Saw a sudden whirling of dark shapes, flapping like cold, expiring birds, and heard the awful jingle of their voices.

'Trick or treat. Trick or treat. It's Hallowe'en. Trick or . . .'

'No,' he shouted and slammed the door against them.

The sudden, brief silence was filled with his own breathing, laboured, slipping close to sobs. Then the angry, disappointed children struck at the door, calling obscenities, ringing the bell. Jason turned and fled back up the stairs, closing the flat door behind him. On into his bedroom, closing and locking that door too. He groped his way to the bed and fell face downward on it. Outside, he heard their piping voices, chanting, mercifully fading. Laughter on the still October air. A hint of mist that night. And on the screen of his imagination he saw Andy, his limbs angular and jerky as he danced that night in the Carradine's garden, while she lay within, burning, to the sound of their muffled laughter.

Amanda had not wanted to go to the party at all, but Tracey had insisted. Tracey was the most dominant girl in their set, confident and outgoing. She had the room across the landing from Amanda's in the Nurses' Home and so they were rather thrown together. Privately, Amanda thought that she would make a better nurse than Tracey, but she had to admit that the other girl had a much better social manner. Because of this she tended to fall in with Tracey's schemes or, as on this occasion, allowed herself to be bullied into activities Tracey thought would be good for her.

She wanted to be more confident with strangers, less timid generally, but parties always seemed to accentuate her gaucheness. They overwhelmed her and she always ended up as now, sitting alone, nursing a glass of unwanted and unpalatable white wine. Only this one was worse than ever because being confronted by the sight of Julian Shillingworth had sapped even her will to try.

Everyone else seemed to be standing. They thronged around her, talking in loud voices, laughing a lot. Someone's carelessly flicked cigarette ash dusted her skirt. The heat from the many candles, grouped and spotted around the room, was unpleasantly dry and their smell . . . Seeing Julian made it impossible not to think about it. Until then she had managed to keep her mind occupied, off the special, sinister significance of that day. She had completely forgotten that Tracey's cousin was at college with Julian, although they had discovered this tenuous connection when, in her early days at the hospital, Amanda had occasionally seen the twins. And then Tracey had so many cousins that there was no reason for her to think of Marcie when the party was mentioned . . .

But it was wrong of her to blame Julian, she thought, feeling hemmed in by the legs that crowded against the settee on which she sat, hunched and trying to make herself invisible. He had been as startled as she. It had been horrible. That long – to Amanda it seemed endless – moment when they had stared at each other, knowing exactly what the other must be thinking. As though there was some shameful complicity between them, something intimate and shared. Marcie had seen it, and Tracey. Marcie had been cold and formal, unwelcoming, while Tracey had squeezed her arm and whispered something about being 'a dark horse'. And she could never tell her, never tell anyone, what she and Julian shared and why it had made them both tongue-tied and guilty, almost afraid of each other.

She had often imagined it. Going into a room or even some public place and seeing one of them. That's why, for a while, she had tried to keep up with the twins and Vanessa, only it had been too painful, too awkward. Eye contact between them was dangerous and lack of it inhibited the conversation. By some mutual, unspoken agreement, they never referred to *it*. That meant there was only the catching up to do, the exchange of news of what they had been doing since they had all left the Crescent. It was impossible even to reminisce about the times before . . . before Lois.

Just facing the name in her head made her feel shaky and she sipped the sour wine, partly to cover her own panic, partly in the hope of steadying her nerves.

Mostly, of course, she had been terrified of walking into a room and confronting Lois. Or a hand falling on her shoulder in a cinema queue or in a crowded pub, turning her eyes to the mocking face. American accents, heard on the top of London buses or in summer-crowded shops made her feel uncomfortable, as though they must know, were watching out for her . . .

'Hey, come on.'

Hands were reaching for her, taking her glass away, trying to pull her up. She shrank away, back into the cushions. A space had formed in the centre of the room. People made a circle around it, around a table with a bowl on it. It was like a scene from some scary film: a ritual for witches and devils.

'Come on. Apple-bobbing.'

A face obscured the bowl, the space now. A nice face. One she dimly remembered. Some boy Tracey had introduced her to earlier. She could not, for the life of her, remember his name. And as she recalled this much she knew that Tracey had sent him to find her, had perhaps bribed him with a promise of a date, to make her join in, partner her.

'No . . . really . . . I . . .'

He pulled her to her feet, smiling, and she staggered a little. He put his arm around her and led her forward into the light.

'Here,' Tracey said, bounding forward. 'Let me fix your hair back.'

'No . . . Honestly, I don't . . .'

The boy held her arms, laughing into her face, and Tracey clipped her long hair back, fastened it at the nape of her neck so that it could not fall into the water. People crowded forward, crowded around her.

'Hands behind your back. No cheating,' Tracey said, pulling her wrists together behind her and pushing her towards the bowl. The boy stood on the other side of it and bent his face towards the still water where candleflame was reflected, dazzling.

'No, please . . . I don't want to . . .'

The bowl was circular, pumpkin yellow.

'Oh shut up and enjoy yourself,' Tracey said and bore down on her shoulders so that she was forced to bend and saw the pallid, imperfect image of her own face floating amid the candlelight. Somebody dropped an apple into the bowl to shouts and cries from those who pressed forward to get a better view. Water splashed onto her face as candlegrease had splashed onto Lois's. She recoiled and cried out. The boy's mouth pursued the apple. Someone – Tracey? – pushed her forward again as they had pushed Lois, pushed her face into the blazing birthday cake, pushed her across the room to the great pumpkin lantern that blazed and hissed with a hundred candles, rising to meet her face, her flesh, to burn her . . .

'No . . . !'

She lashed out with her hands, hitting the bowl. It rose up, water splashing onto the party clothes of those who had crowded close to watch. Some screamed. Others cursed. She saw them fall back, saw the apple roll away on the wet floor. Saw the boy's startled face, staring at her, mouth open.

'No. I can't, I can't, I'm sorry, I . . .'

She could not speak as sobs constricted her throat. She covered her face with her hands, tears welling, feeling ashamed as Julian forced his way through the crowd.

'What's the matter with her?'

'She's bloody mad.'

'Is she on something?'

'It's all right.' Julian's hands pulled her against his chest. 'I understand. I'll see to her.'

She heard other voices, Marcie's, Tracey's, as he led her through the crowd.

'Take me home. Please, Julian, take me home.'

'Yes. All right. Hang on. Did you have a coat?'

She was alone but for whispering voices. Julian's and Marcie's. Almost silent with pent-up anger. Then he was back with her, putting her heavy cape around her shoulders and leading her out. She felt cold air on her hands which still covered her face. A door slammed behind them.

'I had to park up the road a bit. Come on.'

She kept her hands clamped over her steaming face, trusting Julian to lead her. She heard the clink of keys, the creak of a door opening.

'Come on, get in,' he said.

She took her hands away from her face and felt her way into the old car. Peering through the dirty windscreen she saw streetlights like lanterns, other parked cars, all dancing with her tears. The door slammed behind her. Julian's shadow flitted over the windscreen. He opened the door on her right, got in.

'All right?'

'Yes. I . . .' She began to search for a handkerchief.

'Here . . .' He reached unceremoniously across her, pulled a battered box of tissues from the shelf beneath the dashboard. 'Use these.'

'Thanks.'

He waited. It was cold in the car.

'Please,' she said. 'Let's go.'

'Fasten your seatbelt first.'

'Oh, yes. I . . .' She felt foolish, became aware of the blood burning in her cheeks. She was clumsy and he, catching his breath impatiently, had to fasten the catch for her. She sat still, sniffing, dabbing at her tears. When they stopped for a red light, she glanced at him.

'I'm sorry. I couldn't help it. It was partly seeing you there, I think.'

'It wasn't any fun for me, either,' he said angrily, and ground the gears as the light changed. Then he felt bad about taking it out on her and said: 'Sorry. I didn't mean . . .'

'I know. It was just that suddenly . . . I couldn't help remembering . . . And when they tried to force my head down into that bowl I . . .'

'All right,' he said. 'I know. I've had Jason reminding me all week.'

'Jason?'

'Like you he won't let it go, won't let himself forget about it.'

'It won't let me forget,' she said miserably.

She felt him relax a little in the seat beside her and ease back on the accelerator.

'I know,' he said and sounded like a man who had given up, given in. 'She always did spoil everything, didn't she? But we mustn't give in. We've got to stop it. All of us.' He sounded angry again, as though he spoke through gritted teeth.

'How?' she asked and turned towards him.

He shook his head. He didn't know.

Andy took refuge in a pub. It was a cold night with frost already dusting the pavements with glitter when he left the cheap cafe where he had taken his evening meal. Shoulders a little hunched against the cold, hands dug into pockets, he walked. He no longer noticed his loneliness. The alternatives open to him were three: his dreary room with the hissing gas fire and the weight of his own numbed thoughts; the movies, which would at least be warm; the pub, where warmth could be stoked with alcohol, but which he could barely afford. On a warmer night he would have been content to walk for two or maybe three hours, scarcely glancing up from the pavement. But the cold soon ate through his thin clothing, prompting him to get under cover, into the warm. The cinema he came upon, in common with most others in South London that night, was showing John Carpenter's *Hallowe'en*. He sheered away from the dazzling façade as soon as he read the title of the film. Down a side street where television sets droned from closed houses, into a main street where a pub beckoned.

It was warm inside and quiet for a pub. A single long bar, backed by Victorian mirrors, stretched the length of a barn-like room. Andy was not known there. He could not remember having been there before. He studiously avoided finding a 'local', a regular pub where, in a short space of time, he would be recognized, get on Christian name terms with the barman. He preferred the anonymity of being a stranger in a strange pub. Andy eked out his pints of lager, watching. A group of boys crowded around the Space Invaders machine, playing endless games until their money ran out. A group came in, bought one noisy round of drinks and then left for a party, clutching bottles of wine, cans of beer. It was then, after their loud exit, that Andy became aware of the man watching him. He stood at the far end of the bar, spoke occasionally with two others, perched on stools. He had a slow, calculated smile which he used sparingly. An expensive camel-coloured overcoat hung like a cape from his shoulders. A heavy gold bracelet decorated his right wrist. Several times his eyes met Andy's. Andy looked away. Once, the man seemed to be toasting him as he drank from his pint glass, his eyes knowing and blue over the rim. Andy stared fixedly at the door. After a while, the two men slid from their stools and left, calling 'goodnight' to the man who sauntered slowly down the length of the bar. Andy drained his glass, looking at the man's profile in the mirror.

'Have one with me, squire,' he said. 'Dead in here tonight, isn't it, Jim?'

The barman came with a brimming glass for the man, took Andy's wordlessly and filled it.

'But then you wouldn't know, would you? Haven't seen you in here before, have I?'

'No,' Andy said.

The man's voice was low and soft. He spoke with care, as though language held dangers for him.

'Be seeing you again, though, shall we? This isn't a bad boozer.'

Andy shrugged.

'Thanks,' he said, taking the top off his pint.

'Cheers.' The man edged closer. 'At a loose end, are you? New around here?'

'Just having a drink.'

Andy remained drinking with the man, answering his questions with monosyllables or not at all. The man did not seem to mind. When Andy offered to buy him a drink, he waved him aside, insisted on paying, urged him to have something stronger, a short. Suspicion hardened into certainty about the man's intentions, interests. He dropped enough hints, cautious and unexceptional, while his eyes became bolder. They met Andy's with a cold hunger, moved more and more frequently over his body.

'I wonder you're not off to some party,' he said. 'Or perhaps you are, later.'

'No.'

'Girlfriend give you the elbow, did she?'

'No.'

'You're better off without 'em, son. But then I reckon you know that, don't you? Drink up. Have another.'

Andy stayed, accepted drinks from the man, feeling ashamed and excited. He was frozen, incapable of decision. He did not know how to leave or what he would do if the man made some overt, concrete proposal. He wanted to melt away, become invisible, and yet he also wanted the man to make decisions for him.

'I don't know about you, but this place is getting me down. Present company excepted, of course. Drink up and let's go to my place for a nightcap.'

Andy drained his glass, zipped his jacket. The man looked pleased and called goodnight to the barman.

'It's not far,' he said as the cold night air bit. 'My old jalopy's just around the corner. You'll be glad of it, I should think. Not dressed for this weather, are you?'

The car was large and expensive, gleaming silver in the lamplight. The man paused, searching for his keys. Andy stood watching him, shivering a little with the cold.

'Just one thing, sunshine . . .' the man said, holding the keys loosely, turning to face Andy. 'You are going to come through, aren't you?' Andy stared at him, blank. The man moved closer, intimately so. 'I mean, what's it going to be?' The man's hand, discreetly hidden by his body, the car, brushed against Andy. 'What's it going to be, eh? Trick or treat?'

The words, accompanied by soft, nervous laughter, exploded in Andy's head. His skull felt very large and empty, the words bouncing around inside, amplified and echoing. He saw the man's face change. Saw the look of shock and pain wrench his features into ugliness. The man doubled over, clutching himself. The car keys fell tinkling onto the pavement. The man's eyes rolled up towards him. He had seen that look before. It was as though the man had borrowed her expression and pinned it on. Frightened, Andy backed away. The man, still clutching himself, groped with one hand towards the fallen keys. Before his fingers touched them, Andy began to run. He ran up the street, into darkness, away from the look on the man's face, the words singing over and over in his head.

Eveything about him felt small and cold and shrivelled, useless.

'God!' Adrian exploded as soon as they were in the car.

'Ghastly,' Cassandra agreed.

They looked at each other. Cassandra hoped that her husband would laugh and so banish the tension, but he did not.

'Shall I drive?' she offered.

'No thanks. I'm not *even* smashed.'

'I know. They were a bit parsimonious with the dreaded mulled plonk.'

'That I don't hold against them,' he said, starting the car. 'It was completely undrinkable.'

'I am sorry, Ade.'

'All I can say is, if that's a representative example of your old school chums . . .'

'I promise you she was quite palatable at school. It must be that ghastly wet she's got in tow.'

'I just hope this American one is going to be an improvement,' he said crossly.

'Oh she's not really a schoolchum. I only knew her for a few weeks. Funny, gauche little thing. I rather enjoyed impressing her.'

'And how is she going to impress me?'

'Favourably, of course, darling. And do try to think of her as a pen friend . . .'

'How did you come to start writing to her, anyway?' he asked, changing lanes dangerously.

'It was Mummy's idea, actually. Just a sort of courtesy note when we heard about the ghastly thing that happened to her. You know – "Awfully sorry and get well soon" sort of thing. Apparently it meant a great deal to her and we just sort of kept on writing. Anyway, I promise you she's not a bit like Stella . . .'

'I bloody hope not.'

Cassandra tensed a little. He probably wasn't in the right mood but she felt she really ought to remind him again. He could be such a dunderhead when he liked.

'You will remember, darling Ade, won't you, that she is horrendously disfigured?'

'Well, I suppose she can't help that,' he said, softening.

'Most certainly not. It's a tragedy. But she's bound to feel awkward about it and we must all try not to notice.'

'I hope to God she won't frighten the infant, that's all.'

'Ade!'

'Well, ugly people are so unrelaxing. They make me edgy.'

'Is that why you fell for me?'

'Definitely. Mind you, you're unrelaxing in quite a different way.'

'Promises, promises,' she teased.

'You wait and see.'

'Let's just get home and have a decent drink.'

'I'm doing my best. Bloody traffic.'

'Actually, I think you're going to like Lois. It'll be such fun showing her round and everything.'

'You're too soft,' he said, squeezing her hand. 'You and your lame ducks.'

'Hark who's talking! Look what we shell out each month to keep your Nanny in a style to which she should never have been allowed to become accustomed!'

'I love Nanny.'

'I hated mine. All of them. I know, let's make a pact. You be super to Lois and I'll buy something absolutely scrumptious for Nanny's Christmas box.'

'Present,' he corrected. 'Okay. Done.'

'I do love you, dearest Ade.'

'Me, too. Darling Cass.'

That was all right then, she thought. Anyway, she planned to keep Lois well out of his hair. She was pretty certain he'd be furious if he knew the half of it. But it had been such fun, planning this visit and snooping and everything. It had quite bucked her up. And though he didn't realize it, that was good for the Marital Ade, too. She hugged his arm and laid her scented cheek against his shoulder.

'Nearly home,' he said.

'Mm. Bliss. Ghastly party.'

'Ghastly,' he agreed.

It was almost eerily quiet backstage. For the umpteenth time Vanessa looked at her watch, then at her carefully made-up face in the harshly lit mirror. Her eyes were too small and, in that light, the art of her make-up was exposed as mere technical compensation. She got up and switched off the battery of naked bulbs that surrounded the long mirror. He wouldn't come now, she thought, and if she waited much longer she'd run the risk of being locked in. The thought made her shudder. She loved the theatre, its smell and noise and bustle, but with the curtain down and the cast gone it was an unsettling place: a place denied its proper function. Damn it! She could have gone to the party after all. She picked up her fun-fur jacket and shrugged it on, looked around one last time to check that she had got everything and then let herself out into the long, dustily-lit corridor.

Vanessa knew that she was lucky to be in the chorus, to be in one of the few hit shows of the season. Bookings were solid through Christmas and tickets were on sale right up to Easter. And in a chorus of only ten – six girls and four boys – she had a chance to shine, to be noticed. He'd noticed her, Max Krieger, the star who had travelled with the show after two years on Broadway, where it was still running with a new male lead. Of course, the company disapproved, thought she was being taken for a ride, suspected she was on the make. But she consoled herself with the thought that any one of them would have done the same if Max had crooked his finger at them. They were jealous that she was getting on, being so young and new to the business. But she was good. Besides, she and Max clicked. She liked him. She was very fond of him. Too fond, perhaps. Suzie, her flatmate, would say that she was crazy to hang around on the chance that he could get away, slip back and collect her. Mad to give up the chance of a party . . .

She felt her way gingerly down the first flight of stairs. The bulb had gone. She made a mental note to tell Bert, the stage doorkeeper. The stairs were precipitous, worn and scooped by the tramp of many gypsy feet over the years. She heaved a sigh of relief when she reached the landing and started down the second flight, properly lit.

Max was having dinner with the producers and someone from Twentieth Century Fox who had acquired the film rights. Vanessa badly wanted to be in the film, preferably in Sally Grant's cameo role. She was already understudying it and she took singing lessons twice a week. She believed that she was already better than Sally in the big show-stopping number that made the part so desirable. And he'd said:

'Don't go to the party. Wait for me. I'll slip away and come fetch you. We'll have dinner . . .'

Lately, Max had insisted that they play their relationship down in public. It was unsettling for company morale. He didn't want to be carpeted by the producers with the film coming up. There'd been talk of Al Pacino for the lead and then his New York replacement had pulled a crop of good notices. It was in both their interests to play it cool. Max had indicated that he did not see why she shouldn't be in the film, either. But first he had to secure his own part. She understood and didn't believe that he had stood her up, but even so . . .

She reached the third flight, her heels tapping on the worn stone. Only one more to go, thank God. And at the bottom of the third flight somebody rushed out at her. Somebody jumped out of the shadows and flung something at her. It all happened so quickly that she did not even start screaming until the intruder's footsteps were fading away, echoing in the empty theatre. Her screams cut through that silence and rose in volume and terror as she pulled her hand away from her face and saw the blood, red and sticky on her fingers.

It made her gag. It made her stomach churn and rise up into her throat, heaving. She remembered the taste of it, that potion of loyalty they had forced her to drink. She saw droplets of blood, squeezed from their thumbs into the fake chalice. She remembered, with loathing, William holding her, forcing her mouth open and Lois, her face half-covered by a ghostly green mask, tipping the blood into her mouth. It *was* blood. She had always known that, no matter how much they lied, and here it was again, all over her. Her blood?

She collapsed against the metal rails that bounded the

stairs, her screams stifled now by the violent reaction of her stomach.

'You all right, miss? Here, hang on . . . Good God what a bloody mess . . . Here . . .'

The stage doorkeeper, Bert, panting, pulled her to her feet, held her at arm's length. Red stained one side of her face, clung to the shaggy pile of her jacket. For a moment he thought she was cut, wounded, but the smell and coolness of the red liquid quickly reassured him.

'It's only prop blood, love. Come on. Come down to my box and we'll soon sort you out.'

She was weeping now and making sick choking sounds. She leaned heavily on him, let herself be led, trembling, to his warm and safe little box which smelled of pipe smoke and dust. She struggled out of the jacket and thrust it away from her in disgust. Weeping, she cleaned her face with tissues, scrubbed it until the skin felt raw. Bert made her a cup of tea.

'Now, then, what happened, love?'

'I don't know. Thanks, Bert. I was just coming down the stairs and . . . somebody jumped out at me. I didn't see anything except a shape, a figure . . . He . . . he . . . threw something at me . . . blood . . .'

'There, there.' He patted her shoulder. Poor kid. He felt sorry for her but she had no business to be hanging around at that time of night. Besides, he had a pretty good idea what all this was about.

'Didn't you see anyone? He ran down the stairs.'

'Somebody streaked past the window there just as you started screaming. Like you said, it was so quick . . .'

'He was wearing a mask,' she said. 'I remember now. A Hallowe'en mask.'

'Ah well, that explains it, dear, doesn't it?'

'How do you mean?'

'Well, you're not at the party, are you? And you should

be, by rights. It was one of them, one of the boys no doubt, playing a trick on you.'

'Some trick . . .'

'Yes, well . . . Things get a bit out of hand sometimes.'

'I don't know.' She shook her head. 'I could have fallen, hurt myself.' Instinctively she reached down to rub her ankle.

'Still, no harm done.'

'No harm . . .? Look, hadn't you better call the police?'

'What for, love? What would I say?'

'If somebody got in here . . .'

'Nobody got in here as shouldn't be here,' Bert said firmly, on his dignity. 'It was one of the boys, playing a joke. Besides,' he went on, fixing her with an eye that said that nothing to do with the affairs of the company escaped him, 'if I called the boys in blue out, I'd have to report it to management and they'd want to know what you were doing here at this time of night.'

'I had a headache,' she said quickly.

'Well, this little upset won't have helped. I'd best call you a cab, don't you think?'

Vanessa looked at him and saw that it was futile to argue.

'Yes. Thanks.'

'That's right.'

But who . . . why should anyone hate her so much that they would plan and perpetrate such a vile trick? Surely professional jealousy could not go so far?

'Taxi'll be right along. Here . . .' He held out her stained coat.

'No.' She shook her head. 'I don't want it. Throw it away.'

'As you please, miss,' he said, stiffly professional again. Cleaned up, it would do very nicely for his grand-daughter.

Bert escorted her to the stage door. She still felt sick and wobbly at the knees.

'If I was you, miss, I wouldn't make too much of this.

Whoever it was'll soon realize it wasn't funny. You won't have any more trouble. An anonymous bunch of flowers more like, by way of apology.'

She wanted to say, 'How do you know?' but she nodded as though agreeing with him. Perhaps he was in on it. Perhaps the whole chorus had planned . . . But how could they know how she reacted to blood? No, she thought, feeling dizzy as Bert bundled her into the ticking cab, there was only one person who hated her that much, had that knowledge and that terrible, evil ingenuity. That infallible sense of timing, too. Hallowe'en. Lois Carradine's birthday. The start of it all, the nightmare she thought she had escaped. But Lois was thousands of miles away, as good as dead as far as she was concerned. The question formed and froze in her mind: Wasn't she?

One

Early November was unseasonably mild that year and Lois, whose childhood memories represented London as a grey and lowering place, found her perceptions of the city transformed. In the clear, mature sunlight, against startlingly blue skies, the capital took on a lightness and sparkle that delighted her. The weather entirely suited Cassandra's bubbling mood and after five days in her scarcely interrupted company, Lois felt that her trip was even more successful than she had dreamed possible. When she returned she would make Stryker eat his words.

Cassandra was at the root of all her moods. She loved everything about her; the house in an elegant terrace off Sloane Street; the costly, solid and tasteful furniture; the discreetly stiff Nanny and the melancholy-looking Spanish couple who cooked and chauffered and waited at table. She even loved the baby, Sasha, whom Cassandra allowed her to hold occasionally, when Nanny wasn't looking. She even thought she could love Adrian because he so clearly doted on Cassie. But especially and above all she loved Cassandra who had taught her to apply make-up more skilfully and more thickly than she would ever have dared so that, in repose at least, her face did not make Adrian wince any more. She was so grateful she could have yelled or cried out loud. Stryker had often said that she needed friends, should try harder to cultivate people . . . Now she knew the real truth of his words. How badly she had needed a girlfriend, someone close in whom she could confide, with whom she could discuss make-up and clothes, men and babies, without feeling disqualified by her ugliness. She felt, for the first time since she had been a little girl, that she belonged, was loved and wanted.

Spontaneously, wrapped oblivious in the warmth of her own thoughts, Lois turned a skipping pirouette beneath the amber-leafed trees of Green Park. To passers-by, a few lounging onlookers, she seemed a child, a latter-day Alice grown too large, expressing her naive delight in the world, this Indian summer. Secure beneath the mask of her new make-up, Lois caught the eye of a young man who grinned at her, and grinned back.

Yet for all her pleasure in Cassandra's company, she had seized upon this, her first chance to be alone. She needed to think, to get her head straight about certain things. For beneath the steady pulse of happiness there was a discordant, troubling beat.

On her first full day in London, when they were safely alone, Cassandra had presented her with a slim, new manilla folder. Inside, on carefully typed and photocopied sheets, were the names and present addresses of her enemies, together with a few sketchy notes about them. Cassandra had been thrilled with the results of her 'little research project', hungry for Lois's gratitude and pleasure. Lois had done her best to gratify her. Alone in her room at the top of Cassandra's house, she had studied the pages and wondered at herself that she felt only numb and slightly bored. She had, after all, begged Cassandra to track them down. She could not do it. She had known that. Even if she struck lucky, they would never answer, would be afraid to answer. Besides, then, she had wanted to have the advantage of surprise on her side. Now . . . Cassandra, with the aid of 'a darling little man, frightfully discreet and not in the least bit seedy' had traced the Shillingworths and the Hunters, the divorced Beattys and the remote Mercers. They had even tracked the Youngs to their hiding place but they – bewilderingly to Lois – claimed to have no knowledge of their son's present whereabouts. How they had fled the Crescent, Olton, each other! The parents, Lois guessed, because they were afraid of what their children had done, might do again if left in each other's company. And the children, she thought, with something like sadness, because they could not look at each other without guilt or fear.

It had been relatively easy, after that first day, to push the question of the folder and its strangely lifeless contents into the background, the shadows. Cassandra had arranged so many treats, cramming each moment with chatter and expeditions but, without her having said anything specific, Lois knew that the honeymoon was, if not over, drawing to a close. That very morning Cassandra had made an appointment for her with Mr Valentine, the Harley Street specialist, and then had hinted, with a surreptitious wink, that Lois had other, equally important business of her own to pursue.

She was afraid, she realized as she turned back towards the Piccadilly gates of the park, of disappointing Cassandra, who had gone to so much trouble, who had 'felt it wise to keep the whole thing hush-hush from darling Ade, who could be the teensiest bit stuffy on occasions'. But she was even more afraid to break the spell of these magic days. She felt protected from the world, consoled, lapped, cosseted. She thought that Stryker would want her to stay that way awhile, bask a little. Besides, she was no longer sure that she wanted to pursue that part of her plan. Something told her that her present happiness could not last, but she did not want to be the one to shatter the bubble, let ugliness and pain in.

Was that so wrong? she asked herself as she walked from shade to sunlight to shade again and heard the roar of traffic become intrusive, urgent as she came in sight of Piccadilly. She couldn't stall any longer, that was for sure, but then, for reasons she did not want to examine, she was scared to tell Cassandra the truth, to confide her indecision, her new reluctance to pursue and confront them. But surely, when she had not yet explored London or gone shopping for the clothes Cassandra insisted she must have, it would be understandable that she should leave it awhile. She need only say . . . that she wasn't ready yet. Cassandra would want her to be at her best, her most poised and confident.

She hesitated a moment at the park gate, orientating herself. Fortnum and Mason's was that way, to her right. She was due to meet Cassandra there at four, for tea. And as she walked she thought that maybe Cassandra would not bring it up again. But in case she did, she made herself rehearse her excuses, knowing them to be lame, fearing that her sharp-eyed friend would see through them. If all else failed she would plead the need to think first. Then she realized that she had wasted the whole afternoon, her thinking-time, and had got nowhere.

Disappointment with her own indecision showed on her face as she walked into the store and made her way to the restaurant, but she brightened up the moment she saw Cassandra waving at her from a table bang in the middle of the room. She waved back and made herself walk steadily, upright and cool, like Cassandra, through the crowded room, aware of the appraising eyes of other women, a few, elegant young men on her. Probably, she thought, a lot of them knew Cassandra and were intrigued by her new friend . . . She almost spoilt the whole effect then by reaching up nervously to pat the swathe of hair Cassandra's hairdresser had teased and lacquered to fall across the right side of her face. She caught Cassandra's disapproving look in time and turned the gesture of habit into a stiff wave.

'Darling, I'm absolutely exhausted. Those beastly women went on and on and on. I thought I'd never get away. But did you have a wonderful time? What did you buy?'

'Nothing.' Laughing apologetically, Lois sat down. 'I

couldn't make up my mind. I just window-shopped. To be honest, I walked in the park.'

'Oh.' Cassandra sounded disappointed. 'Well, there's lots of time,' she said, trying to retrieve the situation.

'That's just what I figured. And the park is so beautiful, I couldn't resist.'

'Lucky you. Really, if I don't have some tea this minute . . .' She twisted her head from side to side, waving for a waitress. 'Take my advice, darling, and don't get involved in charity work.'

'What exactly were you doing?'

'Trying to arrange a masked ball to raise funds but we couldn't even agree . . . Oh there you are,' she said, turning to the waitress. 'Tea for two, with lemon – You do like lemon, don't you, Lois? – and lots and lots of scrummy cakes. I don't care how fattening. I deserve them.'

Lois's doubts melted. She sat straight in her chair, her eye fixed on Cassandra, basking in her chatter, her beauty and poise. She felt the bubble close around her again and wished for it to harden into glass, immure her forever.

'Talking of which, darling, I'm reminded of something a mite delicate. You won't think me horrid, will you?' Typically, Cassandra did not wait for Lois's assurance, but hurried on, fishing in her bag as she talked. 'The thing is, though I don't expect you to have noticed, indeed I'd feel absolutely mortified if you had, but actually I've rather neglected poor Ade since you came and, well, he is awfully possessive and so, I wondered, if you'd mind terribly amusing yourself this evening, so I can make it up to him?'

'Of course not . . .' Lois said sensing a shadow, a minute blemish on the perfect, clear sphere of her happiness.

'Well, actually, thanks to a spot of string-pulling on darling resourceful Ade's part, you won't have to entertain yourself at all. Here.'

She pushed a small envelope across the table towards Lois.

'Whatever is it?'

'Go on, take it. They're impossible to get. Rumour hath it that one has to pay in Krugerrands, but fortunately Ade put a little money in so he managed to swing it. And I thought it would be absolutely perfect for you because every other American I know never seems to get to see the really big Broadway shows and anyway it is frightfully good. We went to the first night, of course. And then, one of the previews was a benefit for one of my charities so I had to sit through it twice and I didn't mind at all. So I know you'll love it.'

The ticket was pink, a little slip of paper, printed in bold black with seat number, the time of performance, the date . . .

'That's not the reason . . .' Lois said, holding the ticket in trembling fingers.

'Oh you *do* mind. I was so afraid you would. But it's not really unreasonable, is it, of Adrian to want me to himself just now and again? To be absolutely frank, darling, if you promise not to breathe a word . . .'

'No. That's not it at all. Of course I don't . . .'

'One hesitates to use the word "kinky" of dear Ade, but the thing is – now promise not to laugh? – he likes to do *it*, you know, in bizarre places. On the stairs, in poor Philomena's kitchen . . . But with someone staying . . .'

'I mean,' Lois said, her voice rising, 'that I don't . . . I mean, this is the show Vanessa's in. Vanessa Hunter.'

'Oh? Is it? Well . . .'

'Don't pretend with me, Cassie, please. I couldn't bear that.'

'Oh all right. But don't you make a scene. Drink your tea. People are looking.' To subdue them, Cassandra turned her haughtiest smile like a beacon on the room. 'That's better,' she said as Lois raised her cup and sipped.

'I'm sorry. I'm so very sorry.'

'Honestly, everything I said was true. Cross my heart

and hope to die. But I will admit that I also thought – just fleetingly – that a nudge in the right direction wouldn't come amiss. Oh don't look like that or I shall feel absolutely conscience-ridden all evening. After all, where's the harm? You can scarcely confront her when she's cavorting around in a leotard with a whole host of others, now can you? I thought it would break you in gently, sort of get you over the first hurdle.'

'It was very kind. All of it. And I do appreciate that you and Adrian . . . I'm going to make myself scarce in future.'

'I wouldn't hear of it. And neither would Ade.'

'It's just that I've enjoyed these last few days so much . . .' Lois reached across the table and put her hand over Cassandra's.

'I know. And it is awful of us to send you off all alone. I could have got masses of eligible young buffoons to squire you but even the wizard Ade could only prise one ticket out of them. Honestly.'

'I appreciate it. And I'll tell Adrian so. But it doesn't matter. I'm used to doing things alone. I like it.' Her chin came up. For a moment, she even managed to look proud of her self-reliance.

'Oh gosh. Now I *do* feel awful,' Cassandra said, squeezing her hand.

'No. You're right. You're right about everything. And I appreciate it. It's time I got out of the sun.'

Cassandra smiled, not understanding what she meant. She supposed it didn't really matter. Besides, she really had to think about poor Ade. He'd been frightfully patient and longsuffering but then if Lois was going to be dreary about Project Revenge, as she liked to call it . . .

'We'd better go,' Lois said. 'It'll take me ages to dress because I intend to wow 'em in the aisles tonight.'

'That's right. Steal her thunder, darling. Take my advice and wear that filmy green one. It's the perfect colour for you . . .'

*

Lois let herself into the house very quietly, after midnight. There was a strip of tell-tale light under Cassandra's and Adrian's door and she walked on tip-toe, afraid to disturb. In her own room, at the top of the house, adjoining Luis's and Philomena's flat, she switched on the bedside lamp and undressed slowly, putting her clothes neatly away or folding them into piles for the laundry. Catching sight of herself, naked, in a long glass, she thought suddenly of her friendship with Adrian. Her skin tingled. Suppose his fancy had lit that night on the guest room, hers? She looked at the bed, smooth and untouched, and felt guilty. Yet she would like to experience that sort of intimacy. Men had never wanted her. Those few who had not shown revulsion or pity when they looked at her, she had run away from. It was her private joke that being *virgo intacta* at her age must qualify her for some kind of award. It didn't seem funny somehow, not then. She pulled a severe cotton nightdress quickly over her head and got into bed, drawing up her knees to form a platform on which to rest the thick, red and black bound notebook she used as a diary.

Ever since she was twelve, when Daddy had given her that cassette recorder and she had gotten into the habit of talking into it, telling it of her plans and dreams, her fears, like a friend, she had kept a diary. Except when she was too ill. Stryker approved and encouraged her. In the last few days, though, Cassandra had eclipsed the diary. Only a few hasty notes, effusions about Cassandra and her home, her baby, her husband – *Adrian is very blond and very handsome*, she read – covered a scant page since she had arrived in London. She turned to a blank one and smoothed the leaf flat. Stryker would approve now. Stryker would say that this was therapy. And because she was angry and sick of therapy, of Stryker and trying to make sense of everything she wrote:

I want to know what it's like to have a man inside me. I

keep thinking of C and A making love all over the house, so happy, so able to give. Why can't I be like that? I am jealous of them. I want to know what it feels like. I want to be a woman, be loved.

She leaned back, let the pen lie idle along the spine of the open book. It had scarcely ever bothered her before. Why now? Well, that was obvious, she thought. Would Stryker approve? Would the fact that she felt curious and horny be pronounced another of his famous 'breakthroughs'? Screw Stryker, she thought, and picked up her pen again.

I saw her tonight. Vanessa. Vanessa Hunter. I would have known her anywhere. She has grown beautiful. Her eyes are still too small. I recognized her the moment she came on, dancing with a bunch of other dancers. I felt curious. I felt weird. I couldn't believe that she didn't see me, sitting there, staring up at her. Like there was a spotlight on me instead of her. I really believed that she must, that she had to see me, and when nothing happened on her face, when the smile never wavered, when she never lost the beat of the music, I felt like I was invisible, dead.

The show is good, I guess. I liked it a lot. I liked Max Kreiger and Judy Horniman who play the leads. And the girl who sang. 'I'm getting on' was terrific! It was a very good show. I must tell C in the morning. And thank A again.

There is a little alleyway beside the theatre, right off the main street. There were a whole bunch of people there, waiting around, watching the stage door. I just walked up and down, watching them, but then people began to look at me like I was a hooker or something, so I went into the alley, into the shadows, sort of on the edge of the group of people who were waiting for Max Kreiger and Judy Horniman. One guy had a bunch of flowers which he gave to her. After the stars came out and signed autographs, most of the people went away. I ought to have gone with them but my feet wouldn't work. I stood there, pressed up against the wall, out of the light, and knew that I wouldn't be able to move until I'd seen her.

She came out with another girl. I saw her quite clearly. She stood for a minute right under the lamp outside the stage door, holding the door open, waiting for the other girl. She didn't look in my direction. If she had she would have seen me. She was dressed like a dancer. Leg warmers over tight jeans, a plaid jacket. Her hair sort of looped-up in two grips, either side of her head. And she looked just the same as she did when I last saw her, holding up the red candle, red like blood, flicking it under my nose, holding it so it singed my hair . . . Her friend came out and they turned into the alley, away from the main street. I watched them walk to the end of the alley, turn left. I didn't think about it, I didn't plan it. My feet just started walking. I wasn't even tailing them. Not consciously. I could see the candle, see her face in its light and shadow, flickering, and I just kept walking.

The alley runs round behind the theatre, narrow and cluttered with trash cans. Out into another road where I saw her at once, on the sidewalk, holding on to her friend's arm, laughing. Then she looked left, right. When there was a halt in the traffic, she ran across the road, calling something to her friend. She ran lightly. I envied her. Envied her lightness, slimness, prettiness. I went across after her, cars hooting and honking and some guy bawling at me. She turned back, attracted by all the noise, but she didn't look at me, didn't see me. She went into the subway where it was very brightly lit. I guess she already had a ticket because by the time I got down there she was already through the mechanical gates, making for the escalator. I didn't know what ticket to buy. I couldn't remember if her address was in C's folder or not. Even if I had remembered, I wouldn't have known which station . . . So I bought any old ticket.

Enough to carry me I don't know how many stops. And I walked down the escalator, on the left side, like all the little black and yellow notices tell you and then I didn't know which platform she was on. There was a train standing at one, going East. The doors shut and it started to move. I went out onto the platform and I saw her. Just as the train was getting up speed, I saw her, through the glass. She was sitting down and she turned her head and she saw me. She saw me through the window but the train carried her away before I could do anything or see how she reacted. I was on the wrong line and it took me ages to get home. I had to change twice and I got one of them wrong.

Once she was safely inside the flat with the gas fire on, the remains of the gin in a tumbler, Vanessa forced herself to look at it calmly, logically. What had she really seen? A woman on the platform. A woman hurrying, hoping to get on the train before the automatic doors closed. No. She was searching, looking for something, someone. She had thick brown hair. Dark, chestnutty hair. A good colour. It was well cut and cared for. It hung down over the right side of her face. And the left side was thickly-coated with make-up, the eye accentuated. A woman. Just any old woman . . . Vanessa screwed her eyes up tight, concentrating, telling herself there was nothing to be afraid of. And her memory showed her the thin line of elastic running along the hairline. Elastic to fasten an eye patch in place. An eye patch not seen but somehow shadowed there under the carefully contoured tumble of hair.

She remembered further back then, her hand gripping the glass hard enough to crack it. All the parents gathered, all the children in a silent, shamefaced group. Sylvia Shillingworth taking the chair, of course, and telling them all in her cold, plummy voice:

'Apart from her other injuries it is thought that she will

lose her eye. Even if they manage to save the eye itself, she will certainly be blind. Blind in that eye, that is.'

And her mother getting up, ghost-white, saying she didn't think the children should hear all this. And she was running to her mother, clasping her and her mother was holding her and saying:

'Oh Vanessa, Vanessa . . .'

Holding her tight, taking her side but underneath it all, so loud and so clear that she could hear it inside her head:

'Oh Vanessa, how could you? How could you?'

She started, gin slopping wildly in her glass as Suzie came in, still wearing the abbreviated spangled costume in which she danced nightly at the 32 Club beneath her old fur coat.

'What on earth's the matter with you? Don't tell me. Krieger trouble?'

'No.'

'So why do you look dreadful?'

'Nothing.' She took a large gulp of gin which burned her throat and made her shudder. 'I think I'm seeing things.'

'Oh. Is that all? Too much of this, my girl,' Suzie said, taking the glass from her hand and draining it. 'There. Now don't say I never do anything for you. And it's your turn to buy a new bottle,' she said, picking up the empty one and dropping it into the waste bin. 'Since there's no more booze, I'm going to turn in.'

'Good idea.'

Vanessa followed her slowly out into the hall.

'Post,' Suzie said, thrusting a couple of envelopes at her.

'Thanks. 'Night.'

She carried the two envelopes, one long and white, containing her bank statement, the other square and flat and brown, into her room. She opened it without interest – it looked like a circular for thermal underwear – and drew out a single square sheet: a photograph. A black and white photograph of a ballerina. She did not recognize the dancer. On glossy paper, such as is used by the better magazines. A portion of the picture had been torn away. A ragged, jagged torn line bisected the ballerina's uplifted leg. Her arabesque was broken, cut off, ugly.

Vanessa gasped and pushed the picture from her, watched it flutter onto the bed. She knew then, knew without any shadow of doubt, that the woman she had glimpsed earlier was Lois Carradine and, bending to retrieve the photograph, she thought she knew what she intended.

But Stryker would want more than that and under his tutelage she had developed the habit of using her diary as an aid to analysis, as a rehearsal or preparation for what she would say at their next or some future session.

I wanted her to see me and recognize me. I'm almost sure she did. She must have. I hated her. I hated her so much for being pretty and happy and having friends and everything. I felt weak. I had to sit down. I sat on a bench on the platform while another two trains came and went. I don't know how long it was before I was able to get up and look at the map-thing and work out my route. Even then all the names swam before my eye and melted into each other.

Oh none of that matters. I hated her for taking away from me my eye, my face. For making me so that no guy ever looks at me without wincing like Adrian or without pity, like Mr Stryker. Men will like her, want her. She is young and pretty and talented, dancing in a big show. It doesn't matter that her eyes are too small. I hate her. I wish she was dead or as ugly and unwanted as me. I remember her holding that candle and the look in her eyes. She was the first, I'm sure of it. She was the one who started it. She was the first to burn me, hurt me. And the look in her eyes – I've never forgotten. It was like she knew how pretty she was going to be, how clever and successful and she burned all that out of me. She took all that away from me and seeing her tonight . . .

Wait. This is important. I told Mr Stryker I was curious about them. Well, now I know about her, at least. There are no scars. Nothing. She's fine. She's doing great. It was written all over her. I was a fool even to think that they would remember or feel guilty. They'll all be like her, carefree, forgetting. They've all forgotten. I'd like to make her look, just for one minute, at my face, as it really is. I'd like her to see . . .

She was crying. Tears splashed onto the page, blurring her scrawled words. The cavity that was her right eye ached and remained dry, withered up, no longer human. It ached so much that she dragged herself out of bed and swallowed two pain-killers. On the floor below she heard Sasha wake and cry, Nanny go to him.

She got back into bed and shut the diary away in the drawer of the night-table, put out the light and lay down. If they could forget, maybe she could. But why should she? After all, she'd got something permanent to remember. They'd seen to that. She would never ever be able to forget or forgive them. She didn't even want to. Without that she would be nothing, a shell people could overlook. At least her face made her different, got her noticed.

Cassandra accompanied her to Harley Street and waited while she saw the consultant. Mr Valentine was very kind and gentle. He spoke to her in a fatherly way that reassured and almost overcame her fear of doctors. Afterwards, Cassandra made up her face for her in the plushly-furnished waiting room.

'Well, what did he say?'

'Oh he was very nice. He said he was hopeful . . .'

'That's wonderful.'

'Only he needs to do another examination, take a tissue sample. He wants me to go see him at his hospital.'

'Super. Which one and when?'

'I don't remember. He wrote it all down.' Lois pulled a sheet of paper from her pocket and handed it to Cassandra.

'Oh but, darling, don't you see? This is a sign, a positive omen.'

'Of what?' Staring into the mirror, Lois patted her hair in place.

'Don't you recognize it?'

Curious, Lois took the sheet from Cassandra's hand and read it.

'It's where your little friend Amanda Beatty is doing her training.'

'Oh.'

'Come on. Let's see if we can get a cab. I'm famished.'

They found a taxi in Wigmore Street. Cassandra gave the address of her 'very favourite little restaurant' because they had to celebrate.

'You can kill two birds with one stone,' she said, settling back into the seat.

'What do you mean?'

'Don't be obtuse, Lois . . . Oh, sorry. I forgot how medics scare you. Poor darling. Never mind. All over now. What I meant was, you can go and see nice Mr Valentine again and renew old acquaintances, all at the same time.'

'Yes,' Lois said, turning her head away to look out of the window. 'I guess I can.'

As soon as she saw Jason waiting for her by the entrance to Kensington Gardens, Vanessa regretted having contacted him. She hesitated, wondering if she dare turn away, hop on a bus, but he spotted her, raised his arm in a signal and came towards her.

'You look great,' he said, his smile unable to dispel the worried frown that gave his face a morose, hangdog look.

'I am really,' she said, feeling awkward. She had acted on impulse, out of panic, and now she would have to pay for it. 'How are you?' Her voice sounded falsely bright.

'Oh . . .' He shrugged. 'Look, do you want to sit down somewhere or . . .' He looked around vaguely at the trickle of people passing through the gates.

Vanessa did not want to sit. She sensed that if they did, conversation, the whole meeting, would become even more difficult.

'Let's go to the Flower Walk,' she said. 'It's always nice there.'

He matched his long stride to her shorter one, walked with rounded shoulders, head bent. Like a gangling schoolboy, she thought. God, what on earth had possessed her?

'Where's Julian?'

'Oh, he's fine.'

'No, I said *where* is he?'

'Oh . . . He's got a lecture.'

'But you haven't?'

'I cut a lot.'

'Oh. Why? Don't you like it?'

He shrugged.

Vanessa looked at the flowers. Bedding dahlias encouraged to linger by the warm weather, chrysanthemums of all kinds, their softer, autumnal colours more suited to the season.

'Aren't you going to tell me about it?' he said.

'Of course. I don't know where to begin.' It all sounded so crazy now and, even if it wasn't crazy, she felt that it would be pointless to share it with Jason. If only Julian had come, she thought and immediately felt mean.

'You saw Lois,' he prompted.

'I think I saw her, yes. I'd just got on the tube, you see, and I just happened to glance out of the window. The train was moving. The thing is, Jason, I can't be sure.'

'You seemed sure enough on the phone.'

'I know. But I was scared. I panicked. I really shouldn't have bothered you . . .'

'Why me . . . us?'

'I told you. I couldn't remember the name of Amanda's hospital. I'd put your number in an old address book. I was surprised when you answered, really. I thought you might have moved.'

'No. We're still there.'

They walked for a while in silence, a silence which Vanessa found oppressive and a little embarrassing.

'What was she like?'

'Oh . . . it was only a glimpse.'

'But you recognized her.' He stopped, turning in front of her to block her path.

Vanessa looked up into his face, startled by the urgency in his voice.

'I think she was wearing an eye patch. I could only see one side of her face properly. Her hair was sort of combed forward, as though to hide . . .'

She had not realized he was holding his breath until he let it out in a long sigh. He stepped aside, began to walk on.

'It was the photo that clinched it,' she said, hurrying to catch up with him. 'But now I'm not so sure. Maybe I jumped to the wrong conclusion.'

'Did you bring it?'

'Yes.' She stopped and drew the envelope out of the large red and white tote bag slung over her shoulder. She handed it to Jason.

He drew the photograph part way out of the envelope, far enough to see the ragged tear bisecting the dancer's leg.

He stared at it without expression, then slid it back into the envelope. He turned it over and peered at the postmark.

'It's all smudged,' Vanessa said. 'You can't make anything of it.'

'What are you going to do?' he asked, handing the envelope back to her.

'I don't know. What can I do? Nothing.' She pushed the envelope back into her bag. It seemed sick now rather than menacing: the sort of thing any sensible person would shrug off, ignore.

'You could go to the police,' he said.

'No, thanks. Anyway, what could they do? People in the theatre, girls especially, get all sorts of funny mail. They'd say it was a crank, forget it.'

'But it's not. It's her,' he said and she knew that he was absolutely certain.

'We can't really know that . . .'

'You don't want to believe it. You did, when you were frightened, but now . . . You're just like Julian,' he said angrily.

'How am I? What did he say?'

'I haven't told him. But I know what he'd say. He'd just dismiss it, say we were being morbid.'

Vanessa felt uneasy at being coupled with his certainty.

'He might have a point. I've been jumpy lately, ever since . . .'

'Stop it,' he said. 'Don't make excuses. It won't go away. *She* won't go away. You've got to face it.' His tone, the fervent look on his face alarmed Vanessa. She wished more than ever that she had not come. 'I've thought about it a lot,' he went on, his voice quieter, almost matter-of-fact. 'How she must look. There'll be skin grafting, of course, but on an area that big, well, it's bound to look patchy. Even if she didn't lose the eye, well, it wouldn't look normal, so obviously she'd wear a patch . . .'

'Stop it,' Vanessa said. She felt sick. 'You sound . . . fascinated. Almost as though you'd . . .'

'Like to see her?' he said with a funny, almost dreamy smile. 'No, I wouldn't go that far. But I've been expecting this. I suppose in a way it's a relief . . .'

'What?' Vanessa said, her heart suddenly hammering in her chest so that she felt out of breath. 'Expecting what?'

'That she'd come back,' he said reasonably. 'She was bound to, one day.'

'But why?'

'Don't be naive, Vanessa.' He was suddenly haughty, dismissive.

'Me? Now hang on a minute . . . If anyone's being naive, morbidly naive . . .'

'That's right, go on. Pretend that nothing happened. You helped to maim her, blind her, but of course that doesn't mean anything. You weren't responsible. That's no reason for her to come back.'

'Christ!' Vanessa said softly and turned away. He frightened her more than the glimpsed woman, the torn photograph. She felt as though a kind of madness was closing around her.

'I'm surprised though,' he said, raising his voice to get her attention, 'that she started on you first. I always thought she'd go for the strongest or the weakest. William or Amanda.'

'I don't want to hear any more,' she said and began walking more quickly.

'Then why did you ring me?'

'I told you. Panic. It was all going round and round in my head and I thought I had to tell someone. I must have been crazy.'

'You had to tell one of us but you don't want to face up to it. Not really. You hoped I'd laugh at it, dismiss it as a coincidence.'

'Which is what it probably is. A sick joke. I was probably mistaken about the woman . . .'

'No Vanessa.' He shook his head slowly. 'No way.'

'How can you be so sure. You can't be.'

'Because I've been expecting it. I've *thought* about it. In a way, I'm prepared. I knew she'd do it in her own inimitable style,' he said almost smugly. 'And that . . .' He jabbed his finger at her bag, the envelope. 'That is definitely her style.'

Vanessa could only stare at him, her mouth hanging slightly open. It required an effort to tear her eyes away from his, shining and certain. Mentally, she shook herself.

'I have to go.' She pushed back her cuff and looked at her watch.

'All right. But keep in touch.'

'No. I don't think that's a very good idea. I'm sorry, Jason. It's nothing personal. It's just that there's no point in going over it all again and that's all we ever seem to be able to do.'

'But you must,' he said, gripping her arm with strong fingers. 'It's not just you . . . It's all of us. You owe it to us. Forewarned is forearmed.'

'I don't know what you're talking about.'

'Lois. She'll contact us all in time, somehow. We must be prepared. We can learn from you . . .'

'Are you in touch with the others?' she asked, imagining suddenly a regular series of meetings, a sick kind of club or gang, she thought despairingly, just as they'd once been.

'No.' He shook his head and his fingers loosened about her arm. She pulled free of him. 'But we'll all get in touch now, one by one. It's inevitable.'

Not me, Vanessa thought. Oh God, no! I've learned my lesson. You can't go back. It's madness.

'I really do have to go. I'm sorry.'

'But you will let us know, when she gets in touch again?'

'I don't believe she will. I don't think she has.'

He smiled then, the sort of smile people use against children who are being stubborn and foolish and are bound to get their little fingers burned.

'I must go. There's my bus . . .' She glanced towards the road. ' 'Bye, Jason. I'm sorry I . . .' She began to run, weaving in and out of the strolling people who admired and commented on the flowers. With relief, she turned towards the road and saw that a bus was indeed coming. She did not care which bus, any bus so long as she got away from Jason.

And the terrible thing about it was that he did make a certain kind of sense. Huddled in her seat on the top deck, Vanessa smoked a rare cigarette and admitted to herself that it was possible. After all, she had jumped to the same conclusion as Jason. So if he was mad . . . Even before the photograph and the woman with hair brushed across her face. That night, Hallowe'en, she'd thought it then. As though it had been lying ready in her subconscious, waiting for the right moment to rise and form consciously in her mind. No one else could know about her and blood. No one else had that sense of timing. The whole thing was designed to announce Lois's return. There was no other possible explanation.

She wished then that she had been kinder to Jason. He was clever. He had thought about it, prepared himself. But it had to be crazy. No one would go to those lengths . . . But if she were in Lois's shoes, if she were scarred and ugly . . . And she knew why Lois had chosen to contact her first. It was because she knew that Vanessa had hated her more than any of the others. Always, even when they pretended to be friends. She had hated her. And she still did.

Oh God, she thought, there has to be another explanation. Please, please let there be another explanation. And it seemed as she stared miserably out of the window, her cigarette burning to ash in her fingers, that she could see Jason smiling, waiting for the terror that was to come, that had already begun for her.

Two

There was one part of it all that she could not remember fully and clearly: an emptiness that nagged at her mind. The doctors, Stryker, everybody said that she must have lost consciousness with the pain and the fear. She believed this to be true, for it was definitely after Vanessa had held the candle to her hair, after they had bundled her across the room and forced her face down into the flaming pumpkin lantern. After that she thought she had been alone. Their voices went on chanting in sing-song, but that was the tape, the goddamned tape her father had found and kept and used to play over and over nights while he got drunk . . .

Happy birthday to you
Happy birthday to you
Happy birthday, dear Lo-is
Happy birthday to you

Their sweet little piping children's trebles . . . Then the tape stopped. She remembered that.

Spurred by the memory, she got up and walked to the window. The sky was heavy and grey, pressing down on the rooftops. Cassandra had been wise to take an umbrella with her when she went out. Lois turned back to the bed where the folder lay, open.

She had thought she was alone, had struggled to pull her raging face out of the lantern. Her hip hurt where she had fallen from a horse earlier in the day. She remembered, she distinctly remembered hearing a step. Someone had knelt or crouched beside her, pushed her over onto her back. She had not been alone. But there was no other sound in the room. No, that's wrong, she thought. It was silent but for steps, the soft sound of a person moving calmly about, as though engaged on some perfectly ordinary task. While she lay burning, suffering. Someone turned her over so that she lay on her back and could breathe easier. Then there had been more pain. The sound of breathing, a sort of grunt. More pain. An agony in her right eye.

Lois raised her right fist and pressed it hard against the socket of her right eye. Her nails bit sharply into her palm. She kept her lips and teeth clenched together, against the cry of misery and pain that rose in her throat. She stood like that for a long time, shaking, until the spasm of memory and fury passed. She let her breath out, lowered her hand, forced her fingers to unfold, relax. She was breathing heavily. Downstairs, faint, Nanny's voice lulled and cajoled.

For a time she had believed it was Vanessa, Vanessa who had stayed with her or returned after the others had run away. Had returned to inflict that final, dreadful pain and damage. In turn she had accused them all, individually, of that gratuitous cruelty. Any one of them was capable of it.

She moved slowly back to the bed and turned the pages in the open folder, not reading them. William's absence struck her now as sinister. Of course his parents were lying. That did not surprise her in the least. After all, Doug Young had his own grudge against her. She smiled a little at *that* memory. But their lie, in such contrast to the bravado-innocence of the other parents, argued that they had something extra to hide, a bigger fear. Oh yes, she felt sure of it. William had remained behind with her. William had driven that last deadly candle into the seared jelly of her eye. She'd had good eyes, pretty teeth . . . So if there was any point in it at all, it was William she wanted. And there was no address for William. Nobody knew where he had gone. Liars, she thought, closing the folder and knocking it angrily to the floor. It fell with no audible sound. She needed a crash, a bang to assuage the turmoil of her feelings.

She began to pace up and down the room, from bedhead to opposite wall, diagonally across to the window where, in a sudden gust of wind, raindrops pattered and exploded against the glass. Would Cassandra understand that? That it was William she needed, William alone she trusted to tell her the truth? She did not bother to answer her own question for she knew it was futile. Cassandra had already rung the detective, her 'frightfully discreet little man'. He thought it probable that William had gone abroad, possibly to Australia.

'Of course, he'll keep on trying, but really, darling, there's absolutely nothing more I can do for you. It's up to you. The ball is firmly in your court.'

After that Cassandra had suddenly become very busy. All her dinner parties became dull business affairs, for Adrian's friends and colleagues. Lois would find it dreadfully boring and, in any case, Adrian simply had to keep things hush-hush. And when they weren't entertaining Adrian's friends, they went out to dinner, to parties and the theatre. Lois would have made an odd number at table. There simply wasn't a third ticket to be had. Twice she had overheard phone calls in which Cassandra arranged to meet her friends in restaurants and dress shops when she had told Lois that she was going to one of her boring committees.

Lois stopped at the window, leaned her hands on the sill, looking bleakly out at the rain. It was as though she had done something, behaved in such a way that Cassandra felt compelled to punish her. But when she tried to talk to her, Cassandra was like quicksilver, changing the subject, avoiding the issue, pretending the old affection. Damn it to hell, she wasn't a kid to be taken up and frozen out at will. And it hurt. It hurt inside. She pressed her hot cheeks to the cool glass, listened to the raindrops hit and shatter. It was because she had failed Cassandra. Cassandra thought she was afraid, afraid to face them. But she wasn't. Why should she be? It was all much more complicated than that, only Cass would never give her a chance to explain. She judged and condemned and imposed her own punishment.

Well, Lois did not need her. She pushed herself away from the window. She was grown up, used to being independent. There were other people in the world besides Cassandra Foss. She sat down at the dressing table and began to arrange her hair, brushing the right side forward from the parting, checking her make-up as she did so. She would show Cassandra she wasn't afraid. She would show them all.

It was almost ten a.m. before Amanda got off duty. There had been an emergency theatre case in the night which meant that she and Staff Nurse Jones, her senior, had had to remain on the ward to make their reports direct to Mr Mullins, the Registrar. Almost two hours of hanging around, bone-weary, fighting off sleep, not daring to nap. And the Day Sister complaining that she and Jones were getting under her feet and criticizing the dressing Amanda put on Mr Grieves. She had almost cried and now she thought she was too tired to sleep.

Overnight, the mild weather had changed. Emerging from the always warm hospital, she caught her breath as the wind whipped her cape, tugged at her cap. Rain splashed her face. The whole world had changed. It was only about two hundred yards to the Nurses' Home, a square, new tower block that echoed the functional design of the hospital, but there was no cover and her legs felt too tired to run. She huddled under the portico, outside the main entrance, feeling miserable, dreading another night on duty.

'Aren't you in bed yet?' Nurse Jones bustled up beside her. 'Why do you think I told you to clear off? I want you fresh and bright for tonight, my girl. Not waiting for someone, are you? It's sleep you need.'

'No.' Amanda shook her head. 'The rain . . .'

'Oh don't be so stupid, girl. A drop of rain won't hurt you. Come on.' She tucked her arm through Amanda's and pulled her out into the weather. 'Thank your lucky stars you haven't got to drive yourself to Putney, like me. You juniors don't know you're born. Go on . . . See you tonight.'

Jones gave her a little push and, clutching her cape more tightly around her, Amanda found the strength to trot the last hundred yards. Panting, stumbling a little on the steps, she pushed against the swing doors and entered the Nurses' Home.

'You're late, Nurse Beatty. Busy night?' The warden, Miss Pringle, poked her bespectacled face round the glass partition marked *Reception*.

'Yes. And we had to wait for Mr Mullins. He wanted a personal report.'

'Best get some shut-eye then.'

'I'm going to.' She forced her leaden feet to carry her to the lifts.

'Hang on. Post. And some messages.'

She turned reluctantly back to the desk and took a small, oblong package and a piece of paper from Miss Pringle's hand.

'You're in demand, I must say. Boyfriend, is it?'

'No.' She shook her head. Why would Julian Shillingworth be calling her? After the fiasco of that party . . . *And a lady called in person. Told her you were on duty.* 'Lady?' Amanda queried, looking up at Miss Pringle.

'I only know what's down there, Nurse.'

'But what sort of lady? What did she want?'

'I don't know. It's not my place to know. Anyway, I didn't see her. That's the porter's writing. You'll have to ask him. But he's off duty now.'

'Thanks anyway,' she said, moving away.

'Don't forget your parcel.'

'Oh, sorry.'

The lift took an age to come. Who could it be? she thought. Why not leave a name? And then she decided that it must be her mother. Only she would behave in such a cavalier fashion, would assume that everyone must realize it was she. But she would have telephoned, surely? Though with her mother, it was impossible to count on anything. Especially if she'd had a row with her new man. Idly, as the lift moved smoothly upward, Amanda wondered if she'd got another new man. There had been so many since the divorce that she had lost track. But she hadn't heard from her mother for ages and that usually meant a new affair. And then, when things went wrong, or she felt particularly pleased with her new conquest, her mother usually got in touch with her. Well, she'd ring her later. After she'd slept. And Julian, she supposed.

She let herself into her room and shrugged off her cape, leaving it where it fell. She sank gratefully onto the bed and leaned down to unlace her shoes. It was as she was massaging the throbbing arch of her right foot that she caught sight of the little package where she had dropped it on the bed. She pulled it towards her. It seemed to weigh nothing. She reached up to remove her cap, pulling the hairpins from her hair as she studied the address. It was very neatly printed in block capitals that gave no clue to the identity of the sender. The postmark was blurred, but she thought it was a London one. She could make out letters that looked like S.W.1. No return address. Her fingers automatically stripped off the thin brown paper to reveal a white box. She could not think what it was. Holding the box steady on her knees, she lifted the lid.

It was not until she had screamed and knocked the box to the floor so that it spilled out and collapsed into an almost harmless little heap that she realized the spider, so cunningly arranged on a bed of cotton wool, was dead. But by then it was too late. She could not stop screaming and crying hysterically. It lay there, its eight sinister legs folded up, its body a dry, ugly husk. She could not stop screaming and she could not move.

Ever since his meeting with Vanessa, Jason had been waiting and watching. He hardly left the flat, kept long vigils at the window, looking for a sign. Sometimes this 'activity' filled him with excitement: at other times he was a prey to black despair. If Julian noticed, he said nothing, for his brother had not told him about seeing Vanessa and his own concerns dulled the edge of curiosity. By withholding what Vanessa had told him, Jason felt that he was punishing Julian. It was no more than he deserved. Let him be taken by surprise, Jason argued. The shock, when it came, would jolt him into reason, force him to acknowledge the truth of all Jason had been saying.

So it was with a sense of excited expectation that he heard the postman's three sharp rings that morning and Julian's call that he would go down and answer it. His hand shook as he placed an egg on a spoon and gently lowered it into bubbling water. He was checking his watch to time the egg when Julian came into the kitchen.

'Parcels,' he said. 'One each.' He slid a small square box across the table towards Jason. 'What can it be, do you think?' Julian shook the little box bearing his name by his ear. It was light and made no noise.

Relief flooded through Jason. He *had* been right. It had come at last.

'Aren't you going to open yours?' Julian said, pulling out a chair and sitting down.

'I've got to time this egg.' He turned back to the stove, adjusted the heat beneath the pan. He heard the rustle of torn paper and twisted his head to watch Julian, the muscles around his mouth working with an involuntary tic.

Julian lifted the lid from the little white box, extracted a wodge of cotton wool and then whistled.

'What is it?' Jason's voice sounded hollow.

Julian drew a gold chain from the box, looped it around his finger and grinned at it, obviously pleased.

Jason stared at it, his body tensed, waiting for, willing Julian to understand. Still holding the chain up, he removed more cotton wool from the box and turned it upside down.

'No card, nothing.' He looked up at his brother. 'What's the matter with you?'

'Don't you see?'

'See what? Who could have sent it? Open yours. Maybe there's a message in there.'

Jason put down the spoon with a rattle and picked up the box. He knew there would be no message. The chain was message enough for those who had eyes to see it.

'Well? Get on with it.'

The box contained a silver-coloured chain-link bracelet. Thicker and heavier than Julian's necklet, it resembled a piece of industrial chain and fastened with a small padlock. Jason let it fall onto the table.

'Any message?'

He shook his head, his mouth dry. Obvious, he thought, but then subtlety had never really been her strong point.

Julian grabbed Jason's box and pulled out the cotton wool.

'Nothing,' he said.

'Think,' Jason said. 'Who would send us chains?' For a

moment, he thought he saw a flicker of understanding in Julian's eyes but he only shrugged and repeated that he did not know. 'They're from Lois Carradine,' he said.

'Lois? Don't be ridiculous. How do you know?'

'It's obvious.'

'Not to me. Look, you're not going to start up on all that again, are you?'

'Ask the others, then.'

'Others?'

'Vanessa's already received hers. Go on, ask the others.'

'I'm beginning to be seriously worried about you,' Julian said. 'I think you ought to see a psychiatrist or someone.'

'Chains,' Jason insisted, leaning across the table, his eyes burning into his brother's. 'To remind us of that day in the barn. Our "birthday treat".'

'Don't be so bloody ridiculous,' Julian shouted. 'For one thing she doesn't know where we live and . . . and for another, they only used chains on you. It wouldn't be appropriate for me.'

'I expect,' Jason said sarcastically, 'she found it a bit difficult to find an electric chair small enough to send through the post.'

Despite himself, Julian shuddered.

'I'm going to talk to Mother about you. This has got to stop.'

'Don't believe me. Ask Vanessa.'

'Why do you keep on about Vanessa?'

'I saw her, last week. She's seen Lois, here in London. And she got a photograph, a torn photograph of a dancer . . .'

'So?'

'Don't you see? Are you really as thick as that or . . .'

'All right. So she saw Lois. What did she say?'

'They didn't speak. She was on a train . . . Oh go and ask her . . .'

'No.' Julian picked up the chain, poured its fine links in

a steady stream from one hand to the other. 'No. I'll do better than that. Since Vanessa's obviously as crazy as you, I'll try someone else. I'll try Amanda.'

'Fine.'

'But before I do, tell me why you're so certain that Lois would bother to send us . . .'

'To remind us. To frighten us.'

Julian opened his eyes wide.

'I'm not frightened. I like it. I shall wear it.'

'It's a warning,' Jason shouted, banging his fist down onto the table.

'Of what?'

'That she wants revenge.'

'Oh . . . Now I know you're mad. Revenge? What for?'

'Go and ring Amanda. You'll see. Maybe you'll listen to her.'

'I will.'

He went out of the room. Jason looked at the pan on the stove. The water had almost boiled away. The egg would be hard now. He didn't want it anyway. He couldn't eat. He switched the stove off and poured himself a cup of tepid tea, sat miserably at the table, staring at the bracelet. It was apt, he thought, even witty in its horrible way. Julian came in again, pulling on his anorak.

'Well?' Jason asked, hungry for news, confirmation.

'She's on night duty. Not back yet.'

'So what are you going to do now?'

'I'm going to my nine-thirty lecture. And that's another thing . . . You're not doing any work. You're going to flunk your exams.'

'So what?'

'Jason . . . I mean it. I'm worried about you.'

'Will you try her again later?'

'Yes,' Julian said, exasperated. 'If it will please you. But I'm also going to ring Mum. Somebody's got to get you sorted out.'

'Just piss off and leave me alone.'

'With pleasure.'

He went out, slamming the door, the front door. Jason looked at his tea, then at the bracelet. He picked it up gingerly, as though it might hurt him, and let it swing back and forth before his eyes, catching the light in bright and mesmerizing flashes. Deep down he was glad, glad that it had begun.

'I've always hated them,' Amanda sobbed, twisting on the bed, trying to escape Tracey's strong, restraining arms. 'When I was a little girl I could never bear them . . . never . . . And once they locked me in a cupboard . . . You know? A sort of broom cupboard thing . . . whitewood . . . They locked me in and it was full of them . . . spiders.'

'Shush,' Tracey said. 'Try to lie still now.' Bearing down on Amanda's shoulders, she turned to Flower McKenzie, who was hovering at the foot of the bed, an anxious look spoiling her pretty face. 'Go and see what's happened to that bloody houseman,' Tracey said. 'And be quick about it. All right, love, all right. It's gone now. Come on, Amanda . . .'

'And worms . . .' Amanda twisted her head from side to side. 'Oh it was so awful . . . They were all over me . . . running . . . The cupboard fell over . . . and . . . no . . . I can't . . .' She sat up, shaking her head wildly.

Tracey drew back her right arm and slapped her hard across the cheek. There was a moment's silence, stillness. Amanda stared at Tracey, her mouth a round O of surprise and shock. Then she began to wail.

'That's better. Come on. Lie down.'

Amanda's body was limp now, obedient. She turned onto her side, her face pressed into the pillows. Sighing, Tracey stood up and watched her shoulders, back heave with sobs of relief.

A young houseman came bustling into the room, his white coat flapping. In a low voice, Tracey told him what had happened.

'She's on nights. I reckon she's exhausted as well,' she said.

'All right.' He went to the bed and spoke to Amanda in a quiet, gentle voice. 'It's all right now, Nurse. Come on, just turn over for me. I'm going to give you a mild sedative, make sure you get some sleep, okay?' She made a frail attempt at protest, but her sobs were beyond her control now. Tracey took her arm and bent it down, held it firmly. The doctor swabbed the white crook of her arm, measured the drug into the hypodermic, holding needle and phial up to the grey light, and swiftly pierced her vein. 'Good night, Nurse. Have a good sleep. You'll be as right as rain . . .' He nodded at Tracey. 'Stay with her for a bit and then see if you can arrange for someone to cover for her tonight. I don't want her on the ward. I'll look in about seven. She should be awake by then.'

'Thanks,' Tracey said, and went through the automatic motions of making her friend comfortable.

In a few minutes she was drawing long, steady breaths, hiccuping a little as her sobs subsided. Her eyelids fluttered and closed. Her hand became quiet and relaxed in Tracey's. She pulled the counterpane over her. She waited a little longer, watched until Amanda turned onto her side, snuffling. Then she went to the corner of the room and moved a chair out of place. She had kicked the dead spider under it when she came in, attracted by Amanda's screams. Using a medical tissue she picked the thing up and carried it out of the room. Flower McKenzie was waiting in the corridor.

'How is she?'

'She's okay. Hang on, let me flush this down the loo.'

'Ugh,' Flower said, shrinking back.

'I'd like just ten minutes with the bastard who played

this little trick,' Tracey said as she flushed the lavatory. 'Callous sod.'

Cassandra was wearing a new red dress that flared softly from her hips, setting off her long, elegant legs. She did not smile when Lois came hesitantly into the drawing room.

'Have a drink,' she said, raising her own glass in which ice cubes tinkled invitingly.

'No. No thanks. You look very glamorous. Is that new?'

'Mmm.' Cassandra turned, making the skirt swirl out from her legs, and walked to the window where she stood, staring out.

'Something wrong?'

'No. Not really. How about you? Did you have a super day?'

'Not bad.' Lois felt rather excited. She sat down, cleared her throat. 'Actually, I went over to the hospital. I tried to see Amanda Beatty.'

'Oh?' Cassandra turned around, came towards her, her eyes bright with interest. 'And?'

'Well, I didn't get to see her . . .'

'Why ever not?'

'She was still on duty.'

'Who said?'

'I don't know. Some guy at the Nurses' Home.'

'Hmm,' Cassandra said dismissively. 'Avoiding you, more than likely.'

'No, I don't think so. How could she be? I didn't call first or give my name or anything . . .'

'Oh well . . .' She moved away again, restlessly.

'I mean to try again . . .' Lois said. Cassandra made no sign of a response. 'What is wrong? I know something is . . .'

'Oh I'm so bloody bored . . .' Cassandra burst out, walking again to the window.

'Bored? I can't think . . . I mean, how can you be? You've got so much . . . you keep so busy . . .'

'Oh well you wouldn't understand. But I am. Thoroughly and completely, absolutely bored out of my mind.'

'Oh.' Lois felt helpless, inadequate to the situation.

'In fact, I've decided to go away for a few days. A long weekend. Nothing special, just down to see Mummie.'

'Oh . . . that's nice.'

The years rolled back, like a mental curtain. Lois recalled everything Cassandra had ever told her about her home: the stables, the horses, the lake in the garden, the Orangery where dances and parties were held for her elder brother and his Sandhurst friends. Then, a mere child, she had longed to visit Cassandra's home, to be a part of that strange, beckoning world. Cassandra had promised that she could, just as soon as she had learned to ride. But she never had. She'd had just one lesson before *it* happened, before they . . . She pushed the ugly thought aside and looked up at Cassandra, who was staring at her. Her heart skipped a beat. Maybe . . .

'What are you thinking?'

'Oh nothing . . . Just envying you, I suppose.'

'You ought to travel while you're here. See something of the countryside . . .'

'Yes. Maybe I will.'

'Anyway, I shall be off in the morning.'

'Sure. Are you taking Sasha and Nanny?'

'Of course. One would scarcely be welcome at home without. My mother is disgustingly into babies.'

'Well, naturally . . . Grandmothers . . .'

'They have their uses, I suppose. Oh where the hell is Ade? We're going to be hours late.'

'You're going out?'

'Yes.' She went to the telephone, picked up the receiver then changed her mind and slammed it angrily back down. 'Do go and tell Philomena if you want supper . . .'

'Sure. But I won't bother her. I'll get something out.' Her feet dragged. She wanted to cry.

'I say,' Cassandra stopped her, her voice high and brittle, 'I suppose it'll be all right leaving you alone here with Adrian?'

Like someone accepting defeat, a sentence, Lois pulled herself up straight and said:

'I'll move out if you like.'

'Oh no, don't be ridiculous. You'll hardly see anything of him, I expect. Just keep out of his hair, there's a pet.'

Lois nodded and went to look for Philomena. If she'd had any courage, any dignity, she thought, she would have insisted on going. Never outstay your welcome, her mother used to say in her uptight English fashion, and she could no longer kid herself that she was welcome. She'd look for somewhere, a proper room, not an hotel, while Cass was away. It would give her something else to do.

The young houseman returned that evening, after Amanda had woken up, and insisted on examining her, even though she protested.

'Been overdoing it a bit, haven't you?'

'Not really. It was a long night last night. Mostly it was the shock . . .' Her face crumpled a little. He thought she was going to cry again, and patted her hand.

'Don't think about that. Look, I'm going to give you a few sedatives, low dosage, just to calm you down. Get one of the girls to go over to Dispensary for you. Take one tonight and then one three times a day. Eat, rest and try to relax. I'll get the duty houseman to see you on Monday morning.'

'But I'm on duty . . .'

'No you're not. Until Monday night, anyway. Get out. Get some fresh air. Enjoy yourself. But don't overdo it, okay?'

'Thank you.'

'There's your prescription . . . And don't worry.'

She lay back when he'd gone, feeling weak and silly and useless. Her head was still a little muzzy from the sedative. She hoped all this would not affect her chances of qualifying. Nurses had to be tough, able to take pressure, and she very much wanted to be a nurse.

Tracey came in.

'Three days off, you lucky beggar. Oh, look, you haven't touched your tea. It'll be stone cold by now. Shall I get you another one?'

'No, thanks. I don't feel like anything.'

'Now that won't do. You've got to eat something before bedtime. What's this?' She picked up the prescription. 'Valium, eh? Now you just make sure you take them.'

There was a tap on the door. Another nurse, Lucy, put her head into the room.

'There's a phone call for you, Amanda. What shall I say?'

'Who is it?'

'Julian somebody.'

'All right. I'll come. Ask him to hang on.' She pushed back the bedclothes and lowered her feet slowly to the ground, feeling a little dizzy.

'I see,' Tracey said in a loaded voice, crossing the room to fetch Amanda's dressing gown.

'It's not like that,' Amanda said tiredly. 'This is important.'

'I hope Marcie thinks so,' Tracey said darkly, helping her into her robe.

'Don't go on, Tracey, please . . .'

'Come on. Steady as you go.'

The pay phone was fixed to the wall at the far end of the

corridor. Lucy had left the receiver dangling. Another girl was waiting impatiently, clinking a pile of change in her hands.

'Hello? Julian?'

'Hello, Amanda. How are you?'

'All right.'

'I rang this morning . . .'

'Yes. I got the message. I'm sorry, I wasn't very well. I've been asleep all day . . .'

'Oh. I'm sorry. Well, I won't keep you then. It's just . . . Listen, Amanda, this is going to sound crazy, but I wonder if you could settle a sort of argument I've been having with Jason?'

'I don't know. What argument? Julian, I . . .'

'Did you . . . I mean have you received anything . . . unusual through the post . . .?'

She felt faint suddenly. The colour drained from her face and she leaned against the wall.

'Yes,' she said in a very small voice. 'This morning . . . Somebody sent me a dead spider . . .'

And the tears started again. Tracey ran down the corridor and supported her. Gratefully, Amanda hid her face in the other girl's shoulder.

'Tell him to piss off,' Tracey said to the waiting girl, who stared round-eyed at Amanda. 'Come on, love. Back to bed.'

'What?' Jason demanded. 'What did she say?'

'She's not very well,' Julian said and replaced the receiver carefully.

'What did she say?'

Julian squared his shoulders, tucked his shirt more tightly into his jeans.

'Somebody sent her a parcel this morning,' he said. 'A dead spider.' He waited, trying to think what he would say, how hang on to a reasoned argument, but Jason said nothing. He just stood there, smiling triumphantly.

'Come on,' Julian said. 'I want to talk to you.' He felt sick.

Three

There were so very few reasons to go home that Andy often put it off until bedtime. He did not think of it as 'home' at all: it was 'the room'. A limbo place, outside his life, any concept he had formed of his life, and since it embodied this sense of detachment it had become a place where strange and forbidden, unpleasant things could happen. He did not like to think about those things. When he went to work – he was a carpenter with a South-East London building contractor – he left them locked in the room, like stale air. One exception, one regularly recurring practical reason to go back there early was the need, instilled in him by his Scots family, to keep clean. So, when the big blue launderette bag was full of soiled clothing, Andy went to the room, straight from work.

The Mercers had been the first to leave the Crescent in Olton after the events of Lois Carradine's thirteenth birthday and Andy had been the only child involved to be beaten with his father's belt. The family returned to Scotland, rather in the mood of an animal who slinks back to its lair or other secret place to lick its wounds. Andy was in no doubt that he was the cause of this: the upheaval in his and his brother's schooling, the downward turn in his father's career, necessitated by the move. Above all, he was the source and centre of the family's shame. Long before that fateful Hallowe'en, Mrs Mercer had learned how Andy preyed upon the girls, bullied and wheedled them into letting him do disgusting and unmentionable things. At first she had protected him from his father, but once Lois had been found and rushed to hospital, Ella Mercer abandoned her son. Just what his mother knew of those secret games, what she had told his father, Andy never learned. There was no discussion, no chance to defend himself. Ella Mercer had connected the two events, believed that Andy had plotted and perpetrated the attack on Lois out of revenge, because she had told on him. Worse, she believed that she had a sexually deviant and violently delinquent son on her hands, and so his father had produced the belt and sold their house for less than it was worth in order to punish and escape their shame. Scotland, they said, where the tawse was still in use and moral standards still counted for something, would straighten him out.

Andy accepted it all in a pervading mood of dumb misery. To his parents' cautious but growing relief, their remedy appeared to have worked. Quite simply, there was no more trouble. Occasionally Ella looked at her adolescent and quickly growing son and remembered with a pang how lively and bright-smiling he had been, but any regrets she felt were short-lived. His parents counted it a blessing that he did not appear to make friends or develop any absorbing interests. The lack of both meant that he was content to stay at home, where he could not get into trouble. And soon they had the alarming rebellion of their younger son, Luke, to contend with.

Never academically bright, Andy had got through the required years of schooling unscathed and had been smoothly apprenticed to his uncle as a carpenter, carpentry and the construction of gadgets being the one thing in which he had maintained an uninterrupted interest. When his apprenticeship was finished and he could not find a job, it was his parents who had suggested that he go south, where work was more abundant. The resurgence of old fears, any doubts they had about him were dismissed with a bleak shrug: he was of age now, his own man. They were no longer responsible. And secretly, feeling ashamed, they thought that if he was going to revert to his old ways, they would prefer him to do so at a safe distance. Ella, who tried to be optimistic, told herself that surely they could depend on him now. He had given no trouble for years, had outgrown those awful impulses. Quite what they were, of what his sins consisted, had grown hazy with time and the fastidious reluctance to examine them closely. As for Andy, he accepted this move as he had the earlier one. It had never occurred to him to ask exactly what Lois Carradine had told his mother about him all those years ago. He had other problems.

The room was on the first floor of a late-Victorian villa, one of many built by local merchants and shopkeepers not in imitation, but in order to create their own vision of, the spaciousness and style of the mansions of the rich. The result was dour and somehow mean-looking. The landlord, a Mr Czerniak, did not live on the premises and asked only two things of his tenants: that they pay their rent on time and not bother him about repairs and other irksomely expensive details.

Andy squeezed past the four overflowing dustbins crammed between the dusty privet hedge and the front bay window to reach the door. The hall contained, on its curling, colourless linoleum, three padlocked bicycles – the tenants, hardly knowing each other, certainly did not trust each other – and a flimsy cane and wicker table. Whoever was down first in the morning dropped the day's post on this table. Over the years its surface had become littered with advertising literature – free offers, coupons, mini-cab and plumbers' cards – like a paper dust which spilled onto the floor. Andy received very little mail and only ever expected the weekly letter from his mother. He would probably not have noticed the slim pad-a-bag at all had he not knocked it to the floor before flipping through meagre piles of envelopes. He bent and picked it up, only at the last moment recognizing his own name, printed in faceless capitals. He turned it over, squeezed it – it yielded softly to his fingers – and carried it up the first flight of stairs to the room.

It was one of those rooms that seem to absorb light, never get completely warm. In an automatic ritual, he put on the central light, lit the gas fire, switched on the bedside lamp. The room contained a double wooden bed which he had not made properly for two weeks. Opposite its foot, behind an eau-de-nil, hinged, folding screen-like partition, which he never closed, was a small sink, Baby Belling stove and a food cupboard. Andy filled and plugged in his one luxury – an electric kettle, gift of his mother – and spooned cheap coffee powder into a rinsed-out mug. Then he turned and attacked the mess of the bed, pulling off the pale blue sheets and shaking the too-soft or too-lumpy pillows from their soiled cases. He bundled these up together and stuffed them into the waiting laundry bag.

The kettle had not yet boiled, so he picked up the packet from the single easy chair, sat, and rested it on his knees. He noticed, without really realizing that he did so, that the stamps were not Scottish. He looked at it, read his name and address carefully and then looked at the kettle. He was not curious about the package, felt that it could not really be for him, since only on his birthday did he receive parcels. It would be a mistake which it would be boring to rectify, or unsolicited goods which, if he did not return them instantly, would involve him in a hassle with some follow-up salesman. Steam issued from the spout of the kettle which then switched itself off with a sharp, plastic click.

Andy got up, the parcel slipping to the floor, and poured water onto the coffee powder. He added three spoons of sugar, direct from the crumpled packet and, since he had no refrigerator in which to keep milk fresh, stirred in a spoonful of dehydrated milk granules which slowly, greasily dissolved. He carried his coffee to the window and stood looking down at the shabby street. It was already dark.

One street lamp cut in and out in an irritating orange rhythm, a parody of the flickering neon signs that sickly illuminated so many mean and lonely Hollywood hotel rooms. Cars passed. People went in and came out of houses. Faintly, he heard a radio playing. The plumbing pipes gurgled and built up into a roar, announcing that someone was taking a bath. Sniffing, he smelt frying bacon. He waited for the coffee to become cool enough to drink, his mind floating empty, vague. Absently, his left hand rubbed gently, but with growing insistence, against the crutch of his jeans.

Alone in the house – Philomena and Luis had the night off, Nanny and the baby were away with Cassandra – Lois found it easy to pretend that it was hers. She fixed herself a rare steak with fresh salad, washed down with lots of real orange juice, which she ate in the kitchen. The act of washing up, wiping clean the sparkling surfaces, gave her a greater sense of possession. Afterwards, she went upstairs and peeped into the severely aseptic nursery. If the baby were hers she would want more colour, more things to delight the eye: a mobile in primary colours, rainbow-patterned wallpaper she had seen in a shop somewhere recently. Nanny, of course, would find such things frivolous, but then if Sasha really were her baby she wouldn't have a Nanny. She would do everything for him herself. For the first time in her life Lois considered the possibility of a baby, her baby. Did she want one? She thought then that she did, but quickly realized that she could not imagine a baby without a doting father, like her own. The fracturing of her childhood had destroyed Daddy and ultimately took him away from her. Bitterness welled in her. Those doors, taken for granted by pretty, assured women like Cassandra, were closed to her: locked and bolted.

The thought drove her out of the nursery and, perversely, drew her to the master bedroom. Because of Adrian, she had had no more than glimpses of that room. It was a silken den, frilled and delicate. All the colours were pale, various shades between oatmeal and a kind of muted gold. Mirrors increased and sharpened the light. There was a looped and ruched canopy over the bed which invited thoughts of luxury and eroticism. Lois was tempted to test the bed, but the thought of Adrian deterred her. She could not imagine sharing that bed with him and no more acceptable, personal substitute came to her mind. She stared at it and knew that it was definitely not a bed in which a person could sleep alone.

Downstairs, she felt more comfortable. She sat on one of the two large settees and imagined herself mistress of the house. Of course she was poised and charming, wore her hair looped back from her face to fall delicately over her shoulders. She raised her hand to touch it and felt, with the sensitive tips of her fingers, the ridged and wrinkled skin of her face. The sensations on that side of her face were dulled. You had to feel it or look at it in a mirror to know how it was, yet that didn't make it any easier to forget. Embarrassed, she finger-combed her hair forward again. She would wear beautiful and elegant dresses, classic cuts in good stuffs that proclaimed taste and wealth. Nothing showy or gaudy. And real jewels at her throat instead of the locket that Daddy had given her. She touched the locket, warm from contact with her skin, and felt ashamed that she could imagine, even in such a harmless way, ever taking it off. She got up and moved around the room, touching polished surfaces, looking at the silver-framed photographs of Cassandra and Adrian and Sasha. The pale green curtains were closed tight against the winter night. The carpet was a maze-garden of delicate pink, green and cream, stretching to the glossy parquet surround. She wanted a room like this, wanted to be the sort of person who could create such a room. She thought, momentarily, of her haphazard apartment in LA. The thought brought her down and she pushed it away from her, tried to imitate Cassandra's elegant, swinging walk as she went to the sideboard and surveyed the gleaming array of decanters and bottles. She poured herself a very small brandy because she liked the shape of the fragile-looking balloon glasses, and almost drowned it with soda. She sat down again, spreading her imaginary skirts and sipped her drink. She would be witty and able to talk lightly on any subject, have a perfectly tuned laugh, like rippling wind-chimes, like . . .

She started as the front door slammed. She was halfway out of her seat when Adrian opened the door. His face was flushed and, on seeing her, his expression altered to one of disappointment.

'Oh,' he said and came slowly into the room, dropping his briefcase on a chair beside the door.

'I was just going up . . .' Lois said, standing, feeling awkward as though he had seen her game, knew that she had taken possession of his house.

'No, no. Be an angel and pour me a drink.' He flopped down into one of the sofas, easing off his Gucci casuals and loosening his tie at the same time. 'Scotch,' he called as Lois went to the sideboard.

'You thought Cassandra was back, didn't you?' Lois asked as she poured the amber liquid into a Waterford tumbler.

'Well, she has been known to change her mind rather suddenly.'

Lois held up the glass, asked him if that was okay. He told her to put a splash more in.

'Thanks,' he said laconically, reaching up to take the tumbler from her. Dark, strong-looking hairs showed where he had opened his collar. Lois looked away, picked up her drink. 'Oh do sit down,' he said. 'You're making me nervous. I've had such a bloody awful day.'

Lois sat, unconsciously prim, opposite him.

'You miss her very much,' she said, not looking at him.

'Well, naturally . . .'

'I could see on your face when you came in . . .'

'But I'm jolly glad to see you,' he said, heartily. 'The worst thing about Cass being away is not having anyone to chat to after the daily grind.'

Lois ducked her head, feeling gauche, afraid that she might colour up.

'Let's have a good old chat, eh?' He stretched his long legs out, sprawled.

'Can I ask you something?'

'Fire away.'

'Is Cass . . .? Have I done anything to upset Cassandra?'

He pursed his lips, rather full, fleshy lips and seemed to consider the question. His eyes, however, moved restlessly over her, as though, she thought, checking her out. It made her feel uncomfortable.

'No. I'm sure not. Anyway, she's said nothing to me.' He sat up, put down his drink and took a cigarette from the onyx box on the glass table between them. 'Cass is a creature of moods, you know. She blows hot, blows cold, and she bores very easily. You mustn't take any notice.' He lit the cigarette with a heavy, fluted table lighter and blew smoke at her. 'You know what your trouble is?'

The question, reinforced by his stark blue eyes, took her off guard.

'I wasn't aware I had any trouble,' she said, trying to turn it away.

'You're too damn sensitive. Sensitive to a fault. You mustn't take Cass's moods, anything, come to that, personally.'

'It's just that I'm very fond of her. I feel . . .' But she was not sure that she could express what she felt and suddenly it seemed disloyal to be discussing Cassandra in this flat way, as though this was not her home, her husband, her domain.

Adrian lay back against the cushions again, his Scotch resting on his chest. Lois gulped at her drink, wanting to finish it, get upstairs out of his way.

'It's a damn pity about your face,' he said.

It was a shock, like being slapped or spat upon. Strangers – and she regarded Adrian very much as a stranger – never mentioned her face outright. She put up her hand to cover it. Adrian saw this and said:

'No. I mean . . . You'd be an attractive girl if . . .'

'Please,' she said, her voice on the edge of tears.

'There you go again, you see? Too sensitive. What I'm trying to say is . . .'

Lois stood up quickly.

'I'm sure you mean well but really I'm very tired and . . .'

He got up, intercepted her as she moved to the door. Lois could not look at him.

'I didn't mean to upset you. On the contrary, actually.' He took a step closer to her. She felt his hand on her back, pressing her towards him. Gently, he raised her chin. 'You *are*,' he said, with honey in his voice, 'a very attractive girl.'

'No I'm not.' Lois shook her head, dislodging his hand from her chin. 'I'm scarred and ugly. I know that.'

His other arm went around her, hugging her. She smelled Scotch and stale aftershave.

'Beauty is in the eye of the beholder,' he crooned. 'And I think . . .'

'Please . . .' She got her hand up between their perilously close bodies and pushed against his chest. His embrace tightened.

'Come on,' he said. 'Where's the harm? I get damn lonely . . .'

She knew what he meant then. His hand moved down, onto her rear, stroking, kneading. She braced her hands against him again, but did not push or attempt to wriggle from his enclosing arms. He pressed against her, moving his hips sinuously.

'What about Cass?' she said, because she wanted to know. The idea of hurting Cass through him had sprung strong and tempting into her mind. And there was curiosity fluttering underneath all coherent thought, her body wanting to know.

'While the cat's away . . .' he said, with a soft laugh, his breath ruffling her hair.

'She'd hate me,' Lois said.

'My dear girl, she won't know.'

He tugged her closer still, grinding his body against her.

'No,' Lois said. 'No, I can't.' She pushed hard, finding his arms, his assumption about her, the easiness with which he was prepared to cheat on Cassandra repugnant. She pushed him hard enough to make him, unbalanced as he was, stagger backwards. The arm of the settee caught him behind the knees and he fell, bouncing on the cushions. Lois ran to the door, got it open. She was not crazy enough to think that he would pursue her, that he was serious about her. She looked over her shoulder and saw him pull himself up. His face was cold and bitter over the back of the settee.

'Stupid bitch,' he said, the words made worse by the lack of venom in his voice. 'You ought to be begging me for a quickie instead of playing the high and mighty. Considering the way you look,' he added, turning from her and reaching for his drink.

Oh no, no, no . . . The voice, hers, burst in her. Please, please God let him not have said that. It hurt. It hurt more than she would have thought possible, much more than she was prepared for. Her uncertain vision blurred by a rush of tears, she rattled the door open and got out, sobbing.

Hearing the door, Adrian turned his head, his mouth open ready to tell her to come and sit down, not to be so sensitive. He saw the door close, heard her rapid steps across the hall, turned back to his drink and shrugged. *C'est la vie.*

Andy ate a hamburger and a portion of overcooked French fries while his clothes passed through the cycle of the wash. He transferred them, a damp lump, to the drier and read someone else's abandoned newspaper until the machine stopped revolving. He had left the fire on in the room while he was out and its glow fell upon the forgotten package, making it the first thing he saw before clicking on the light. He sorted his clothes, folding the few items that needed ironing. The sheets he dumped back on the bed, thinking that he would make it later. He bent over and picked up the package. There was a strip opener running down one side, its tab standing free of the squashy, padded paper. He pulled it, inserted his hand inside and pulled out a scrap of cloth. It was pretty, white, printed with small pink roses. He shook it and the shapeless piece of cloth resolved itself into a garment: a pair of panties, a child's undergarment, edged in shiny pink ribbon. He smoothed them flat on his knees. He did not understand. He searched and shook the opened bag but there was no letter, no message. He let it fall to the floor, looked down at the innocent article of clothing and saw it become sinister.

He remembered, remembered the upright of the ladder pressing hard into his left shoulder as he tilted back his head, having difficulty in catching his breath. He had let his eyes crawl upward from her knees. The pale, smooth thighs, slightly parted. To the leg of her knickers gripping and indenting the flesh. There was a narrow little band of pale green trimming edging the legs, the waist. Above them, her bare stomach, the hollow of her navel. And between her legs where the knickers were drawn taut, a voluptuous hump. He gazed at the memory as he had gazed then at the girl, holding her skirt high, to show him as he had begged to be shown. And then with a shift, like a breeze ruffling the still surface of a pond, he saw her face, looming over him. Half a face. The bottom smothered in a makeshift surgical mask, her eyes devouring his rudely exposed body. They had pulled his underpants down, giggling, and she had bent over him saying that it, his penis, was the cause of all the trouble and they would have to cut it off.

Please, Lois, no, no . . . Please.

I really ought to do it, Andy. For your own sake. To stop you being dirty and chasing after the girls, frightening them. I ought to do it to stop you going mad and blind. To stop you getting hairs on the palm of your hand. To stop you weakening your backbone . . .

He wished she had, for what she had done to him that evening was much worse. Andy began to cry, fat tears spilling from his eyes, splashing onto his hands and the pretty sprigged knickers which still lay in his lap. He picked them up, buried his face in them as the terror and the shame of what he was welled unbearable in him.

Lois did not dare leave her room until she heard Adrian shouting something to the help, followed by the front door slamming. All night long she had imagined that he would come to her room, try to force his way in. She had wedged a chair under the door handle to keep him out and she had not even tried to sleep until the dawn came up, and then it was impossible. She had packed her bags, strapped and locked them. She had cried a lot, cried out of misery and fear. During the night she had written in her journal, trying to make sense of it all, trying to be honest. Among other things she had written:

Because I am ugly he thought I would let him. That's what hurts. And makes me so angry. Damn him to hell! What right has he to think that, to assume that, I'd be glad to . . .? When you are an ugly person it's like you don't have any inside. Other people's qualities, their inner beauties and strengths, shine in their faces. But when your face doesn't work properly, when people hold their breath to look at you, they can't see beyond the ugliness. They say the eyes are the windows of the soul. With only one eye they think I have only half a soul, or a very small one, or maybe no soul at all. Because I am ugly, I am of no account, fit only to be used by Adrian for a 'quickie' when his wife's away and he feels horny.

He doesn't love Cassandra and I wanted to hurt her. I thought, when I realized he was making a pass at me, that I wanted to hurt her. It was the only way I could think of. But I didn't know it until he touched me, put the idea into my head. I wanted to hurt her because she has been cruel to me. I wanted to revenge myself on her. The possibility of doing that was the only attractive thing about him. But I couldn't go through with it. I guess I don't hate her that much. I don't hate her at all. I was just sore at her. I want to be around her, be her friend and have her think well of me. I wonder if she knew that I had pushed Adrian away, if she would like me again?

Stryker would say that that is only another revenge ploy, a way of getting back at him. But I'm scared she wouldn't believe me and I don't want her to hate me. As for him, why shouldn't I get my own back on him? He asked for it.

Later, as she lugged first one and then a second suitcase down into the hall, she wondered how she could explain her leaving to Cassandra without mentioning Adrian. She had offered to leave, could always say she thought it best. But she was not a good liar, especially not to Cassandra. But what if she knew about Adrian, knew how he was? Suppose Cassandra asked her, asked did he try something on? And, worst of all, suppose he had really wanted her or had worked harder to make her think he did? She was afraid she might have let him, just to see, to know . . .

She picked up her coat from the bed and pulled it on. She had a big hat to mask her face, protect her from the rain. She looked around the room, stripped now of all trace of her. If they wanted they could pretend that she had never been there, had never brought her ugliness into their beautiful, shining lives.

Damn it, she would not cry, would not.

Downstairs, she explained to Luis that she wanted to leave her bags there, would collect them or send for them later. Sure, sure, she'd explained everything to Mr Foss. She left no message. Everything had been spoiled and that only honed her regret to a cutting edge as Luis gently closed the handsome front door behind her.

The first agency she tried was polite but unhelpful. It might have been her mood but Lois thought she recognized the sort of stonewalling technique that said she was unsuitable. At any other time she might have been angry but right then it just seemed inevitable, her lot. She tried other agencies but they could offer her nothing but a share with two, three, four others. There were mixed houses and all-girl flats, even two men who wanted a non-smoking, non-liberated girl to share. Lois was almost tempted to try that one, just to show them. *Here I am, guys, the original Miss Scarface. How d'you like them wounds?* A fat girl with braids explained the position to her. If she did not want to share, she would be better off looking at noticeboards in areas like Earls Court, Barons Court, Hammersmith. She might find something there, but really the agencies didn't handle single rooms much any more. It was all to do with the Rent Acts. Lois thanked her, touched by her kindness. She set off, determined to find something. She had to, because she could not go back to the Foss's and she could not present herself for vetting by two, three or four other people, male or female. She could not bear their embarrassment, their eagerness to get her out of the house or flat because, sorry though they might feel for her, they simply could not live with someone so ugly. She could not face that.

She saw two rooms, both in back streets, in mean houses that looked as though only ghosts lived in them. The first was no more than a closet. The grey partition wall wobbled when the occupant next door walked across his or her share of the sliced-up room. The second was vast and cold and very dirty. The myopic landlady said of course it would be thoroughly cleaned before Lois moved in. She promised to let her know.

An old man selling newspapers beside a board where rooms were offered advised her to telephone first. Half of them, he said, were not genuine lets anyway and those that were got snapped up quicker than you could say knife. Ring, he said, and save on shoe leather. Lois thanked him and accepted a pile of change from his capacious pocket. She called a host of numbers but either there was no reply or the rooms were taken. One man, speaking in an accent she could not place, said she should come round anyway, have a bit of a chat. He might be able to think of something, if she was a friendly sort of girl, like. He started to ask other questions, and she hung up, feeling sick and remembering Adrian.

The rain, which had slackened off, dried up, started again, a steady drizzle. Lois walked, looking for a likely hotel, trying to make her numbed mind work. Suddenly, she began to recognize where she was and, turning into a main street, she saw the tower block of the hospital, Amanda's hospital, rising into the rain. Suddenly she felt better just because there was something familiar around her. It seemed an age ago since she had visited the hospital, made her appointment, tried to see Amanda.

It was as though there had never been any hesitation, no reason to hesitate. More than anything in the world, she wanted to see a friendly face, talk to someone she knew. The idea seized her and blotted out, as nothing else had done, what had happened and the years between. She increased her pace, almost running, her left hand clasped to the crown of her floppy felt hat. She stopped at the far gate, the entrance to the Nurses' Home, transfixed by what she saw. Something about the slight figure in the beige raincoat and bright headscarf spoke to her across the years. Just so she had hunched her shoulders against cold or damp mornings, waiting for the school bus at the curved foot of the Crescent. She had always held her left shoulder a little higher, to keep the strap of her satchel in place, her hands stuffed into the pockets of her school coat. Now it was a smart shoulder bag that bumped against her hip as she hurried along. Hurried towards Lois, head down, against the rain.

Lois felt as though a layer of skin had been stripped from her body when the girl – unmistakably Amanda Beatty – hurried past her, without a word or sign. She caught her breath as though she had been punched in the solar plexus. But then her mind began to work, saving her from the rejection Mr Stryker said she went looking for and therefore always found. Of course Amanda would not recognize her, not after so long, on such a day, her face all but hidden by the hat's drooping brim. She spun round, saw Amanda ahead of her, hunched and hurrying, head down. She yelled her name.

'Amanda! Hey, Amanda Beatty.'

The traffic was thick on the main road, running fast in a flurry of spray. The noise, the roar and hiss of engines and tyres, drowned her voice. She began to run and she gained steadily on Amanda. She ran until she felt she could reach out and tap her on the shoulder.

'Amanda, Amanda . . . please wait . . .'

She slithered to a stop as Amanda turned, brought her head up, her expression uncertain. Lois smiled, waited for the light of recognition.

'Amanda? Remember me?'

She took a step towards her, just one small step, holding out her arms. She did not hear what Amanda said, if she said anything. She saw her mouth open in an ugly, growing O. Maybe she screamed. She backed off, collided with someone, who protested. She turned and dashed straight out into the road.

'Oh my God . . . Amanda . . .'

Somebody caught her arm, pulled her back. She saw the big red bus go into a slow, inevitable skid, its back end slewing sickeningly towards the pavement. But Amanda was ahead of the bus, running, her arms flailing. For a moment Lois thought it was going to be all right, but she had forgotten that the English drive on the lefthand side of the road and that there was a contra flow of traffic. The bus, by braking, certainly missed her, but the small white van did not. It slid, slewing water from its locked wheels, right into her. Lois saw her rise, twist and fall, heard the ugly crash of metal against metal as a car bashed into the back of the van and another into the back of the car and another into the back of that and so on, in a cacophony of screeching and banging. And the rear end of the bus mounted the pavement and someone pushed her hard, shouting to her to get out of the way: did she want to be killed? Pushed her so that she found her feet moving, unevenly at first, then steadily. Walking, walking away from the accident with only its terrible noise to pursue her.

At about the time they were carrying Amanda into the

hospital on a stretcher, Julian Shillingworth was sitting in Vanessa's cluttered living room. He felt awkward. Ever since he had talked to Jason about what he feared was happening and had decided that he would talk to the others personally, there had been frequent times of regret. Part of him still wanted to laugh at it, dismiss it all as nonsense, while another part had been persuaded and frightened by Jason's certainty. If only for Jason's sake, he thought, resolving to go through it once again, he had to get to the bottom of it.

The room made him uncomfortable as well. It smelled of perfume and cosmetics, was draped and littered with soft and intimate articles of female clothing. The effect was almost stiflingly feminine and Julian felt like a clumsy intruder. Then there was the fact that Vanessa had been very reluctant to see him at all and had, apparently, forgotten the appointment. At least, he assumed she had since she answered the door wearing a silk kimono, her hair a tousled mass of curls, as though she had just risen from her bed. He found her distractingly attractive and that, somehow, made his mission seem even more ludicrous. He and she, at least, were not children, trapped in the past.

'Here you go,' Vanessa said, coming into the room with two steaming mugs of coffee. 'And I suppose you'll want to see this.' From a pocket concealed in the folds of her kimono she took the torn photograph of a dancer and dropped it on the table. Julian stood and smoothed it out. In the cold light of day it did not look particularly sinister. From his own pocket, he took the chain and bracelet and dropped them onto the picture. Vanessa glanced at them. 'Not much, is it?'

'Don't forget there was the dead spider . . .'

'Yes. That does alter things a bit,' she admitted. 'But what about Andy, William?'

'Mother's trying to get Andy's address for me. Nobody seems to know where William is.'

'Lucky William,' she said, sitting down and tugging the skirts of her kimono around her long legs. 'But you're going to contact Andy?'

'Yes. I have to, for Jason's sake.'

'He scared me,' Vanessa said. 'I thought he was mad but . . . I don't know, when I thought about it, well, he made a kind of sense. More sense, anyway, than the idea that all this is coincidence, unconnected.'

'I know. I feel the same. It's logical, what he said, yet the whole idea is mad . . .' His voice tailed away. 'I almost didn't come this morning.'

'I almost didn't open the door.'

They looked at each other and laughed. Julian sat down, felt easier. Vanessa watched him, smiling over her mug of coffee.

'There's just one thing strikes me. All this . . .' He waved at the table where the trinkets and photograph still lay. 'There's an inconsistency.' Vanessa raised her eyebrows, but said nothing. 'The reference to chains, the spider, that all links back to Lois. But the picture . . . that's got nothing to do with . . . then,' he finished lamely.

'I know, I thought of that. Except that she was always jealous of my dancing. She was supposed to come to classes with me once but she never did. It could be that.'

'Mmm. Look, I don't want to worry you, but yours, on the face of it, does look more like a threat.'

'I *had* noticed,' she said, suppressing a shudder.

'Whereas ours, Amanda's are just like reminders.'

'Maybe it's my turn first.' She tried to make a joke of it, and failed. 'Actually,' she said, in a low, rapid voice, 'there was something else.' She told him about the figure on the stairs backstage who had thrown 'blood' at her, on Hallowe'en. 'It was horrible,' she concluded.

'That certainly makes more sense, but could it have been Lois? I mean, could she have got into the theatre?'

'That's the trouble. Sometimes I think it's impossible,

that it must have been a practical joke of some kind, somebody in the company, going over the top, you know? And then I think only she would know . . . As for whether she could have got in there, well, I suppose it's possible. The stage doorkeeper ought to be on duty at all times, stopping people, of course, but . . .' She shrugged. 'It could happen, especially if someone was determined enough.'

'But you said it was a man,' Julian reminded her.

'I *thought* it was. It was all so quick . . . Anyway, now you know. What do you make of it?'

'Not a lot,' he admitted. 'Except that both your incidents are different. And then you saw her.'

Vanessa put her hand to her forehead, rubbing it, pressing her temples.

'I thought I did. Now . . . I mean, she was on my mind. I can't swear to it. It was just a glimpse. I panicked. I should never have told Jason, any of you . . . I wish to God I hadn't.'

'No, you were right. Something's going on and we ought to do something about it.'

'Like what?' It was a challenge and he saw how very frightened she was, underneath.

'Well, if we can get enough evidence, I think we should go to the police. In fact, you could probably go now. I mean, something like chucking blood at you amounts to an assault, surely, and this . . .' he gestured to the picture, '. . . could be taken as a threat.'

'No.' She shook her head, making the loose curls dance. 'They'd only say it was some crank . . . Julian, I don't want to have to tell them about . . . you know . . . and without that, what possible motive could she have?'

'I don't think any of us relishes the thought,' he said quietly.

'So, we do nothing.' She stood up, as though dismissing him.

'No. I'm going to get hold of Andy, William if I can. If we put it all together, we may have something. And then, you've had two incidents. Maybe there'll be more for us. I think we have to wait and see.'

'Okay. But I don't want the police dragged in. I don't want all the fuss.'

'If there's a danger . . .' he said.

She wanted to deny it, dismiss the very possibility. She looked at him, with scared eyes.

'Do you think she's mad?'

'If she's doing this, she must be.'

'Then we made her mad.'

'No, I don't think . . .'

'Yes, we did. We must have. We've got to face that.' Vanessa sighed. 'I never think about it, never think it through, you know? I mean, what it must have been like for her, after . . .'

Julian nodded. He knew what she meant and he did not know how to express it. He wanted to say that he did not think they could win either way. Jason thought about it too much and ended up starting at shadows, while they, by pushing it away, became impotent and frightened.

'Perhaps it's all in our heads,' he said.

'Just a hefty dose of guilt, you mean? Well, there's that, certainly.'

Neither of them wanted to talk about that. Vanessa looked at her watch.

'Look, I don't want to throw you out but I've got to get to the theatre . . .'

'I should be going anyway. Thanks for seeing me.' He picked up the bracelet and necklet and slipped them into his pocket. 'I'll keep in touch. I'll let you know if I get hold of the others.'

'Okay.'

'And Vanessa . . .'

'Yes?'

'If there's anything else, you will tell me? Especially if you won't go to the police?'

'Thanks,' she said and nodded. 'You're very sweet.'

She checked into a hotel off Cromwell Road. How she came to be in that area was a blur in her mind. She had just kept on walking. The hotel was clean and respectable and not as expensive as many. She had to get off the streets, anyway, find somewhere for the night. She asked them to get her a taxi and went to pick up her baggage. Afraid that Adrian or, worse, Cassandra might be there, she asked the driver to go collect her bags. Then, installed in her room, she made herself take a long hot bath. All the time, although she did not realize it until later, her mind was prompting her to keep busy, keep occupied and when there was nothing else obvious to do, she unpacked her smaller valise, then walked up and down the room, trying to hold thought at bay. She did this by asking herself, over and over, what Stryker would say. *He'd say: Face it, Lois. Get your head together and sort out just what you really feel about all this. Lay a few ghosts, huh?*

So she picked up her notebook and huddled against the head of the bed, writing quickly between long periods of thought.

I shouldn't have run away. Walked away. I should have stayed and seen what happened to her. I didn't think. It was panic. I just didn't . . . No. Okay, yes, I panicked a little, but that wasn't really it. It was like there was a monster on my shoulder. Something ugly and terrible. Okay, okay. My face. No. When I saw it happen and it all seemed to happen in slow motion, like something out of a Peckinpah movie, I realized there is a curse on me. Just by being there I caused her to run across that street, into all that traffic. I wanted to see her so much. I felt so glad and positive about just finding her like that. It felt like an omen. A good omen. Like it was meant. Isn't that weird? And then as I watched her run into the street I knew that it was me. Just by going near her, them, I bring something terrible, make something awful happen. I don't mean to. I don't think I meant to. I don't know. I ought to be glad I feel this way. But I can't. It happened. Whether I wanted to or not, it was me made her . . . I made that accident happen, like I made Adrian think I was an easy lay, just waiting for the chance. It isn't my face, not really. My face is an excuse. It's what goes on inside me. Something dreadful people see and fear and have to run away from or take advantage of. I am an ugly person inside. You don't know, Mr Stryker, how lonely that feels. Maybe you were right. I shouldn't have come. But I didn't do anything. Nothing bad, anyway. It was enough that I was there, said her name. And, oh my God, she might be dead by now.

Trembling, she asked the hotel switchboard to please connect her with the hospital. She kept being transferred from one place to another because she did not know what to ask for. All the time she waited, listened to muffled voices or the muted ring of another extension, she became more convinced that Amanda was dead and that it was somehow all and entirely her fault.

'Ward Seven South. Sister speaking.'

'Please, I want to know about Amanda Beatty? She's a nurse there, at the hospital. She was in an accident today . . .' Her voice sounded small and gruff, tight with resentment and fear.

'Who's calling, please?'

'A friend. Just a friend. I'm not a relative or anything . . .'

'Miss Beatty's quite comfortable. She's sleeping now.'

'Oh thank God . . .'

'Would you like to leave a message?'

'She will live, then?'

'Oh yes.' The Sister's voice brightened. 'She's in no danger. Now, if I can just have your name . . .'

'No.' Lois put the phone down flat. To give her name would be to extend the curse, to kill her for sure.

So what do I do now, Mr Stryker? Get the hell out of it, back off? For their sakes? Because I carry around with me this bad luck and worse? You can see the sign of it on my face, okay? But they did that. They made me the way I am. Why should I be sorry if she got killed? Go on, tell me?

Stryker did not come to her aid and, as she stared at the blank cream wall of the ordinary London hotel, she knew that no one ever would.

Andy never answered the phone because he did not expect to receive calls. He seldom even noticed it ringing. The third time another tenant shouted his name up the stairs, he roused himself and went out onto the landing.

'You Andy Mercer?'

'Yes.'

'Phone for you.'

The young man went into his own ground floor room, slamming the door. Andy walked down into the hall, picked up the dangling receiver of the wall-mounted pay phone.

'Hello?'

'Is that Andy Mercer?'

'Yes.'

'Hello, Andy. This is Julian Shillingworth. How are you?'

'All right.'

'Long time . . . We must get together some time.'

Andy said nothing. He could not fit the voice, burring in his ear, to the child he remembered. He wondered if you could tell the twins apart now and realized that he did not care. He concentrated on what Julian was saying.

'. . . so we wondered if you'd received anything odd or unexpected through the post recently.'

'What?'

'If you . . . Have you received a packet or anything unexpected through the post?'

'No. Nothing.' His cheeks burned.

'Are you sure? Because, as I said, we all have, Amanda, Vanessa . . .'

'I don't know what you're talking about. What's all that got to do with me?'

There was a pause. He heard Julian take a deep breath.

'We think, just possibly, Lois Carradine might be here and trying to, well, scare us.'

Now it was Andy's turn to be silent. He saw the package again, its awful, accusing contents and realized that it made sense only if she had sent it. His heart sank.

'So we thought if we all pooled our information, stuck together, if you like, we could do something about it. That's why it's important that you . . . Andy, are you sure you haven't received anything?'

'No. I told you. Nothing.'

They knew. He hooked the receiver on its rest. Somehow they knew. Unless they'd done it? A sort of joke. He stared at the telephone as though expecting it to ring again. He would not answer it. They definitely knew. Of course it wasn't Lois. Lois hated him, had wanted to cut off his cock, make him . . . He ran up the stairs and shut himself in the room, panting. Made him what he was. The thought insisted on finishing itself. He could not bear to be in the room, be alone. He pulled on a jacket and went out, almost running, from the phone, their awful, mocking knowledge.

Four

The best thing that had ever happened to Marge Beatty, after her divorce, that is, was getting Amanda off her hands. Though why the girl wanted to be a nurse she simply could not fathom. It wasn't as though she'd take advantage of all those dishy young housemen and distinguished doctors. Then again, children were never really off your hands. Whenever there was a crisis, it was always 'Mummy' – oh how she hated that name – who had to mop up.

These not unfamiliar thoughts went through Marge's mind as, a stiff gin and tonic by her side, she dialled the number she had copied from her daughter's address book. It still surprised her, slightly, that Amanda had kept up with any of those horrible kids from the dreary, dead days of Olton. In that, as in so many other ways, she supposed Amanda was like her father. He was a great one for reunions and keeping up with old friends . . .

'Hello? Is that Julian?'

'No. This is his brother . . .'

'Oh, hello . . .' She could not for the life of her remember his name. They were always indistinguishable anyway. She could remember their mother, though – the glassy bitch – all too easily and clearly. 'Listen, this is Marge Beatty. Remember me?' With reluctance she added, 'Amanda's mother.'

'Oh yes. Hello, Mrs Beatty. How are you?'

'Fine, dear. Well, I would be if . . . Listen, don't get alarmed but Amanda's had an accident. I've just left her at the hospital . . .'

'Oh, I'm sorry. What happened? Is she all right?'

'Oh, she got herself run over somehow. Yes, she'll be all right. A fractured pelvis, they think. Cuts and bruises, you know . . . Anyway, she particularly wanted me to ring you . . . Well, your brother, actually, but I suppose it doesn't make any difference, really, does it?'

'Julian's not home,' Jason lied. He could hear his brother splashing and humming in the bath.

'Never mind. She just wanted you to know. Do you think you could go and see her, or something?'

'Yes, of course. Did she . . .'

'Oh that *is* sweet of you. And there's just one other thing. She was burbling on about that awful Carradine girl . . . Do you remember her?'

Jason had been expecting it, something . . . He caught his breath, nodded his head, forgetting that he was on the phone.

'Hello? Are you there, dear?'

'Yes. Sorry. What about Lois?'

'Amanda just said to tell you that she'd seen her. That's all. Frankly, I think she was hallucinating. They pump so many pain-killers and things into you these days . . .'

'No. I'm sure she . . .'

'Well, she wanted me to tell you . . . tell Julian, and I have, really, haven't I?'

'Yes. Do you know . . .'

'Now I really must rush. I've got a thousand things to do. Lovely if you can go and see her. 'Bye now.'

'Mrs Beatty . . .'

But she had gone. Jason put the receiver down slowly. He felt triumphant. Here it was, proof positive. Even Julian would have to believe now. And Lois had tried to kill her, he thought. She must have. Making it look like an accident. Just as he had been warning them . . .

He hammered on the bathroom door.

'What is it?'

'Amanda's seen Lois.'

'What?'

'Open the door.'

He stood back, breathing deeply, trying to steady his jangling nerves and pounding heart. He saw the blackness again, that special kind of darkness that had been caused by the improvised hood pulled over his head. He remembered how it felt to climb in that darkness, how he had tipped forward into that greater, more terrible blackness, the chains jerking at his legs as he swung at the end of his fall.

'What is it?' Julian's hair stuck to his head, making his face look larger, more bony. He held a towel around his waist.

'Amanda . . . That was Mrs Beatty on the phone.'

'I didn't hear the phone . . .'

'She said Amanda's been run over. She's in hospital . . .'

'Oh Christ, no.'

'Listen . . . She said to tell you she had seen Lois.'

Julian pushed the door wider. Steam billowed out into the chilly hallway. He gripped the towel tighter, bunched at his hip.

'When?' he asked.

Jason shook his head.

'That's all she said. Amanda wanted you to know . . . I tried to ask but Mrs Beatty rang off.'

'You're sure?'

'Of course I'm sure!'

'All right.'

Jason turned away, hurrying.

'Where are you going?' Julian called, stepping into the hall, leaving wet footprints on the cheap matting.

'To see her of course. Get dressed . . .'

'Don't be daft. You can't just barge in . . .'

'Mrs Beatty said . . . She said would we go and see her.'

'Yes, but not now.'

'You please yourself . . .'

'Jason, listen . . . When did she have the accident?'

'I don't know.'

'Well, then . . . Oh, look, ring the hospital. What time is it?'

'Eight . . .'

'You can't visit tonight anyway . . . Go on, phone them, while I get dressed. Then we'll see.'

Slowly, Jason came back down the hall, picked up the telephone. Julian left the bathroom door ajar, heard his brother talking to the hospital as he quickly dried himself and pulled on a towelling robe. He came out of the bathroom, rubbing his hair, as Jason hung up.

'Well?'

'She's comfortable. Only immediate family can see her for a day or two.'

He pushed past his brother, went into the kitchen. Julian finished drying his hair and combed it before following Jason. He was leaning against the sink, drinking from a can of beer.

'Now do you believe me?' he demanded, his eyes glittering.

Julian nodded.

'Unless of course . . .'

'Oh there you go again. "Unless", "if", "but" . . . You're full of excuses . . . What are you going to do? Just sit around until she's killed us all off, one by one?'

'Killed? . . . For God's sake . . .'

'You can't think Amanda really had an accident.'

'What did her mother say?'

'That's what she said, yes, but . . . Why would Amanda be so anxious to tell us about Lois unless . . .'

'Stop jumping to conclusions,' Julian said wearily. 'Vanessa thought she saw her. Now she's not sure.'

'Amanda wouldn't say . . . wouldn't get her mother to tell us if it wasn't true.'

'No. I agree. But that's all we know.' He opened the

refrigerator, took out a can of beer and pulled the tab. A fine mist of foam hissed into the air.

'All you want to see,' Jason shouted.

'We'll go and see Amanda, listen to what she says, then . . .'

'Then what?' Jason slapped his can down on the table so hard that beer spilled.

'We'll see if we have enough evidence to go to the police.'

'Enough? With Amanda lying in hospital!'

'We don't know that that has anything to do with Lois.'

Jason turned away in disgust. Julian hung on to his temper, letting the argument die down, fizzle out, as it always did. But it would not go away. He shivered.

'Come on, Jason, it's cold in here. Let's go in the warm.'

Jason shook his head.

'Jason . . .'

'You go. I . . .'

'It's stupid to stand there getting cold when . . .'

'You do believe me? You will help me do something now?'

'Of course. I told you the other day . . .'

'Only I can't be alone. It's like . . . I don't want to be alone any more.'

Jason turned and staggered towards his brother who, surprised, put down his beer and opened his arms. For a moment, he felt embarrassed, but then it was all right. He hugged Jason, who put his face down on to Julian's shoulder.

'Hey, it's okay.'

'I keep thinking. Before all this began I felt guilty. I used to think what we had done to her. No, let me . . .'

'All right. It's okay.'

'But now I keep remembering what she did to us and . . . and . . . I'm so scared.'

'There's nothing to be afraid of. She can't hurt us now.'

'She has,' he whispered, his voice full of unshed tears. 'You . . . you've gone away . . .'

'Don't be silly . . .'

'Don't, please don't . . .'

Julian held him tight, let him shake and snuffle against him, trying to control himself. Julian felt afraid then, not of Lois or anything outside them but of Jason's need, of the closeness that he had outgrown and knew that he could never truly feel again. Lois had done that to them, perhaps. After that terrible occasion in the barn he had realized that he could never again take responsibility for his brother. He could not bear it. And so he had separated himself, little by little, and Jason had paid the price. Roughly, but not unkindly, he grasped his twin's shoulder and pushed him away. Just then, he hated Lois for what she had done to them, the wedge she had driven so carelessly between them and which had now grown into a sickening gulf.

'Come on,' he said hoarsely. 'There's nothing to be afraid of. You can look after yourself, for God's sake.'

He knew at once that it was the wrong thing to have said, that Jason would interpret it as another rejection, separation.

Jason did not speak. He shook his head, wiped his hand across his face and moved out of reach of Julian's hands.

'I mean . . .' Julian began, but Jason flapped his arm at him angrily, to shut him up.

'It's all right,' Julian insisted.

Jason, still shaking his head, went out of the kitchen. Julian knew that he should follow him, try to comfort him, but he stood where he was and heard Jason's bedroom door close. He pulled a chair out from under the table and sat. Was this what she had wanted, all along, to destroy them slowly, inch by inch? If so, he thought, reaching for his beer, she had almost succeeded.

*

Cassandra was furious.

'Gone?' she screeched. 'Gone where? What do you mean, "Gone"?'

'I don't know, Sweets. She never said a word . . .'

'You never liked her,' Cassandra retorted. She flung herself across the room, wrenched open the door. 'Philomena? Luis? Come here. Philomena?'

'I don't know what you're getting into such a state about,' Adrian said as she whirled back across the room, tearing off her gloves. Upstairs, the baby began to cry.

'No, of course, you wouldn't.'

'What have I done?'

'She is my friend. We had an obligation to her . . . Ah, Luis.' She swept towards the Spaniard, her unbuttoned coat billowing like a cloak. 'Do you know where Miss Carradine went? When she left here?'

'No, Missus.' He shook his head to emphasize his lack of knowledge.

'Well, tell me what you do know.'

'She go. She leave baggage. She say she come back for baggage. Later, is man . . . taxi-driver, he come for the baggage. I give.' Luis grinned, broadly.

'Oh my God!' Cassandra threw up her hands, imploring heaven. 'You gave her bags to a taxi-driver? Are you mad or what?'

'I don't understand,' Luis said, understanding perfectly.

'How did you know it was *her* taxi-driver? I promise you, Ade,' she continued, rounding on her husband, 'if you've contrived to lose her luggage as well, I'll . . .'

'All right, Luis. Thank you,' Adrian said smoothly.

Cassandra tore off her coat and threw it on the settee, glaring at the door which closed behind Luis.

'For God's sake calm down. Have a drink or something,' Adrian said moving to the sideboard.

'Why did she go? Did you say something to her?'

'She was pissed off with you, if you must know.'

'Me? How could she possibly . . . Did you talk about me with her?'

'We had a little chat, yes. She asked me if I knew why you were cross with her . . .'

'And what did you say, beast?'

'That you were an adorable, mercurial creature of moods and she shouldn't take you so damn seriously. I added that it was because you are so gorgeously unpredictable, that we all loved you so madly.'

'Oh Ade,' Cassandra flung her arms around his neck, stood on tip-toe to kiss his lips. 'Did you really?'

'Scout's honour.'

'Oh I *do* love you. And I have been absolutely beastly. I'm grovelling. Look at me. I'm sorry. Truly.'

They kissed, lightly at first, but Adrian's kiss quickly became more passionate, insistent. He stroked her trim behind, pressed her close against him.

'Naughty Ade,' she said. 'Frustrated Ade, I can tell. But you do forgive me? Say you do?'

'I forgive you.'

'It's just that I feel so responsible for her. She's such a waif. I really don't think she'd have made this trip if it hadn't been for my encouragement. And then I have been the teeniest bit off, but I'd made such plans. I was going to make full reparation.'

'You can make full reparation to me,' he said, kissing her neck.

'Yes, I know, darling, and I will. But I can't bear the thought of her all huddled and miserable in some ghastly hotel room.'

'What about me? All alone in that enormous bed . . .'

'Poor darling. Mmm.'

She kissed him again. It would never do to let Ade know how important it all was to her. She could have kicked herself for reacting so violently, without thinking. Fortunately, it was easy to divert him. She nestled in his arms, returning his kisses, her mind already running on how she could find Lois.

'I think I would like a little drinkie, after all,' she said, pulling gently away from him.

'And I want a bloody good fuck,' Adrian said, trying to hold her.

'Ade, darling, language. Later. Cassie promises.'

'Oh all right . . . But not much later.'

'One before dinner and another after. How's that?'

'Fantastic.'

'Pour me a gee and tee,' she said sweetly, twisting away from him and fluffing her disarranged hair. Where would she go? Supposing she'd made it up, gone to live with one of them? That would really make her see red. No. Some measly hotel would be most likely. 'Thank you, darling. Mmm. Lovely. Mummy sends you masses of love, by the way.'

'How is she?'

'Fine. Bossy as ever. I nearly died of boredom. Ade, about Lois . . . No, no, I'm not going to go on, I promise . . . But was she okay? I mean, she wasn't depressed or anything ghastly like that, was she?' He shook his head. 'You're sure?'

'She seemed perfectly all right to me. Just a bit low because you'd been off with her.'

'I should have taken her with me. I know that's what she was angling for.'

'Why didn't you, then?'

'Oh you know what Mummy's like. And then there were all sorts of people in and out. No, it wouldn't have done.'

'Well, she'll get in touch, surely?'

'Do you think? Oh yes, of course. I hadn't thought of that. Oh clever, Ade. Go to the top of the class.'

And if Lois did not get in touch, she would find her. She absolutely would. Then another thought struck her. She looked at Adrian speculatively.

'Ade, darling . . . You didn't, you know, you didn't try anything on, did you?'

'Uh? With Lois? You must be out of your mind.'

'No, of course not. Sorry.'

'I'd find it easier to get a hard on for Nanny than her.'

'Oh Ade . . .'

She threw back her head and laughed.

'Why are you laughing?'

'Oh I'm sorry, darling. But the thought of you . . . you and Nanny . . . Really, it's too bizarre.'

Adrian began to laugh with her. His laughter was tinged with relief that the awkward moment had so easily passed.

'It is good to have you back,' he said fondly.

'Mmm. I know.'

Lois seriously considered going home, telling herself that it would be no big hassle to change her ticket. But then she thought it would be a pity to waste her appointment with Mr Valentine. She would let her decision rest on what he said.

She felt like a criminal going to the hospital, even though she kept telling herself there was no chance of her bumping into Amanda or anyone. Still, she hurried through the big entrance hall and breathed a sigh of relief when she entered Mr Valentine's waiting room.

The consultation was long and, from her point of view, inconclusive. Another doctor came and examined her as thoroughly as Mr Valentine had done in Harley Street. They peered at her through all kinds of instruments and talked together in soft, low voices so that she could not hear. They took her to another room where a tiny skin sample was taken from behind her right ear. Mr Valentine said he would need to see her again. Then he would be able to tell her something definite, what he could and could not do for her. Lois nodded, thanked him. So nothing was decided. She was not really surprised. She knew, in her heart, that she had to make the decision.

She booked another appointment at the central desk and rode the escalator down into the lobby. On impulse, she stopped at the florist's shop, tucked away in a corner of the entrance hall, and bought an expensive bunch of gold and lavender chrysanthemums.

'Could you get these to Amanda Beatty, please? I don't know which ward . . .'

The woman at the reception desk flipped through a sheaf of admission sheets.

'Seven South. You can take them up . . .'

'Oh no, no thank you . . . I really don't have the time. Would you mind?'

'Very well.'

The woman took the bouquet and balanced it on the side of the desk.

'Thank you. I'm grateful.'

Somehow she felt better because, she thought, she had handled herself, things, well.

Between the hours of one and two each day, the patients were required to rest. Venetian blinds closed off the windows and the main lights in wards and corridors were extinguished. Pale blue curtains were drawn around each bed, creating a sub-aqueous bluey grey light in which the patients slept or tried to.

Amanda, still sedated, drifted in and out of a light sleep, frequently starting awake. It seemed that Lois was waiting for her, floating in the shallows of sleep where a soft, insistent wind blew, whipping her hair back from her face. The two halves of her face did not match, like a photograph torn down the middle and hastily pasted together again. One side was burnt and puckered, the skin having the unnatural sheen of charred and melted plastic. Her eye glittered. Half her mouth twisted into a sneering parody of a smile. And she lifted up her arms, stretched out her hands towards Amanda where she lay.

'No!' She jerked awake, tossing her head on the pillow. A rushing noise, like the wind in her dream, made her freeze. The blue curtain swept back, hissing on its rails. She tensed her throat to scream, expecting to see Lois there, maimed and reaching for her. Instead she saw a blur of soft colours and she smelt an odour richly associated with autumn and the dying of the year. The colours resolved into balls, feathered, tight-curling. She heard the sharp crackle of florist's paper.

'Here you are, love. Pressie for you.' Smiling, Tracey laid the bouquet of gold and lavender chrysanthemums across her chest. Their smell became recognizable, fresh and tart and smokey. Amanda smiled with relief and pleasure.

'Oh they're beautiful. You shouldn't have . . .'

'Not me, love. I just brought 'em up. Good excuse to see you before I go on duty. How are you feeling?'

'All right.' Amanda smiled, pulled a face. 'I hurt.'

'I'm not surprised.' Tracey bent over her, smoothing the folded-back sheet with automatic expertise. 'Still, it could be worse.'

'I know.'

'Let it be a lesson to you. If you must quarrel with traffic, pick on a bicycle. It's more your size.'

'Oh don't make me laugh,' Amanda said. 'It hurts worse then.'

'Do you want anything?' Amanda shook her head. 'I'll get someone to fix these,' Tracey said, checking her watch and picking up the flowers at the same time.

'Who sent them?'

'Search me. The old girl on the desk just asked me to bring them up.' She looked among the flowers. 'No card.

Must be a secret admirer. Oh God, Sister'll have my hide if I don't rush. I'll pop in and see you later, love, okay?'

'Yes. Thanks, Tracey.'

Her mother had already sent flowers, and so had her father, who had said that he would come and see her. There was no one else, no one who would not include a card. No one except . . .

'I don't want them,' she said when a junior nurse brought the flowers, poorly arranged in a big vase, and placed them on the bed-table, which arched across her feet.

'What? They're gorgeous. Must've cost a bomb.'

'Yes, but please . . . Put them somewhere else.'

The girl frowned, seeing the pale set of anxiety on Amanda's face.

'Okay,' she said, 'I'll put them over by the window where everyone can enjoy them. Hey up, you've got visitors.'

Jason and Julian, like one person splitting into two, separated at the foot of her bed, advanced one on either side of her. Jason, she thought, looked ill. Julian smiled, offered chocolates and a rather squashy bag of grapes.

'So, how are you?'

'We came as soon as they'd let us,' Jason added.

'All right. It feels worse than it is, really. My pelvis is cracked, otherwise just cuts and bruises. I was very lucky, really.'

'Oh that's good. And they're looking after you all right?'

'What happened?' Jason said.

'Yes. Everyone's been smashing. It was nice of you to come.'

'Your mother said . . .'

'Jason,' Julian said warningly.

Amanda looked from one to the other, her lower lip trembling.

'After you called,' she said to Julian, 'I just thought it best to tell you.'

'Of course,' he said.

'You saw her? It was really her?' Jason sounded excited and apprehensive at the same time.

'Yes.'

'How? Where?'

'I don't know. I mean, just outside . . . I was going out, you see. I'd been so shocked by the . . . parcel she sent that they'd given me a few days off. They said I ought to get out and . . . It was raining. I was just walking along, you know, hurrying because of the rain, when I heard someone call my name.' She paused, swallowed, closed her eyes for a moment.

'And it was her?' Jason prompted, leaning towards her, eager.

'Yes.'

'What did she say?'

'Nothing. She just stood there. She held out her arms . . . I couldn't see her face properly . . . She had this big hat on . . . I was so scared . . .' Amanda swallowed again, closed her eyes.

'Then what happened?'

'I was scared to see her face, you know?'

'She pushed you,' Jason said, quite calmly, as though he had witnessed the entire event.

'Jason . . .' Julian said, looking at him furiously.

'No.' Amanda's eyes flew open. 'No . . . I mean, I don't know. I can't remember anything. The next thing I remember is waking up in Casualty, hurting . . .'

'All right,' Julian said, seeing the tears start to her eyes. 'It's all right now.'

'She must have followed me . . . There was something terrible about her . . . although I couldn't see her face properly . . . Terrible . . .' Two sad, trembling tears squeezed from beneath her fluttering lids.

'She must have pushed you,' Jason said.

'Oh God . . .'

'Shut up,' Julian warned his brother. 'Pass Amanda a tissue.'

Jason fumbled one from a box on the top of Amanda's locker and gave it to her.

'Today,' she said, sniffing, 'I had this bunch of flowers . . . There was no card . . . I'm sure she sent them . . . Over there . . .'

Jason turned to look at the flowers. A passing nurse glanced in his direction, saw Amanda and came quickly to her bed.

'What's the matter, Nurse? These two upsetting you?'

'No.' Amanda sniffled, shook her head.

'What are you upsetting yourself for, then?' The nurse pushed Jason aside, lifted Amanda's limp arm and took her pulse. 'This will never do, Nurse, will it?' She looked from her watch to Julian. 'I think we're still rather tired. Perhaps you'd better go now.'

'All right.' Julian stood up.

'It was her,' Amanda repeated, her face creasing and turning pink.

'We believe you. Don't worry. We'll think of something.'

'I'm going to get you something to calm you down,' the nurse told her. 'Come on, boys, off you go now.'

' 'Bye, Amanda.'

' 'Bye, Julian. I'm sorry.'

Jason nodded to her. He hurried after Julian, plucked at his sleeve.

'She's not tired, she's scared out of her mind,' he said.

'I'm not surprised with you saying Lois pushed her.'

'Well, didn't she?'

'You don't know,' Julian said between gritted teeth. 'She probably just ran . . .'

'You believe what the hell you like,' Jason said angrily, hurrying ahead of him. 'I know. She knows. You'll see.'

Two nurses, moving towards Amanda's bed, looked at them, one alarmed, the other frowning in disapproval. Julian did not argue with his brother, anxious to avoid a scene. They rode down together in the lift, standing far apart, locked in a stiff silence.

Cassandra had drawn an infuriating blank with Mr Valentine's secretary. The only address she had for Miss Carradine was Mrs Foss's own. Mr Valentine was seeing Miss Carradine at the hospital now, so any change of address would be filed there and no, she was very sorry, but she really could not get hold of it. Nor could she tell Mrs Foss when Miss Carradine's next appointment was. She rather thought that would be confidential, like all other information concerning patients.

'Put me through to Mr Valentine, then,' Cassandra had snapped. After all, she had sent Lois to him in the first place. The least he could do . . .

'I'm sorry, Mr Valentine's not in today. If you'd like to call tomorrow, after ten . . .'

Cassandra hung up. Well, that was definitely the last time she'd drum up trade for Herr Valentine. She tapped the receiver with her long, maroon nails and wondered if she dared, if she should . . . What else was there? She knew in her bones Lois was not going to get in touch. And she who hesitates jolly well deserves to be lost, Cassandra thought, and picked up the telephone, dialled the number of the discreet little man who had helped her trace Lois's chums.

'Mr Critchley? Cassandra Foss. How are you?'

He said that he was fine, had been planning to get in touch with her.

'Oh? Why?'

'That young man, William Young? I think I've got something at last.'

'Oh how thrilling. Do tell. Hang on. Let me get a pencil.'

Cassandra listened, made a few notes. She was disappointed that he had nothing definite, but even this – and it was certainly intriguing – would be enough to get Lois's adrenalin flowing again. Cassandra decided she was very pleased with Mr Critchley.

'Super. Yes, do please continue your enquiries. And now I've got another little problem for you . . . The thing is, I've managed to lose Miss Carradine . . . Yes, I know . . . Positively hilarious, isn't it?' Cassandra laughed, brightly and falsely. She told him what little she knew. 'I'm sure she meant to leave an address, but . . . Anyway, if you could just make a few discreet enquiries I'd be tremendously grateful . . . Oh, and Mr Critchley, if you do manage to locate her, don't mention the information about William Young. I want to break the news. Thanks so much. 'Bye.'

William Young. She tapped her pad lightly. Very interesting. He really was a brilliant little man, her Mr Critchley. She had no doubt he would be able to find Lois in a jiffy. Meanwhile, she had to *do* something or she would go out of her mind with boredom.

William. Look at it every which way, as she had done, it all came down to William, Lois concluded. If she could just see him and talk to him then it would be all right, it would be over and she could go home, go to Europe . . . Start to live, she thought, and it was an idea that took her breath away, in a distressing and uncomfortable manner. William would tell her the truth, whether it was he or one of the others who had remained behind with her that night, who had effectively put out her eye. By seeing William she would know how the others felt, for William was the sum of all the others. And she knew she could trust him because, before it all went bad and wrong on her, she and William had been close. Kind of. Not close exactly, but special. They had been alike. William was the sort who got things done. He was not scared and timid, like the others. She remembered his horoscope. He was a Leo. She had thought then, right at the beginning, that he was a natural leader. She had watched him, had seen how it was he who organized the kids in the Crescent, got things moving. All William lacked was imagination, but he had been smart enough to recognize that quality in her. That's why, against all his natural instincts, he had accepted her, let her become the leader of the gang. Oh yes, she and William had been two of a kind and it was William she needed now if she was ever going to clear up this mess and get her act together.

But on the subject of William Young the folder was blank. Once again she thought of simply calling his parents, and once again she rejected the idea. Whenever she thought of them she inevitably remembered that night in the barn when she had caught William's father and Amanda's mother doing it. It made her blush now to recall what she had seen, but it also made her want to giggle. Anyway, it had been worth it because it had secured the barn for them. Marge Beatty and Doug Young were so scared of what she had seen and what she might therefore say, that they had talked the other parents round. But she had not done it for herself but for them, all of them, the gang. Anyway, Doug Young would not help her now. No doubt he would welcome the chance to get back at her. But if she was right, if she really had William to thank for her blindness, and if Doug Young knew it, he would go to any lengths to protect his son. There was no one to protect her, not since Daddy had driven himself off the freeway, taking Mommy with him, and Grandma had died like, even as a little girl, she had always been afraid that she would.

William had always inspired protection. She remembered his birthday, that year of their association and how, after she had let his precious rabbit loose, Doug Young had announced that William could have two rabbits. It was funny, but she had wanted to protect William too. The others, yes, she had wanted to scare them, to let them know who was boss, but on William she had only played a joke. That's all it was, her conscience asserted. A joke. She had let the damn rabbit out, not knowing that it would get lost or run away or do whatever the stupid creature had done. And then she had gotten a dead rabbit from Mr Applegreen's farm and wrapped it up in sheets of newspaper and given it to William to identify when they were all playing pass-the-parcel. It had been a joke. She had no idea that it would hurt him so.

I was jealous of that dumb rabbit, she realized.

She tried to ignore the thought, laugh it off, but it stuck, stubborn, in her mind and irritated in the way that one of Stryker's more penetrating insights had often done. That rabbit had been William's pride and joy. He had loved that rabbit.

When he got the rabbit, she forced herself to admit, he had had less time for her. No time. Damn you to hell, William.

Stop it!

She could not stop it. That's why it had never really been a joke. She had needed to hurt William more than all the others. If she looked at it calmly, she would have to admit that she had done more and worse to the others individually, but there had been an element of a game in all those incidents. She had never acted alone, either. She had plotted and schemed with the others, so that everyone knew what to expect, except the victim. That way no single treat, as she had called them, could go too far, get really heavy. They had all joined in to frighten one another, like a bunch of kids perpetually riding the ghost train.

Except when it came to William's birthday. She had told no one, had planned and organized it all herself. It was one-to-one, between her and William.

Stop it, she ordered herself.

And she had lit upon the rabbit because the rabbit was the best, the cruellest way to get at William. Because she had been jealous of the rabbit.

No!

Yes. Jealous of the rabbit.

It had been William who brought the big pumpkin lantern to her surprise birthday party, the lantern in which her face had been seared and scarred. She could see him now, standing in the doorway, holding it in both hands, so serious, calm and controlled, while her parents stood back and smiled indulgently.

William had been smarter all along.

William had shut the window on her, that first time, at the Hunters' Christmas party, when they had dared her to climb out onto the window ledge and walk along it. When she had thought that she was going to fall and die. William had shut the window, had left her out there until it felt like her legs were going to give and her fingers slip from their precarious hold on the gritty-feeling roof tiles.

William had been ahead of her all the way down the line.

Maybe he was still ahead of her?

No. That could not be true. William had respected her after she had walked the ledge. It was the rabbit that tipped him over, tipped it all around so that the games became deadly earnest and jokes turned to scary and bloody, cold-blooded hatred.

William had wanted to be a vet.

Of course! Why hadn't she thought of that before? Excitedly, she took up the folder and went through it, looking for Cassandra's little man's number. She picked up the telephone and asked the switchboard to call his number. It was answered almost at once. She had to give her name and then a man's voice, quiet, drily precise came on the line.

'Mr Critchley? You don't know me. My name is Lois Carradine and you did some investigation work recently on my behalf, through Mrs Cassandra Foss?'

'Yes, Miss Carradine,' Critchley said, unable to believe his luck. 'How can I be of assistance to you?'

'Well, you know there was one of the names Mrs Foss gave you that you couldn't trace? William Young?'

'That's quite so, yes.'

'Well, I just thought of something. It's a long shot but . . . The thing is, William always wanted to be a vet. A veterinary surgeon? You know?'

'I'm quite familiar with the profession, Miss Carradine, having three cats of my own . . .' He laughed softly.

'Well, I wondered if you could check on the places vets train? I mean, I don't know anything about it, but . . .'

'A very good thought, Miss Carradine. I'm quite conversant with the training procedures and establishments. I'll look into it straight away. Now, where can I reach you, Miss Carradine?'

'At Craigie's Hotel. The number is . . .'

He copied it down carefully, smiling.

'I'll be sure to ring you back, Miss Carradine, just as soon as I'm able. Good day to you.'

He put the phone down, checked the address in the telephone directory and then, still smiling, dialled Cassandra Foss's number.

Cassandra's hand hovered over the white telephone receiver. One of her nails was chipped and she swore softly under her breath. No, it would never do. She stood up, quite decided, even though it was inconvenient. If she went now, as she fully intended to do, she'd have to miss Sasha's playtime, which meant that Nanny would be all pursed-lipped disapproval for days. And then she might not be back by the time Adrian returned. Well, she decided, they'd all have to manage without her for once. Calling to Philomena, she pulled on her coat and took the car keys from the pretty little hall table.

The rush hour was in full spate and it took her three-quarters of an hour to make a journey that should have taken twenty minutes at most. And then she spent an age searching for somewhere to park. Only as she ran up the ugly, mosaic-decorated steps of the hotel did it occur to her that Lois might not be in. If she wasn't, Cassandra vowed, she would simply lie down on the floor and scream blue bloody murder.

The lobby was all mean beige and muted cream, with ghastly stiff displays of plastic flowers. No, Cassandra corrected herself. It was not even beige. It was positively fawn. She marched up to the desk and asked for Lois Carradine. The young woman glanced towards the row of pigeon-holes from which the plastic tabs of keys dangled and said that she would ring the room.

'Who shall I say?'

'Just a friend.' Annoyed by the woman's look of hesitation, Cassandra produced her most disarming smile. 'I want to surprise her.'

'Very well.'

'Tell her,' Cassandra interrupted, 'I'll meet her in the bar. I suppose you do have a bar?'

'Yes, Madam.' The woman pointed to a pale neon sign.

'Super. Thanks so much.'

The bar was red and intended to be intimate. The effect was dingy. Shedding her coat, Cassandra perched on a high, squeaking bar stool, feeling like a cheap tart in a movie, and ordered Martinis thinking they would please Lois. The barman had absolutely no idea and she had to ask him for olives. She began to think that she had had a wasted journey after all, or that Lois was playing hard to get when she saw her, hovering nervously in the doorway.

'Darling! Do come. I've ordered Martinis. Thought they might remind you of home. Come on, let's go over there . . .' She pointed to a corner banquette, fulsomely padded. 'Bring the drinks, barman.' She slipped from her inelegant perch and linked an arm through Lois's. 'Come along. I won't hear a word of protest. And I'm absolutely gasping for a drink.'

Lois let herself be led across the room and sat down heavily.

'Now, let me look at you,' Cassandra said, swivelling towards her.

'How did you know where to find me?' Lois said. She did not know whether she was glad or sorry. She just felt awkward, a little scared.

'Ah, that's my secret. Wild horses wouldn't drag it out of me. Suffice it to say that you cannot walk out of my life without an explanation.'

'I . . . I told you I was going,' she said hesitantly.

The barman brought their drinks. Cassandra immediately ordered two more.

'You said no such thing. You mentioned something about did you ought to go, or something like that, but you did not tell me you were leaving. Nor, I may add, did you tell Ade. He was absolutely out of his mind with worry. And he got the rough edge of my tongue to boot, poor love. Cheers.'

'I can imagine,' Lois said, hoping that Adrian had been through a hell of guilt and uncertainty.

'So, what are you doing here? It's quite ghastly, Lois, really.'

'Shh,' she said, embarrassed, looking around her.

'Well it is . . .'

'I want to find a room. This is only temporary.'

'Too damn right. You are coming home with me.'

'No.' She shook her head vehemently. 'Oh it's very sweet of you, but I really can't impose.'

'Who said anything about imposing? It makes sense. Oh, Lois, I do so want you to. Please say you will.'

'Do you? Do you really?'

'Cross my heart and hope to die.' She sat back, a satisfied smile on her face, which faded slowly to be replaced by a look both petulant and contrite. 'I see. So Ade was right. You *are* miffed at me. He told me all about your little talk.'

'He did?'

'Mm. Ade tells me everything. I'm sorry, darling. I was just in a foul mood. I told you. I get bored. And when I do, I'm absolutely bloody. But you will forgive me, won't you?' She leaned closer to Lois, eager, liquid-eyed. Like a spaniel, Lois thought, or one of those Indian children you see in photographs, begging. She picked up her drink, sipped.

'I forgive you,' she said. 'How could I not? But I won't move back into your house.'

'Oh hell . . . That means you don't forgive me. Not deep down.'

'I do, honestly. There's nothing to forgive. Just a misunderstanding. But, truly, I don't want to be a nuisance.'

'But . . .' Cassandra started to protest.

'Come off it, Cassandra. Remember what you told me about that night you wanted to be alone with Adrian? If I'm not a nuisance, you must admit I'm inhibiting.'

'Oh, Ade can do without his little kinks for a while.'

'No. I mean it.'

Cassandra opened her eyes wide in studied surprise.

'I do believe you're adamant.'

'I am.'

'All right. Never let it be said that I can't accept defeat gracefully, but . . .' She paused while the bartender brought fresh drinks. 'You've got to get out of this place.

You must go to Brown's or the Dorchester. Or the Savoy. Have you ever been to the Savoy?'

'No. And I'm not about to go to any of those places . . .'

'But, darling, you can't stay here. You'll get rampant melancholia in forty-eight hours.'

Despite herself, Lois laughed. She felt herself softening, relaxing, giving herself up to the balm of Cassandra's attention and concern.

'Oh, Cassie, you're impossible. Now listen, I can't afford these places. They're definitely out.'

'Oh what a bore. It's not fair. Everyone should have money.'

'Besides, I want to find a place of my own.'

'All right. I'll see to it. There has to be someone . . .'

'No, Cassandra. Will you please stop? Listen to me, just for a minute.'

'Oh dear, you are frightfully fierce. I feel quite in awe of you.'

'I don't want a room in someone's apartment or to share. I want somewhere I can be by myself.'

'Is that wise?'

'I think it's necessary.'

'You don't want me to help at all? Not even the teensiest bit?'

'No. I appreciate it. I thank you, but no.'

'Very well. I give in. I'm defeated. You may do what you will with me.'

Lois smiled. She felt safe now, free to enjoy the best of Cassandra while remaining her own person, in control.

'It's a jolly good job for you, Lois Carradine, that I'm an honest woman.'

'Now what are you trying to tell me?'

'Well, a lesser mortal might use certain knowledge she just happens to have at her disposal to blackmail you.'

Lois felt her heart skip. Nothing escaped Cassandra. She

knew. She had guessed and she had got it out of Adrian somehow. Lois felt small and dirty.

'Look, I . . .'

'But not me. Much as I long to have you cosily under my own roof, I will not stoop to gain my heart's desire by immoral means. I'll tell you anyway, gratis and for free.'

'Tell me what?' Lois cried, scenting a reprieve, her heart still hammering.

'A little bit of news I got today concerning . . . one . . . William Young.'

Like a pedigree cat licking cream from its whiskers, Cassandra delicately sipped her Martini and smiled.

'William?' What was it she had thought? That all roads, everything lead to William. William was the answer, her best, perhaps her last chance. 'What about William?'

'I know where he's been. I don't know where he is, but I know where he's been. And the divinely discreet Mr Critchley is hot and panting on his elusive trail. Now say you don't adore me.'

Lois opened her mouth to say that she had put Mr Critchley on that trail when she realized that he could not possibly have made any enquiries yet. She stared at Cassandra, open-mouthed.

'Do close your mouth, Lois. You look like an absurd goldfish.'

'What . . . where has he been? I don't understand you.'

'If I tell you, you do realize I'm being . . .'

'Please, Cassandra . . .' Lois grabbed her wrist, jerking it so that Martini slopped onto the table. 'Stop teasing. This is important.'

Slowly, her face closing into a mask, Cassandra eased her wrist from Lois's grip.

'So I see.'

'Where has he been?' Lois insisted, her voice breaking.

'In a word, Redpaths.'

'Redpaths?'

'Uh-huh.'

'Where's that?'

Cassandra told her, succinctly.

'Oh my God,' Lois said.

When the doctors had finished their rounds, a little after eleven a.m., Staff Nurse June Thornton took the mail around, distributing it among the patients. On Amanda's bed she placed three envelopes and a square brown box. Amanda levered herself up on her elbows, her midriff protesting, and opened a card from her father, repeating his promise to visit, a card from Vanessa Hunter, with a row of sprawling Xs and her bank statement. She lay back against the pillows, the untouched box on her stomach. Her stomach tensed. She thought she had detected movement, coming from the box, something alive . . . She stared at it, a cold sweat standing on her upper lip.

Passing back down Ward Seven South, Staff Thornton paused at the foot of Amanda's bed.

'You haven't opened your parcel, Nurse. Come along.'

'No . . . Please . . . Could you do it?'

'Me? Why on earth . . .'

'*Please*, Staff.'

'Oh all right. Though I warn you,' she said cheerfully, tugging at the sealing tape, 'If it's anything good to eat, I shall want the lion's share.'

Amanda managed a wan smile. The staff nurse's competent fingers gently raised the close-fitting lid.

'Oh!'

'What is it?'

'There must be some mistake . . . I'll . . .'

'What?'

Her body protesting, pain flowing down her thighs, Amanda forced herself up and reached for the box.

'No, really Nurse, I don't think . . .'

Their hands collided. The box dropped to the floor, spilling damp soil across the polished wood blocks, and an uncounted number of worms, slewing and squirming in a knot.

Five

'Is that Andrew Mercer?'

'Yes.'

'This is Lois Carradine.'

Tension cracked down the line. Lois held the receiver too tightly. All colour drained from Andy's face, making it look ashen, unhealthy.

'How did you . . . get my number?'

'I hired a private detective.' She had decided to be completely honest, to answer any questions fully and honestly. Just so long as he did not hang up or tell her to get lost.

He made a noise, a sort of grunt. Maybe laughter, perhaps not.

'You must've wanted it very much.'

'I did. Andy, I want to see you. I want to talk.'

The silence was long and got longer. The line crackled, became silent again.

'All right,' he said.

'Oh, thank you.' She could not keep the relief from showing in her voice. 'I appreciate it, I really do.'

Andy did not know how to reply. Her accent, the warmth and rush of emotion in her voice confused him. It was like talking to an alien, like stepping outside the routine of his life and yet, in another way, it did not feel at all odd. In fact, it was a relief. He cleared his throat nervously.

'What was that?'

'Nothing, I just . . .'

'Well, can we meet somewhere? When?'

'I don't know.'

'I'd like for us to meet somewhere we can talk, somewhere sort of private, you know?'

Andy thought that was best, too. Or he went along with it.

'You could come here,' he said. 'If you want.'

'Oh, I'd like that very much, Andy. Thank you.' She tried to keep her voice steady, not to sound too eager. 'When would be a good time for you? I can manage any time, almost.'

He thought. He looked up the stairs to the door of the room.

'It doesn't matter. When you like.'

'Tomorrow then. What time? And you'd better tell me how to get there. Are you near a tube?'

Andy answered automatically, told her what time he got home from work, how to get there.

'I really appreciate this, Andy. I'll look forward to it.'

'All right.'

' 'Bye, Andy.'

'Cheerio.'

He hung up. He stood passively in the hall, feeling an unfamiliar calm. It was a strange feeling, but not unpleasant. The impression that he had somehow stepped into a new dimension persisted. His head felt clear, almost light. It was as though he had been waiting for that call all his life. For years, anyway, he thought as he climbed the stairs and slipped into the room.

He had forgotten the young man. He was propped on the bed, partially unclothed, smoking a cigarette. The good, easy feeling shrank to the back of Andy's head.

'You're obviously in demand,' the stranger said, mashing out his cigarette. 'Mind you, I can see why.' He smiled, shifted on the bed, inviting Andy to join him. 'Who was it? A regular boyfriend?'

Andy shook his head impatiently.

'It was a girl,' he said, not knowing why he bothered to

answer, only that suddenly the words seemed loose in him, ready to spill out. 'Someone I knew years ago, when I was a kid.' He sat on the edge of the bed, let the stranger take hold of his cold hand.

'You bi?' he asked, turning Andy's hand lightly in his.

'What?'

'Bisexual. Are you?'

'No.' Andy shook his head again. 'I can't make it with girls.'

'You're not doing too well with me, either, sitting there with all your gear on.' He tugged at Andy's hand, trying to pull him down into an embrace.

'No,' Andy said, getting up. 'I tried. I tried a lot but I couldn't ever do it. Because of her, the girl that rang. She made me . . . Once, when I was a kid I mucked around with another boy. William Young. But that wasn't important. It's just that when I go with a girl . . .' Andy stopped, hearing his own voice. It seemed that he had not talked so much in years. It was an odd feeling and, for a moment, he had forgotten that he was not alone.

'I'm sure your life story's fascinating,' the stranger said, making the bed creak, 'but that's not what I came here for. Come on . . .'

Andy turned and looked at him, his movements slow, his expression dreamy.

'I feel a bit daft lying here . . .' the stranger said, gesturing at his partly undressed body. 'I mean, some people would find it sexy . . . I've had no complaints . . .' Andy's eyes moved slowly to the red-glowing filaments of the gas fire. 'If I don't turn you on, you might as well say so.'

Andy walked towards the fire.

'I'm sorry,' he said. 'You'd better go.'

'Oh, charming!'

The bed springs squeaked protestingly. Andy squatted down, staring into the fire, extending his hands towards it, to warm them. He heard the stranger dressing, zipping his fly, cursing as he dropped a shoe.

'If there's one thing I despise,' he said, 'it's a cock-teaser.'

Andy looked at him, not really understanding why he was so angry. The good feeling expanded when he looked into the fire, uncoiled through his brain.

'Well, thanks for sod all.' The stranger went out, slamming the door, clattering down the stairs, slamming the front door so that the glass in Andy's window rattled.

He turned back to the fire and said, aloud:

'I feel . . .' But he did not know the words for what he felt. He sat on the floor, drawing his legs up, wrapping his arms around them, his chin on his knees. The firelight put patches of false colour on his face. 'Lois . . .' he said. 'Lois is coming here,' he told the fire and the good feeling grew stronger.

She was crying. With relief, gratitude? She did not know. All that and more, she guessed. But they were good tears, the sort you can smile through. She was smiling, too, even as she mopped at the tears with a wad of tissue.

Andy was not William, she knew that, but after Cassandra had dropped her mini-bombshell, the need to talk, to see one of them had persisted. She had to do it, just to see if she could, just to make sense of the whole nightmare crazy trip. She had to see what it was like.

Lacking William, she had immediately ruled out Amanda. She was still scared of what might happen if she went anywhere near Amanda. And then Vanessa. It was harder to admit why she ruled out Vanessa. Because she was successful, pretty and had a hard, glossy look about her. Because, really, Vanessa had never liked her. Which left the twins and Andy. It made her feel creepy that the twins were still together, living together, studying together.

Their closeness had always overwhelmed her. She had been so alone and they, they had no idea what loneliness was. Possibly, if the twins had been split up, she would have approached one of them, but as it was, apart from anything else, she did not want to be out-numbered.

So she arrived at Andy by a process of elimination. He was not William but then he did not seem as daunting as the others. After all, Andy had liked her. Andy had been her friend when all the others were avoiding her because of William's birthday treat. Sure, he had ruined that by making her take off her bra and show him . . . But that did not seem so very awful now. She could understand his curiosity, if not his desire. And it would now give her the advantage, surely, of embarrassment? She knew, she remembered clearly that though Andy could be stubborn to get his own way, he couldn't take pressure. She had never seen anyone cry like him after that game of doctors and nurses, when she had held his flaccid little thing in a pair of tweezers and threatened to cut it off . . .

Then a terrible thought had come to her: she had been crying like that ever since her thirteenth birthday. Ever since her life had been destroyed, she had lived with that kind of desolation. It was a scary kind of feeling, knowing that she and the boy Andy had that terrible weeping in common. She wished that she could discuss that knowledge with Mr Stryker for it confused her and made her feel . . .

She had made her plans carefully. There would be no sudden, shocking confrontation. She had thought of writing to him, but that seemed too risky. Letters could so easily be ignored or destroyed. She would answer any and all questions truthfully. If he hung up on her, she did not know what she would do.

But he had not. He had said he would see her. He had invited her over. And she was laughing, laughing through her tears.

*

Amanda felt that she had been caught up in a chain-reaction over which she had no control. Staff Nurse Thornton, after she had swept up the mess from the ward floor, told the Sister about the parcel and Amanda's reaction. Sister questioned Amanda, but since this only increased her distress and elicited no answers, she contacted the Sister Tutor in charge of Amanda's training set. This woman, Sister Wilson, had already heard the other girls talking about the incident of the dead spider. To her it was obvious that someone was harassing Amanda Beatty and in a particularly cruel and effective way. Her first thought was to look for the culprit – some enemy or rival – among the other trainees in her set. She talked to several of the girls and questioned Tracey closely. This both reassured and alarmed Sister Wilson. She felt confident that none of the set bore any vindictive grudge against Amanda, but Tracey's account of her behaviour at the Hallowe'en party added to the general picture of distress and nervous strain. As gently and as tactfully as possible, she talked to Amanda, explaining these 'jokes', as she thought it best to call them, were hindering her recovery and affecting her training. Therefore the hospital was concerned. Amanda ought to tell her all she knew, whatever she suspected. Faced with monosyllabic denials, Sister Wilson said in that case Amanda should inform the police and if she persisted in refusing to do this, then the hospital may have to do so on her behalf. These incidents were affecting the other girls. A slew of worms on the ward floor was scarcely consistent with hospital hygiene or good for the other patients. Amanda, tearful, pointed out that she was not responsible and repeated that she could not explain how or why these things were happening to her.

Sister Wilson arranged for her to be moved into a single room off the main ward and requested that her post be vetted: anything suspicious should be handed to the nurse in charge. Then she raised the whole bothersome matter with Amanda's doctor, who had already talked to the girl and who confirmed that there was cause for concern. Doctor Metcalfe referred the matter to Assistant Matron Hume, who had special responsibility for staff. So it was that, one afternoon, the assistant matron made an unscheduled appearance on Ward Seven South. Assistant matron, by virtue of her office, terrified Amanda. Consequently, the visit caused her more distress, which Assistant Matron Hume took as proof that there was good cause to be worried. She was, however, a cautious woman. She was determined that no breath of scandal should emanate from *her* hospital. Therefore, before contacting the police, she decided that the girl's parents should be seen and, being informed of John Beatty's impending visit, she briefed Sister Wilson to lay the whole matter before him.

He stood there at last, beside her bed, tall, rumpled, his hair flecked with silver. Amanda threw her arms around him and wept on his familiar shoulder. The roughness of tweed, the smell of pipe tobacco were more than a comfort: they were the fabric of safety itself. Amanda clung to him, tried to tell him through her alarming tears that she felt safe at last, that she was actually happy.

She seemed to him never to have grown, become a young woman, leading an independent life of her own. Her hair was still baby-soft and silky. The pallor, the red-rimmed eyes, above all the darting hint of fear in her eyes all belonged to the little girl he had tried to protect from the war of his marriage. Had tried and failed, he thought, an accusing lump in his throat.

He held her small hand tightly in both of his and saw her grow calmer as she answered his many questions about her injuries, her progress. She was able to reassure him, for he had uncritical respect for any medical knowledge and to him Amanda's word was as good as any doctor's. He patted her hand, sought automatically for his pipe and then remembered that he could not smoke.

'Well,' he said, 'feel up to a bit of a talk now?'

'Yes, Daddy. Of course. I'm sorry. I just seem to be very emotional. Some patients are. It's the shock . . .'

'Of course, of course. Perfectly understandable. You just take things easy.'

'I am. I just lie here . . .' She smiled and he thought her brave and beautiful and wished that he did not have to ask what now worried him.

'I wondered if you'd heard anything about me seeing sister . . . . your tutor . . . um . . . They said at the desk she wanted to see me, after my visit.' Her hand fluttered and clenched in his. She turned her head away. He saw her delicate throat working as she swallowed and wanted to kick himself for his clumsiness. He should have kept it to himself, dealt with it alone. It was just that he hated going into any situation without being properly prepared. 'I'm sorry, sweetheart. I shouldn't have mentioned it.'

'No.' She jerked her head round sharply. 'I want to tell you about it. I want you to help me. You're the only person I *can* talk to.'

'Of course, I'll help. You know that. What is it? Are you in some kind of trouble?' He looked grave and bewildered at the same time. She had always been such a good child. It was inconceivable to him that she could be guilty of any breach of discipline or etiquette.

'It's . . . things have been happening to me, Daddy. Horrible things. The hospital want me to go to the police and I . . .'

'All right, all right. Please, Amanda, don't cry again. Just tell me about it. Start at the beginning . . .'

She did not know where the beginning was. She feared that it lay in the past, years ago, and she did not want to face that. Not yet. So she told him about the spider and the mysterious woman who had left a message. About how her nightmare had come true and suddenly, there in the open street, in the winter rain, Lois Carradine had called her name. And what Jason Shillingworth had said and how she was afraid, horribly afraid that it might be true.

He heard her out, listened to it all, right up to the arrival of the sod of earth, squirming and crawling with worms. He heard it all and it carried his mind back, reinforced his impressions of her as a little girl. Two incidents in particular stood out, sharp as snapshots untouched by time. A spring morning, the first of the year and he was out in the garden at Olton, digging. Amanda watching him, pensive and pretty at his side. He turned over a heavy clod of earth from which a thick worm slithered.

Kill it, Daddy. Please.

It won't hurt you, Lois had said. He saw her bend down, reaching for the worm, and he heard again Amanda's piercing screams. And then Marge's voice, calling, raucous, from the window. The memory blotted out with Marge's voice, as though a shutter descended in his mind. Then it was Amanda's birthday and Marge was making no effort, no effort at all. His daughter's party had been put back to the weekend because of Marge's precious job. Or so she had led him to believe at the time. He had watched Amanda opening her cards and had seen her blanch at one and thrust it away from her. It was a pretty thing – he could still see it quite clearly – a reproduction of a Victorian illustration. Little Miss Muffet, eating her curds and whey. And when, in an attempt to create some sense of occasion, he had set the cards out on the mantleshelf, Amanda had begged him not to display that one. She could not bear to look at the large spider descending towards Miss Muffet. So, telling her she was silly, he had folded it back to the printed greeting and the childlessly scrawled message:

Have a terrific day, love from Lois XX.

That was the day he had caught Marge out in her lie. She had been to London, spent the day with Douglas Young, her lover, returning laden with clothes, a party dress for Amanda which he, in the only rage he could remember ever feeling, had torn to tatters while Lois and a trembling Amanda watched.

'Daddy? Daddy, what is it?'

'Nothing. Sorry. Nothing at all. I was just trying . . . um . . . to remember Lois Carradine.'

'Oh Daddy, you couldn't . . . you couldn't possibly have forgotten her.'

'No,' he said sadly, shaking his head. Though he had tried. Because it was then that he had decided that he must divorce Marge, get her out of his life. The terrible thing that had happened at Lois's party later that year had impressed him less than the other parents, he remembered. He had just wanted to get Amanda away, out of it. He recalled Marge laughing her cruel, bitter laugh and saying: *Whatever they did to that little bitch, she asked for it.*

'I had a lot on my mind at the time, sweetheart. Your mother and I were . . . um . . . anyway, I never thought you had anything to do with what happened to that poor girl.'

She wanted to say that he had never listened, never asked, and at the same time she wished that she could take refuge in his illusion.

'But Daddy I did,' she said, her voice shaking. 'And now she wants revenge.'

'Oh come now, Amanda. That's nonsense. It's not like you to be . . . er . . . fanciful.'

'Daddy, I am not imagining this. You can ask the twins . . .'

'Well then, if that is the case, the hospital is absolutely right. You must go to the police. They have a duty to protect you. We all do . . .'

'I can't,' she wailed. 'Oh don't you see I can't?'

He touched her shoulder, smoothed a strand of hair from her averted cheek.

'You must,' he said gently, but without any hint of doubt.

'You said you'd help me . . .' Amanda said, refusing to look at him.

'Of course, in any way . . .'

'Then tell Sister Wilson. Tell Sister Wilson that it will stop and that . . . that it will make me ill to go to the police.'

'How can I tell her it will stop when . . .' A sudden, frightening thought occurred to him. He took her chin in his hand and turned her face towards him. 'Amanda, have you told me the whole truth? Everything?'

'Oh, Daddy, surely you don't think I'd lie? Not to you.'

'No, of course not. I believe you . . . that's why I can't . . . um . . . allow you to be at risk.'

'I think it will stop,' she said urgently. 'I think she's finished with me now. You'll see, she'll concentrate on the others, one by one . . .'

'You're just saying that to persuade me . . .'

'No. Listen. I've thought it all out. She wants to punish us all and, for some reason, she started with me. I've had two parcels. I've seen her. But the others have received only one . . . Now she'll concentrate on them.'

'But if she tried to kill you . . . No, it's out of the question.'

'Daddy,' she said, her voice suddenly becoming low and strong, commanding him to listen. 'I tried to kill her.'

The words, of course, were nonsense, silly, childish boasting talk, a form of sickness, but nothing to be taken seriously.

'Now, Amanda . . .' he began, aware that he was floundering.

She continued to stare at him, to fix him with her eyes.

'We all tried. What we said at the time, that it got out of hand . . .'

'Amanda, I will not let you distress yourself like this. I will not listen to . . .'

'You have to. Look at me. I'm calmer now than I've

been for weeks, because I'm telling you. At long last. Daddy, it was never a joke. We planned it. We were so afraid of her that we would have done anything to make her stop. We were . . . mad, if you like. Isn't there something called collective madness?' He nodded, his face working, trying not to hear, to believe what she was saying. He did not recognize her. She seemed older, a stranger. 'Well, maybe it was that. I don't know. I know that we did not think of the consequences. We didn't care. When we walked out of the house that night, we didn't know and we didn't care if she was dead or alive. But if anyone had asked us, I think we would have said that we hoped she was dead. I know I did. Andy imitated her, I remember. He did this funny little dance . . . jigging around like . . .'

'Stop it, darling, please.'

'. . . just like when we first saw her. She scared us all then. And we laughed . . . Daddy, don't you see?' She reached for his hands and clasped them. 'If they make me go to the police. I will have to tell them all this. It's not just me, it's all of us. I don't have the right. I don't want it.'

'Amanda, I don't know . . . um I don't know what to believe . . . You don't understand what you're asking. Because of something you did as a child which was not, incidentally, murder, which is what you are talking about . . . No, let me finish . . . You want me to stand back and let her kill you? It's preposterous . . .'

'Oh she won't kill us,' Amanda said in that same certain, strong voice that grated on his ear. 'Lois is far too clever for that. She just wants to make us suffer.'

'You can't be sure of that.'

'I *know* her. We all do. Maybe the others will have accidents, too, but she won't do anything that might harm herself. She just wants to torture us . . .'

'Torture you? Whatever for . . .?'

'Daddy, I'm pretty, aren't I?'

'You know you are . . .'

'Just think what she must look like . . .'

She waited, she saw the effect of her words working on him. He only remembered the details of Lois's injuries vaguely, but they were sufficient to make him want to push the whole idea away.

'Daddy, I'll make you a promise. If there's anything else, anything at all, I'll go to the police. I really will. But she's finished with me now, I know. She's done her worst.' She put her hands over her face, her shoulders shaking.

'Oh, darling, please . . .'

He felt so inadequate, so helpless. He did not know what to believe. Certainly he could not accept that Amanda had ever done anything out of malice. Nothing cruel or bad. But she was suffering. He could see that and he could not bear it.

'All right. In return for your promise, I'll tell Sister Wilson that I won't countenance them calling in the police.'

'And when they let me out of here, I can come and stay with you? I know it's not very convenient but I'll feel safe there, with you. And she won't be able to find me. Oh please say I can.'

'Of course, of course.' He hugged her tight and felt her grow calm again, a small child, his princess in his arms.

'Thank you, Daddy. I can't tell you what a relief . . .'

'Shush now. No more.'

'You do promise? Promise faithfully?'

'I promise.'

She lay back on the pillows and sighed.

'I do love you. I knew you would make it all right.'

He smiled and hoped his expression hid the fear that had rooted and begun to grow in him.

Sister Wilson seemed to him impossibly young: a mere girl. He considered asking to speak to someone older, someone in charge and realized that to do so would give offence. Apart from anything else, she was in charge. In spite of her youth, this girl was responsible for Amanda's training and welfare.

'I'm sorry, Sister,' he said. 'This is very difficult for me. It's all been a bit of a shock.'

'Take your time, Mr Beatty. There's no rush. We only want to help Amanda, you know. She's a good girl . . .'

'Yes, I know. I do know that. I love her very, very much. I've always felt that . . . um . . . that perhaps Amanda suffered more than anyone when her mother and I were divorced. I've never felt that we were good parents . . . though I've always tried . . .'

'Oh you've nothing to worry about there. Amanda's a credit to you. She's a hard worker, bright and intelligent. It's only this business that . . .'

'Yes. I've talked to her. My daughter, Miss . . . er . . . Sister . . . is consumed with guilt. Perhaps pathologically.'

The sister's eyes widened. He thought for one terrible moment that she was going to laugh in his face.

'I'm sorry, Mr Beatty, but I don't quite follow . . .'

'Because of something that happened years ago, when my wife and I . . . my ex-wife and I were still married. A childish prank . . . a joke that got out of hand. Really, it was nothing. But another girl was hurt . . . and um . . . Amanda feels responsible.'

'She told you this?'

'She made what I suppose I can only call a confession. I should have realized. I blame myself. You see this . . . thing . . . has . . . um . . . obviously been preying on her mind for years. I've not seen as much of her as I should . . .'

'Excuse me just a minute, Mr Beatty, but what has all this got to do with those awful parcels?'

He shook his head, cracked his knuckles loudly.

'She believes that they are being sent to punish her, to make her suffer for her part in this . . . incident I mentioned. I believe . . . this is very difficult for me, Sister, but I believe that it is just possible that Amanda sent those parcels to herself.'

'But she couldn't have! She was in hospital when one . . .'

'The point is, Sister, that this is definitely not a matter for the police.'

'Then who do you suggest . . .?'

'A psychiatrist. I think my daughter is badly in need of psychiatric help.'

Sister Wilson sat back in her chair. The man appeared to be sincere, was certainly upset but he seemed to be talking about someone else, another case altogether.

'You're saying that Amanda is upsetting herself?'

'Exactly. Look, I do know what I'm talking about. I trained in psychology. I took my . . . um . . . teaching degree later. I'm concerned with student welfare and I've been a Samaritan for some years now . . .'

'Look, Mr Beatty,' Sister Wilson interrupted him firmly, 'I'm not doubting your ability, just questioning why you think that Amanda's present highly nervous state should be a psychiatric matter. Personally . . .'

'Her present state is caused by guilt, unresolved guilt over a childhood . . . misdemeanour which, by the by, she is now exaggerating out of all proportion. She believes that the girl who was injured in this prank is now trying to revenge herself.' Seeing the continued look of doubt on the nurse's face, he changed tack. 'Look, Sister, I'm not asking that you take my word for it. I am forbidding you to go to the police because to do so will only cause my daughter more distress. I beg you to get her to a psychiatrist. You must have some in the hospital?'

'Certainly but . . . But what if these parcels go on arriving?'

'Ah . . . there I can help you. Amanda assures me that she does not think there will be any more. This, to my mind, suggests that she is responsible for them, though she will have no conscious memory of her actions. But the fact that she is reassuring herself and me that they will cease is tantamount to an acknowledgement that her cry for help has been heard. Because that's all it is, Sister. Her collapse, the accident, are cries for help. She wants help badly and this is the only way she can tell us. I am sure there will be no more parcels if she gets proper help.'

Sister Wilson heaved a sigh. There might be something in it, though she could not believe that Amanda . . .

'I can't promise anything, Mr Beatty. It's not in my hands. Look, what I'll have to do is to report the substance of our conversation to the assistant matron. She, finally, will make the decision. I think that she will probably want to see you . . . Are you staying in London?'

'Just for the weekend, yes. I have to go back to Durham early on Monday morning. I planned to see as much of Amanda . . .'

'Very well.' Sister Wilson stood up. 'I'll speak to the assistant matron and arrange for you to see her tomorrow.'

'Thank you.' John Beatty got to his feet. 'I hope you don't think I'm being too hard on Amanda? I find it all very painful . . .'

'Of course not. You want to help her just as much as we do. It may be that your insights will help to speed that along, but I can't pretend to you that I don't find it all a bit . . .'

'Far-fetched? Yes, I can understand that. But I know my daughter and I am certain that she is deluding herself into a form of persecution mania. Do you find it any easier to believe that someone after, eight, ten years, would seek revenge for a childish prank?'

'No, I must say . . .'

'There you are then. Oh, and Sister, this is in strictest confidence as far as Amanda is concerned. She is afraid that people will find out about the incident.'

'What exactly was it, Mr Beatty?' Sister Wilson asked, moving to the door. 'It may help us to know.'

'Oh a prank . . . I don't remember clearly. They played some silly joke on a girl at her birthday party and she got burned. It was really nothing, nothing at all. But to Amanda . . .' He gestured vaguely, indicating the enormity the incident had assumed in her mind.

'Well, thank you very much, Mr Beatty. I expect I'll see you tomorrow.'

'Thank *you*, Sister.'

She opened the door for him.

'And not a word to Amanda?'

'Of course not.'

'It's because I know her to be incapable of anything . . . bad . . . that I was able to see what was going on in her mind.'

'Don't upset yourself, Mr Beatty. We'll sort something out.'

He nodded vaguely and went away down the corridor. Sister Wilson remained in the doorway, watching him. Either, she thought, he was as nutty as a fruitcake, or he had stumbled on something much more disturbing than any of them had expected. Still, she could not see Amanda Beatty as a persecution maniac.

She wore a big hat again. Cassandra had forbidden the hats, of which Lois had several, insisting that her hair, if properly arranged, provided sufficient camouflage. But the hat gave Lois confidence and a style which, though not to Cassandra's fashionable taste, was at least her own. She needed confidence and style, everything the social armoury of dress and manners could supply her, for she was profoundly nervous. Her nervousness was increased by the fact that she could not imagine the meeting for which she had so carefully prepared. She had always been able to conjure up the faces of the children who had scarred and maimed her with great precision, but now Andy eluded her. His face in particular remained a blank oval, misted over in her mind's eye. She panicked at the thought that she would be unable to recognize him. She did not know what she would say, how they might proceed together. And the ball was firmly in her court since it was she who had said she wanted to talk.

She was ready too early, inevitably, so she pulled off the hat, careful to disturb her hair as little as possible, and sat down near the window, her journal on her knee.

I've moved. It's not a proper room of my own but the hotel is smaller and cheaper and because I said I wanted to stay a month at least, they gave me preferential rates. The hotel is in a district called Pimlico, near to Victoria Station. It has no elevator or room service, but there is a dining room where you can have breakfast. Most of the other guests are men, commercial travellers, I understand, and people up to see a show or go to a conference or something.

I'm going to see Andy. I'm sitting here all dressed up, ready to go and it's too early. I can't remember what he looked like or imagine how he will look. Do I really want to do this? I thought a while ago, as I was getting dressed, that what I was doing was grotesque. I prepared myself with all the care and nervousness of a girl going on her first real date! Some date! That's what's grotesque about it. That and the fact that clothes, no matter how pretty, can't conceal the fact, the reality of my face. Still I've done everything I can – make-up the way Cassandra showed me, hair, hat, everything.

It all comes down to this one question: do I really want to go through with this? What is it for? You've asked me often enough, Mr Stryker, and now that I'm actually going to do it, I still can't answer your question. Wish me luck instead, huh?

But it did not cross her mind to cancel the arrangement or simply not turn up. At the appointed time she left the hotel and walked to Victoria Station. From there she took a tube which carried her south of the river and changed, after a long, nerve-racking wait, onto a bus that crawled through heavy traffic, crammed with returning, tired workers. Lois, in her hat and smart new clothes, stuck out like a sore thumb. When the other travellers heard her accent, asking the conductor to tell her when she reached the stop Andy had indicated, several people offered help and so she alighted at the right place, found her bearings and set off again on foot. She reached the road without difficulty and slowly approached the house, ticking off the numbers mentally until she arrived at the right one. Its neglected appearance, the straggling, dusty privet hedge and untidy dustbins depressed her. In a way she thought it a suitably arid and hopeless setting for such a meeting. The doorbell shrilled under her finger and she stepped back a little, waiting. A light came on, just visible through the dirty panes of glass set in the door. She heard footsteps, saw a shadow approaching, obstructing the light. The door opened.

'Lois?'

'Andy?'

He stepped back, opening the door wider. He was almost concealed behind it. She stepped into the cold, ugly hall, looking around her, not at him:

'It's up the stairs, first on the left.'

His voice was light with traces of a soft, Scottish intonation she remembered hearing in his mother's voice. She walked forward, her legs feeling like jelly, and climbed the staircase. The door to the room was ajar. She pushed it wide and went in. The light was too dim to show much of the room. It seemed to shade off into darkness. She had an impression of the room as hostile, not just to her, but to all its many temporary tenants who had not loved it or tried to make it their own. She turned at the sound of the door closing and looked at Andy properly for the first time.

He was taller than she and very slender. His hair was fashionably cut, mid-brown, and the face that she was suddenly able to remember had altered and matured. What had been narrow and peaky-looking as a child had become handsomely bony. His dark eyes surveyed her.

'Do you want to take off your coat or something?' He stepped aside as though made uncomfortable by her scrutiny. 'It'll warm up in here. Anyway, you won't get the benefit later if you keep it on.'

'Okay. Thanks.'

She took her coat off and handed it to him. While he hung it on the back of the door she drew instinctively closer to the gas fire.

'That's the only comfortable chair,' he said. 'Sit down.'

'What about you?'

'Oh, I can sit on the bed or on this.' He flapped a hand at a straight-back chair by the table as he moved away into the shadows. 'I didn't know what to get so I got a mixture. There's beer or wine, some Cinzano . . .'

She saw that he was standing in a little kitchen area, bottles and cans lined up on a small draining board.

'You shouldn't have gone to any trouble,' she said, sitting gingerly in the chair.

'What would you like?'

'Wine would be good.'

'Red or white?'

'Red, please.'

'I hope it's okay. I don't know anything about wine.' He struggled with a corkscrew.

'Neither do I,' she said and tried to laugh but the sound stuck in her throat.

He drew the cork with an efficient plop and poured some wine into a smeared tumbler. He brought it to her, held it out at arm's length.

'Thanks.'

He moved away again and she heard him open a can of beer and drink noisily, as though his throat was dry. She took a sip of the wine, which was too cold, and set the glass down near the fire.

'Okay?' he asked, walking to the bed.

'Fine.'

He sat on the bed, his hands clasping the beer can between his knees. They spoke together.

'So, what are you . . .'

'Do you want to . . .'

'Sorry,' Lois said.

'No, you go on.'

'No, really, I was just . . .'

'Do you want to take off your hat?'

In a reflex action, she put up her hand to touch the sweeping-down brim which shaded her face.

'No, I don't think so. I was going to say how are you? What are you doing now?'

'I'm okay. I work as a chippie.'

'Chippie? What's that?'

'A carpenter.'

'Oh. You were always good with wood and stuff. Do you remember that sled you built?'

He blushed darkly, nodded.

'What about you?'

'Oh, nothing. I'm just having a sort of vacation. When I go back home I guess I'll take some classes. I don't know, really.'

He extended his legs, crossed his ankles, one foot tapping the air nervously.

'You been here long?' she asked.

'A year, bit more . . . Look, I wish . . . Take off that hat. I can't see you properly. It makes me feel odd talking to someone I can't see.'

Do you want to see, she thought. She opened her mouth

to refuse or to warn him but something made her close it again. Without saying anything, she reached up with both hands and lifted the hat free of her head. She twisted a little and placed it on the floor, beside her chair. She did not want to look at him but knew that she must. She picked up her glass, drank and then, at last, lifted her head as bravely as she could, and faced him.

He looked at her with no alteration of expression. She saw his eyes moving, exploring her face. She began to feel uncomfortable. Not ashamed or scared, but uncomfortable, simply because she felt exposed. His appraisal made her feel shy and awkward.

'Did we do that to you?' He spoke each word slowly, separately, as though they did not belong together in a sentence. She was about to answer him when she saw that he was crying.

For once in her life, Lois did nothing. She sat quite still and silent and let him cry. He did not do so noisily. It was as though the tears that streaked his face and dripped onto his chest and lap were simply being drained out of him. She knew that she was in the presence of something necessary and inevitable. She knew, also, that he wept a little for her, but this gave her no comfort and certainly no sense of triumph. His tears were familiar, for so she had cried often in her life when she faced her own ugliness and helplessness and saw that there was no hope and no way of altering her fate. After a while he began to sniff and rubbed his hand across his face. He got up and went to a chest of drawers. When he sat down again he had a large handkerchief in his hand, with which he dried his face and blew his nose, but still the tears did not stop. He simply mopped them up. Suddenly, Lois began to talk, though she could not have said what prompted her or why she chose that moment to say what she did.

'I had plastic surgery but the guy who did it was drunk or a butcher or both. He sort of made it worse. Daddy sued him and eventually we got some compensation. They gave me a glass eye but it hurts me and anyway it wouldn't fool anyone. I prefer to wear the patch. Daddy used to say it made me look dashing, like a lady pirate. My Daddy killed himself, and Mommy too, in a car crash. He was an alcoholic by then. I got the money, and then my Grandma died and she was quite a rich lady. I'm seeing a man here in London – he's supposed to be very good – and maybe he'll try to do some new skin grafts. I'm scared of doctors and stuff, though I keep telling myself it won't hurt because I don't have too much feeling on that side of my face anyway. The nerves got damaged somehow. Sometimes when I scratch my cheek there, I can feel it down here, on my jawline. That used to amuse me at first when I was a kid, but now . . .' She shrugged. 'Anyway, maybe Mr Valentine will be able to do something. Patch me up so people don't turn away from me . . .' She paused, looking at Andy. Her throat felt very dry and she drained off the sharp-tasting wine. 'Okay if I help myself?' she asked and got up and crossed the room without waiting for his answer. She poured more wine into her glass. 'Crying doesn't help any, Andy,' she said. 'Though sometimes it's necessary. But don't waste your tears on me. I've shed enough of my own.'

'I'm not,' he said, his voice thick. 'I can't help it.'

'It's okay.' She brought the bottle with her, set it down near the fire and sat again. 'Funny, I've imagined meeting you – not especially you, all of you or one of you – so many times and the one thing I never thought of was that you might cry. I thought you might be scared or angry but never . . .'

'It's because I'm ashamed,' he interrupted. 'Not just of what we did, looking at you, but everything . . .'

'I guess I can understand that. Tell me about it, Andy. When you can.'

'Tell you what?'

'What happened after I blacked out.'

'I don't know . . . I mean I can't . . .'

'Can't remember? Oh come on, Andy. Those tears say you remember everything. Too much for comfort, I guess.'

'No, I mean . . . I don't know when you blacked out.'

'I came round,' she said in a flat, expressionless voice. 'There was someone with me. Not the whole bunch of you. Just one. I think it was just one. But I couldn't see . . . Was it you, Andy?'

'No.' He shook his head vehemently. 'No, it wasn't me.'

'And are you going to protect him or her or are you going to tell me?'

'It was after . . .' He gulped, cleared his throat noisily. 'After you . . . the big lantern . . . you remember?' She nodded her head gravely. She not only remembered, she could still feel it and smell it: molten wax and dry candlesmoke, singed hair, seared flesh, burning, the smell of pain and the sensation that her whole head had caught fire. 'You were very still, just lying there . . . I suppose that must have been when . . .'

'Yes,' she said, 'and after that?'

'William said . . . William told us to wait outside in the hall.'

There was no surprise in it, no shock or relief. Something settled in her, something came together and balanced. She had always known that it must have been William.

'It was very quiet,' Andy went on. 'The kids were nervous, especially Jason. You know how he always was. Amanda wanted to go home. We heard William rewind the tape and start it up again. That's all. He came out a few minutes later and we all went home.'

And in those minutes, he had taken a candle, flaming, and driven it deep into her eye. William. All her instincts had been right.

'Thanks for telling me.'

'I'm sorry . . .'

She shook her head. It was too late for that. Too late for everything, except William.

'Do you know where he is?'

'No. I've not seen any of them since. We went to Scotland. When I came back down here . . . I didn't want to see them.' He blew his nose again. It was very red but his tears had stopped. 'Funny thing, though, Julian rang me up a few days ago. Out of the blue. Just like you. In fact, when you rang I thought it must be Julian, or one of them.'

'Why did he call you? After all this time,' she asked.

'He said they'd all been receiving things, anonymous things through the post.'

'What sort of things?' She raised her head sharply, fixed him with her eye. For a moment she looked almost as she had as a child: sharp and suspicious, commanding.

'I don't know. He said they thought you must be here, in London, and they thought you had sent them. He said they thought you were trying to scare them.'

'Me? How did they know I was here? I haven't seen any of them? What things? Why would I . . .?'

'I don't know, Lois,' he said desperately. 'I'm only telling you what he said.'

'Why did he call you then?'

'He wanted to know if I'd received anything.'

'And have you?'

He got up and went to the chest of drawers again. Lois watched, her heart pounding. It was crazy. Some crazy game that brought it all back, made it seem like only yesterday. Andy came back, tossed something towards her. It fell at her feet, a scrap of cloth which, uncomprehending, she picked up.

'Why it's a pair of . . .' She looked at him, her mind racing. 'Oh I get it . . . Oh my . . .' She began to laugh.

'It's not funny,' Andy said, his voice low and threatening.

'No?' She smiled her crooked smile. 'You used to think it was great.'

'That was a long time ago. I was a kid. I didn't know . . .'

'I bet that's what you all say. We were only kids . . . as though that excused anything.'

'I didn't say it was an excuse. Did you send them?'

'These? No.' She threw the pants away, as thought they disgusted her. 'Of course not. You don't believe me?'

'You knew where I lived . . .'

'Sure, I told you. I know where you all live, excepting William. But I didn't . . .'

'All right. I think I believe you. I thought at the time . . . I didn't tell Julian about them. I said I'd not received anything.'

'Why?'

'I didn't want to get involved. Anyway, I thought . . .'

'But who would know to do this but one of us? Andy, I promise you . . . I swear to you I did not do that.'

'All right. I thought it was the twins. I thought that was why Julian rang up, really. He wanted to get a reaction.'

'But why would he . . .?'

'I don't know. Perhaps we're all a bit mad.'

'I'll drink to that,' she said bitterly.

'There's something you can tell me,' Andy said, sitting down again.

'What?'

'What did you tell my mother? You know, after you . . . On my birthday that time, when you went to fetch her?'

Something in her, some instinct that she recognized as belonging to the child she had been then prompted her to lie. But she had vowed to be honest and he had told her about William. With difficulty, she pushed the impulse away.

'I told her about how you were always pestering us girls.'

'Just that? Nothing else?'

'Okay. I exaggerated. I said you tried to touch us, make

us do things . . . Hell, you can work it out for yourself. I didn't have to say anything much. She could imagine. I just let her imagine. I told her enough to make her think you were worse than you were. I didn't have to go into any details.'

'But why? Hadn't you done enough?'

'I had to make it look good, didn't I? I knew you'd shout your big mouth off about what we'd done to you in the barn, so I confessed. I told her we'd lost our cool and decided to punish you . . .'

'You made a bloody good job of it,' he said bitterly.

'And so did you.'

There was nothing more to say. Andy got up and finished his beer as he walked across the room. His back to her, in the kitchen area, opening another can of beer, he said:

'I can't make it with girls. I've never told anyone this. Every time I try I . . . It's like it all happens over again, in my head. I shrivel up, feeling those scissors, those tweezers you . . . I can't do it. I just can't.'

She thought he was going to cry again. His voice shook with humiliation and fear. She felt his loneliness and his shame reaching out to her, like a third presence in the room.

'I know it's not enough, but I am sorry. I didn't mean . . . I didn't know.'

'Like I said, we were just kids,' he cried, turning to face her. Lois looked away, looked into the gas fire. 'So, do you know what I do? I go with men. I can do it with them, sometimes. I can do it alone or with some bloke I pick up in the streets. Actually, they usually pick me up. I just let them. I hate it. It disgusts me. But it's the only way . . .'

'No,' she said, starting up from her chair. 'There's nothing to be ashamed of. Thousands of men are gay. In California now . . .'

'I don't give a fuck about California,' he shouted, his eyes blazing from the half-light which shadowed his face.

'I'm not one of a thousand men. I'm me and I hate it. I can't bear living with the knowledge of what I've done. Sometimes, I wish . . . No, you bloody listen to this. I want you to know. I sometimes lie in that bed, afterwards, or trying to promise myself that I won't ever do it again, I lie there and I wish you had cut it off. I wish you had.'

Lois waited, absorbing his words, forcing herself not to look away. She waited until he moved, walked to the window and jerked the curtain aside. When it seemed that he had nothing more to say, she went back to her chair, bent over and picked up her hat.

'What can I say, Andy? I guess that makes us even.'

'You could say that,' he said coldly. 'Now that I've seen you.'

'But I still think you could come to terms . . . There's no need to hate yourself just because . . .'

'I'm not gay, as you call it,' he said. 'I'm just impotent and often desperate. I'm not gay, like you weren't born ugly and scarred. We robbed each other,' he said, his tone changing, softening. 'We might just as well have killed each other.'

Lois pulled on her hat, went to the door and lifted down her coat.

'Thanks for seeing me and telling me about William. If you want . . .' She changed her mind as she slipped her arms into the sleeves of her coat and hitched it onto her shoulders. 'I don't expect you'll want to see me again, but if you like I'll leave my address.'

'What's the point?' he said, indifferent.

Lois accepted this even though she thought that, somehow, they ought to be able to help each other. But did they want to? Did she?

'Goodbye, then, Andy. Thanks again.'

She went out, closing the door behind her. Andy remained at the window, holding the curtain aside. He saw her come out onto the pavement and disappear into the cold, dark night.

Once he had opened the rather fat, otherwise quite ordinary envelope and inspected its contents, Julian considered throwing the whole lot away, thus concealing this latest 'reminder' from Jason. He looked at the two shiny black plastic bags which were the entire and only contents of the envelope and wondered what the police would make of this. The answer was obvious: nothing. Unless you knew, unless they were prepared to explain, there was nothing sinister at all in this 'gift'. Bizarre, certainly, perhaps even potty, but threatening . . .? He shook his head. It was eerie. He and Jason had received nothing that constituted a case. It was as though the sender – Lois Carradine, of course – knew that they were the ones most likely to react in a determined and positive fashion and so they were sent jewellery which, Julian felt sure, the average policeman would say they should be glad to receive, and two meaningless plastic bags. Except, of course, that they were not meaningless. It was as if she was goading them, saying, go on, go to the police, tell them the whole story . . . Perhaps that was what she wanted? But why? What would it achieve? The police would shrug and sympathize, no doubt, and tell them not to make too much of it. While the girls, Vanessa and Amanda, received things that were unmistakable, which constituted a threat, caused genuine distress. Because she knew that the girls would be too scared to do anything. It all made a perverted kind of sense. At the same time, it made no sense.

Sighing, Julian picked up the envelope and examined it closely. Just then he heard the front door slam and Jason's rapid footsteps approaching. It was too late to conceal the bags now and Julian resigned himself to whatever Jason would make of them.

He came to a dead halt in the doorway. The two black plastic bags were laid out neatly on the kitchen table and he saw their significance at once. He put down the heavy bags of shopping he was carrying and approached the table.

'No message, nothing else, of course?' he asked.

'No,' Julian said, relieved that Jason was taking it so calmly. 'The envelope's typewritten this time and the postmark is quite clear.' He handed the torn-open buff envelope to Jason. 'Pimlico,' he said.

'So,' Julian asked, after a glance at the envelope, 'are you going to the police now?'

'What with? Two plastic bags are scarcely threatening.'

'Oh? You really think so?'

'Yes, I do. I think she knows . . .'

'Not threatening, huh?' Jason picked up one of the bags, shook it, crackling, open. 'These represent the hoods, right? Those two shoe-bags Vanessa made for us?'

'Yes, of course . . .'

'That she and William made us put over our heads, to blindfold us?'

'Right, yes, but . . .'

'And what happens if you put a plastic bag over your head, eh? You tell me that?'

A shiver of fear went through Julian. He stared at the remaining bag, suddenly seeing it in a new and ugly light.

'No, she couldn't have . . .'

'Of course she did. Look . . .'

Jason gave the bag he held another shake and then pulled it down over his head.

'Jason, for Christ's sake . . .'

Laughing, Jason danced away from the table. His fingers were curled around the bottom edge of the bag, holding it away from his face, but even so, as he drew breath, it flattened tight against his features, moulding them.

'Jason!' Julian hurried around the table, chasing after

his brother. He reached out, grabbed him and Jason let go of the bag, lashed out with both hands, trying to push Julian away. Julian saw the plastic bag drawn in tight, sucked in by Jason's breath, clamped to his face, tight about his throat. He heard a muffled gurgling sound, saw his brother's hands come up, scrabbling against plastic. It seemed, for the longest and most awful moment of his life, that he was frozen to the spot, condemned to stand there and watch, fascinated, as the plastic bag clung and cloyed . . .

'Jason!' He leapt forward, knocking Jason's hands aside. With painful, heart-stopping slowness, he managed to inch his fingers under the bag's edge, against Jason's throat. 'For Christ's sake stand still. Keep still,' he shouted. His own voice sounded small and very far away. He pulled at the bag, tore at it. The plastic warped and stretched but would not tear. 'Blow out. Blow into it,' he shouted, 'but don't breathe in.' He pulled harder, the bag slipping through his fingers. Useless, his hands felt the contours of Jason's face, black and shining, dying. Grabbing hold again of the loose, stretched edge of the bag, he tried to tear it upwards. He drew back his right arm and punched Jason as hard as he could in the stomach. He grunted, staggered back a little, bent over. The blow drove the breath out of him. The bag mercifully inflated and Julian was able to tear it back, pull it off.

Jason's face was death-pale. His lips, the area of skin immediately below his eyes, looked blue. He bent over, clutching his stomach, gagging and coughing.

'You stupid bastard,' Julian shouted, advancing towards his brother. 'Are you trying to kill yourself or something?'

Jason's eyes rolled up towards him. What Julian saw in them – a plea and a challenge – quenched his anger. He turned away, leaned against the table, trembling with exhaustion and fear. Behind him, Jason's breath rasped in his throat and chest. Julian snatched both bags, the envelope, and tore at them, bunched them together and threw them away across the room. He could no longer pretend that she was not destroying them, or making them destroy each other, themselves. He turned, bleak-faced, to Jason, who leaned against the wall, panting, a half-smile like a rictus twitching his blue lips.

Six

In those tense but somehow dead two hours between the end of the matinee and curtain up on the evening performance, Vanessa, avoiding the rest of the company, sat in a run-down coffee bar on the edge of Covent Garden. It was essentially a workman's cafe, a place that had flourished with the market and declined with its going, unable to adjust to the reburgeoning of the district as an architectural splendour and expensive tourist trap. The cafe, with its scratched Formica table tops and thick china suited Vanessa's mood. Like it, she felt left-over, abandoned. The official notice had gone up that morning, announcing that Max Krieger would be leaving the cast early in the new year. He had said nothing to her. It had come as a complete blow and, though she had acted her heart out, she knew that she had not succeeded in concealing her surprise from the others and that they would draw their own conclusions. As she must. If Max was leaving, without warning her, it could only mean that he intended to end their affair. She could not yet admit that there had been distinct signs of a cooling off for several weeks now. She had put those down to his disappointment at not getting the film role. She understood his disappointment, shared in it since it greatly reduced her chance of going to Hollywood, and she had tried to be understanding and patient with him. But she had assumed that he would renew his contract for another six months at least. Her contract, inevitably, was for the run of the show, and so there was nothing for her to look forward to but a clean break. Except that it would not be clean. She was too involved for that. Her emotions were messy and frayed at the edges. He was okay. He could get on a plane, remove himself from all associations, while she had to go on playing the show, every line and note of which would always remind her of Max.

She did not want to cry. She was too angry for that. She wanted to hit him, spit in his face. She wanted to know who the hell he thought he was? He had used her, for the run of his contract. She supposed he had a girl in every show. Perhaps he swapped them round halfway through a really long run, just to keep fresh and on his toes. God, how could she have been so stupid? They had said she was stupid, or on the make. Well, she would admit to both now, guilty as charged. But it had been his lazy smile, his touch, his gentle but passionate love-making that had mattered. Sure, she enjoyed going out with him, being seen in restaurants she could not normally afford. She had liked being collected in his limousine from dance classes and the quick love-making they had sometimes indulged in on afternoons like this, in his dressing room. She had liked the champagne and the flowers, the whole starry, successful bit. But most of all she had liked him. No matter what anyone said, she had not felt stupid or cheap or guilty. And now she felt all those things in muddled, constantly shifting proportions.

The elderly waitress, swollen feet shuffling in carpet slippers, asked her if she wanted anything else.

'Only we're closing up now, love, see.'

She gathered up her bag and walked out into the chill evening. It was already dark. The city was in the grip of that hush, relaxing or melancholy, depending on your mood, between the end of work and the beginning of the night's revels. Vanessa wanted to crawl away somewhere, pull the blankets over her head and pretend she did not exist. But there was nothing for it but to go back to the theatre, make up her face, change into the gaudy silver costume in which she opened the show. For the first time in her life, the idea that the show must go on struck her as an empty, cheap and sentimental cliché. Why should the bloody show go on? She didn't give a damn about it. Just as, a hard, taunting little voice told her, Max Krieger did not give a damn about her.

Anger helped her to square her shoulders and put a bold face on it. She swept through the stage door like the hardened gypsy she was, her face flushed but, she hoped, radiant.

'Just a minute, love,' Bert, the stage doorkeeper, shouted as she hurried past his little box.

'What is it? I'm in a hurry.'

'Parcel for you. And a message.'

She turned back to the window, nearly collided with Sally Grant, and still managed to smile.

'Here you are.'

She took the almost weightless white box without glancing at it. The message, sealed in a satiny white envelope, occupied all her attention. It was from Max. She ran up the stairs to her dressing room, thankful that the other girls in the chorus had not yet returned from Maisie's or The Bistrotheque or wherever they had decided to go that day to gossip away the empty hours between performances. She put the box down and tore open the envelope, read the note by the light of the naked bulbs around the bank of mirrors.

Darling, I know how you must be feeling.
I couldn't tell you. I only made up my
mind last night. This changes nothing.
Why did you run off? I wanted to explain.
Dinner after the show, okay?
Love you,
M.

She wanted to believe it. Oh how much she wanted to. *This changes nothing*. But it did! It meant not seeing him, not sleeping with him. It meant months and months of grinding out the same steps, chanting the same tired songs with nothing to look forward to . . . God, she was going to cry. She threw the letter down, then grabbed it up again, crumpling it into her bag so that none of the others would see it. Her eye fell upon the square white box. What did he think he could buy her with, she wondered? She had a damned good mind to return it unopened. But curiosity got the better of her. Whatever it was, she'd smash it or throw it back in his face. She prised the tight-fitting lid off and peered inside. At first it didn't make any sense. An artificial flower, perhaps? She tugged one peaked corner and it came free of the box. It was a handkerchief. A man's square, good quality linen handkerchief. And it was soaked and splotched with still damp, still warm blood.

Lois looked at her watch for the third time. She was seated at a table for two in Joe Allen's, in the heart of Covent Garden, and was feeling increasingly embarrassed. The restaurant was full and she had been waiting for half an hour. Cassandra had booked the table and though Cassandra would never win any prizes for punctuality, she was not normally this late. Because she felt she ought to, Lois summoned the waiter and ordered a second Campari soda.

Cassandra had wanted to see her at once the moment she had told her about meeting Andy Mercer. Lois had stalled, put the date off for a few days, partly because she wanted time to think and absorb that meeting and partly out of a sudden rush of resentment. Something so crucial to her did not seem a fit subject for gossip. She told herself that was mean, that Cassandra was genuinely concerned for her, had been centrally involved in this whole trip, yet the quite unpleasant idea that Cassandra was, partially at least, sensation-seeking persisted. And so she had decided to be selective in what she told Cassandra.

As the days passed it became obvious that this would not be difficult. The meeting with Andy had depressed Lois and then moved her. The lessons she had learned from it were unexpected and obvious. She could almost hear Stryker saying, 'I told you so', or, 'What did you expect?' Most of all it had given her a perspective on the whole situation, on Andy and therefore, by implication, on the others. Quite simply, she had no relationship with any of them. This was self-evident, but she had not realized it. It now seemed crazy to her that she should have felt that surge of warmth and expectation on seeing Amanda that day. No wonder the girl had fled in shock and surprise. What she had mistaken as, assumed to be a relationship, was an accidental bonding by circumstances. This was made clear to her by obtaining the answer to one of the questions that had brought her to London in the first place: how did they feel about what had happened? She saw now that Andy at least was punished, yet she felt neither gratification in the fact nor responsibility for it. It seemed to her silly and unnecessary that he should resent what she took to be his own sexual nature. But that was his problem. It affected her only in the sense that it made her see that other people could look similarly at her situation. Others might say that she had not made the best of her lot, that her feelings about her face, the loss of her parents, were a problem of her personality rather than a natural outcome of the events themselves. This did not make her feel any better about it, but she felt that something narrowing and tethering had snapped, leaving her freer and with the real possibility of being more in control of her life. Her curiosity had been satisfied even, in a sense, disappointed, but it was a gap plugged and consequently no longer of interest. She had no curiosity about the others, with the exception of William, and she feared that what Mr Critchley had found out and Cassandra had told her already answered her questions about William.

Towards William she now felt a mixture of fear and rage. She still wanted to see him, confront him, but her motives had subtly altered. It was not to study him, to find out how he had lived with what he had done, but to test her own anger. She wanted to know how much she hated him and to what lengths, if any, that hatred would carry her. She knew that by thinking this way she was treading a dangerous line. Again Stryker's image came to her, thick with disapproval and ill-concealed alarm. Furthermore, it made her feel strange and detached, for she had become the subject of her own experiment. The whole thing then, she had asked her journal, was it a quest to find out about herself, not those who had harmed her? It was a rhetorical question, one that simultaneously excited and frightened her.

She looked up suddenly from her untouched second drink. A clamour at the door, Cassandra's unmistakable voice cutting across the restaurant chatter, announced her friend's belated arrival. Thanking waiters, waving them aside, the object of all attention, Cassandra bore down on the table and Lois.

'Darling, are you absolutely furious with me? I'm *so* sorry. I can't tell you . . . Oh thank God you've got a drink. I had a vision of you sitting here for hours without a thing. I must have one, too. Waiter, would you be an absolute angel and get me a very strong Screwdriver? Bless you. Oh, Lois, you've resuscitated those beastly hats. Does that mean you're utterly crushed? Unbelievably cast down? Darling, you must tell all, just as soon as I've explained.'

Somehow, during all this, Cassandra had managed to kiss Lois's cheek, shed her fox coat to reveal a livid green wool suit and sit down.

'Not that you'll believe a word but every syllable is gospel – Brownie's honour,' she resumed, looking speculatively around the room. 'Oh, look, there's Felicity Kendal. Isn't she absolutely divine? Every bit as pretty off-stage. So fresh-looking. Anyway, darling Lois, I promise you I was ready in bags of time. I was so organized, my dear, you simply wouldn't have recognized me. And then, just as I got to the front door, would you believe . . . of all things . . . a nose bleed! My dear, I positively fountained. There was no stopping it. And, of course, wouldn't you know, I was wearing white? A scrumptious new dress bought specially for today and now probably ruined. Will it dye, do you suppose? But it wouldn't be the same. It was a sort of white cut, if you see what I mean. So, of course, I had to lie down and have Philomena bring me piles and piles of hankies . . . Poor darling Ade won't have a thing to wipe his nose on unless I remember to buy him some more. I was simply streaming. Philomena thought I was dying, poor lamb. And then I had to change and fix my face and could I find a cab? Would you believe that there wasn't a single bloody cab my side of Sloane Square? And then the traffic!' At last, Cassandra paused to sip her cocktail. Lois seized her chance.

'But are you all right? Why didn't you call? You should have cancelled.'

'Oh nonsense, though it's awfully sweet of you . . . No, I get them occasionally, nose bleeds. I was always having them as a child. My Nanny said they were good for one. Cleared the head, or something. But I am most dreadfully sorry. I'm amazed you waited. Oh do look, there's Nicky Henson. Isn't he an absolute dish? I love it here, don't you?'

'Sure. But are you really okay?'

'My nerves are completely shot and I'm ravenous. Otherwise, absolutely fine. Now, what are we going to eat?'

The meal ordered, more celebrities spotted and commented upon in a voice so loud that Lois was too embarrassed to even glance in their direction, Cassandra at last turned her attention to her friend.

'Now I'm going to be completely and utterly *stumm* while you tell all.'

'There's not a lot to tell. It was all kind of sad, really.'

'But what was he like, the little sex maniac?' she asked with a giggle.

'Just an ordinary young guy. He's rather good-looking in a sort of uptight kind of way.'

'Did you . . . Oh no, you couldn't have.'

'Have what?'

'Well, I was going to say, did you fancy him? I mean, what a twist that would have been . . .'

'He's gay,' Lois said, with acid in her voice, feeling sick at Cassandra's idea.

'Like most of the male population in here,' Cassandra said. 'Such a waste, don't you think? I mean, those two over there . . . But I'm digressing. Do tell.'

'He minds. He was very upset about it.'

'Being queer, or you?'

'Both, I guess. He cried.'

'Well, it serves him jolly well right. I hope you didn't go all maternal and forgiving.'

'No.'

'So?'

'That's it.'

'Oh come now. There must have been more than that. You're holding out on me.'

'No. I can't explain. I'm glad I saw him but . . . it's no big deal.'

'How frightfully disappointing. But did you get masses of juicy gossip about the others?'

'Not really. He hasn't seen any of them for years. There was one thing, though. Something odd . . . I wanted to ask you what you thought about it.'

'What? What? I'm all ears.'

Hesitantly, because the more she thought about it the more unpleasant and sick it seemed, Lois told Cassandra about Julian's phone call to Andy and the packet he had received.

'Gosh! How thrilling! It's like something out of an Agatha Christie. Who on earth do you suppose would . . .'

'They think I'm doing it,' Lois said bleakly.

Cassandra caught her breath. Her carefully arched eyebrows rose, her eyes widened. Then she giggled.

'Oh Lois you haven't . . . What an absolutely amazing wheeze.'

'Of course I haven't . . . For God's sake, is that the kind of person you think I am? You think I'm sick or something?'

'Shh, darling, you're drawing unseemly attention . . .'

'You can talk. What about the way you . . .'

'Lois,' Cassandra hissed. 'Keep your voice down and your temper under control. Of course I didn't think it was you . . .'

'Well, I'm glad to hear that . . .'

'But who would blame you? They jolly well deserve it. I think a little reminder of past sins wouldn't come at all amiss.'

'It's horrible, ugly,' Lois retorted. 'It's like anonymous letters or something . . .'

'Oh, well, if that's the way you see it . . . I think it shows a great deal of imagination. I mean, there's no harm in it, is there? It's just a sort of visiting card, a little goad in the right direction . . .'

'It harmed Andy,' Lois argued. 'It made him feel awful.'

'Well, if you say so. It's a wonder he didn't wear them from what you say.'

'Jesus Christ, Cassandra, you are a bitch.'

'I beg your pardon?' Her face was chalk white, so white that her carefully applied make-up looked like so many streaks and blotches of unnatural colour. 'How dare you speak . . .'

Lois opened her mouth to apologize, retract, but her

temper set and hardened. She would be damned if she would take it back. It was true.

'I mean it. I know you've been very good and kind to me and helped me, but what you've just said . . .'

'Excuse me,' Cassandra cut in. 'I had no idea you had such affection for the little monsters who turned you into a freak. What are you after, Lois? Nobel Peace Prize or the Mother Theresa Award for Forgiveness?'

She did not even want to cry at being called a freak. She had always feared the word, had known that one day someone would use it to her face. It had been one of her more macabre jokes, discussed with Mr Stryker, that she could always get a job in the freak show. America's Most Injured Woman, Scarface, The Walking Road Accident . . . It hurt. It stung, but she knew it was not true. She stood up, aware that people were looking at her.

'For Christ's sake sit down . . .' Cassandra hissed again.

'Up yours,' Lois said. She did not care that people were looking at her. Let them look and jeer. Let them see how ugly she was. Cassandra was a whole lot uglier, inside.

She strode through the crowded tables of gawping people. The head waiter, frowning, moved towards the door.

'Mrs Foss will get the check,' Lois said and enjoyed saying it.

The cold air hit her and it felt good. It felt clean and decent. She walked quickly, letting her anger carry her along. Her head was full of things she wished she had said to Cassandra. Like she was a snob and deserved her two-timing husband. Like that she hated her and was a damn fool ever to have been dazzled by her. But by the time she reached the elegant Piazza, her anger had spent itself. She felt alive, sparkling, full of energy. She went down the steps to one of the sunken cafes and ordered herself a great big confection of ice cream which she ate with relish and followed with a strong black coffee.

Though she continued to feel good, her mind returned to the question of the mysterious 'reminders'. What had the others received? She wished now that she had asked Andy, not out of idle curiosity but because if she saw some kind of pattern, an explanation might emerge. But maybe Andy was right after all and he was the only one. Why would the twins suddenly pick on him, after all this time? Because he had stayed away from them? Because they did know, somehow, that she was here . . . But that was easy because Amanda knew and could have told them . . . And they wanted Andy to think she was doing it. Why? To scare him off, prevent him telling her about William? Then again perhaps, like Cassandra, they saw it as a joke. Because this much was true: only one of them could have sent those panties. And maybe the twins weren't lying. Maybe they had received something. If it was one of them – by which she meant the whole group – he or she would be sure to send themselves something, or pretend that they had received something. And after what Cassandra had said, she could easily see that they would believe her capable . . . But who, which of them would do a thing like that? Not Amanda, surely. She just was not mean enough.

Lois got up and paid her bill, strolled slowly through the Piazza, occupied with her own thoughts. Vanessa? She couldn't imagine the twins doing . . . Was Andy crazy enough, unhappy enough to make something like that up? For a moment, that seemed possible, the most likely explanation. But then, as she left the Piazza and turned towards Long Acre, another thought came to her and stopped her in her tracks.

There was someone else who knew.

Someone beside them and Mr Stryker.

Cassandra Foss.

Cassandra knew and Cassandra thought it was funny, thought it was as harmless and intriguing as something out of an Agatha Christie thriller. From which she might have got the idea in the first place?

Lois felt weak with shock. After all, Cassandra got bored easily. Cassandra had been so eager for her to find them and had been disproportionately annoyed when Lois had hesitated to contact them. Lois suddenly saw herself as a crazy scarred doll or glove puppet, being manipulated to alleviate Cassandra's boredom. It made her feel sick. And it made her feel responsible. If she was right then what she had felt about Amanda's accident was true for all of them. By her very presence, she brought fear and pain. Her mood turned black and horrible. A weight, cold and relentless, pressed on her spirits. And underneath it all was an insistent tug of fear.

The doctor examined her with more than usual care and thoroughness, or so it seemed to Amanda.

'Well,' he said, 'that all seems to be progressing nicely.'

'Will I be able to go home soon?'

'Oh you know better than that, Nurse. You'll be discharged as soon as you're well enough. We . . .'

Laughing, Amanda joined in the familiar litany.

'. . . don't keep people in hospital beds unnecessarily, especially when there are long waiting lists.'

The doctor smiled.

'It's good to see you smile. How are you feeling, in yourself, I mean?'

'Oh I'm feeling much better, really. I think it was just the shock . . .'

'Well, I'm glad to hear it. Even so . . .'

'Yes?' A look of alarm crept into Amanda's eyes.

'I want you to have a chat with someone. Mrs Valerian.'

For a moment Amanda was unable to place the name. It hung at the back of her mind, taunting her. Then, with a rush, she said:

'But she's a psychiatrist . . .'

'One of the very best and a very busy lady and you're very lucky that she's willing to see you . . .'

'But I don't need a psychiatrist. Whose idea is this?'

'Mine, Nurse. Do you want to challenge my competence?'

'No, of course not . . .'

'Now look, you've had a rough few weeks. Don't forget that you were exhausted and overwrought before the accident. A shock like that, on top of everything else, is bound to make you feel depressed . . .'

'It's because . . .'

'Listen, Nurse. I just want Mrs Valerian to have a chat with you in case there's anything else impeding your recovery. It's a precaution. Just a once over. Think of it as having your eyes tested, all right?'

'All right.'

'There's a good girl. I'll see you tomorrow, then. Oh, and, Nurse, don't worry.'

It was connected with not going to the police. She knew it. She slid down the bed, pulled the covers up to her chin for protection. Sister Wilson had paid her a brief visit, had told her that, after discussing the matter fully with her father, they had decided not to call in the police at the moment. She had blessed him then for making everything all right as she had known he would, as he always had. But now they wanted her to see a psychiatrist. Amanda knew that there was nothing wrong with her. Nothing at all. Daddy must have told them something about Lois. About the worms and the spiders, the blood and the dead rabbit, the whole terrible year of association, culminating in the candles. Her head whirled and hurt so that she could not remember exactly what she had told her father. She had felt better after talking to him. Now they wanted to drag the whole thing out of her and she could not bear that. She would rather die than . . . She saw it all so clearly and simply. Once she had told them about her part in what had happened to Lois, they would say that she was mad and violent and they would not let her go on training as a nurse. They might even lock her away forever . . . Then another worse thought came to her. Perhaps this was just what Lois had planned – to drive her mad. Perhaps she had succeeded. Perhaps she had thrown herself deliberately under that car. She was going to be punished forever and ever and no one would believe her. She felt herself trapped between Lois's implacable thirst for revenge and the whole unstoppable machinery of the hospital. And she knew that she could not get out.

Somehow Vanessa managed to get through the evening performance. Before she went on, she was sick in the lavatory. Her vomit tasted like blood, the blood Lois had forced her to drink as the first initiate into the gang. Retching, she dropped the handkerchief into the sanitary towel disposal unit and then washed her face in cold water. The show was a nightmare blur of colour and noise in which she participated mechanically. The only good thing about the whole awful experience was that she was able to avoid Max Krieger. As soon as the curtain came down, she dashed out of the theatre and hailed a taxi. She could not face going home. For one thing she was too scared, especially since Suzie was dancing a week's cabaret out of London. And then Max would be sure to ring or perhaps even call round and she felt hysterical at the thought of facing him. She needed to be calm, to be able to think when she saw him. She gave the twins' address to the taxi driver.

Julian answered the door at her third ring, a dressing-gown pulled hastily over his pyjamas.

'Vanessa! What on earth . . .'

'Can I come in? Please?'

He helped her up the stairs. She saw Jason hanging over

the banisters, watching her. She told them about the handkerchief and suddenly she was sobbing uncontrollably. Jason went out of the room and returned with a couple of screwed up plastic bags. She could not take in what they were telling her. Julian poured her a tot of neat whisky and made her drink it. Everything tasted foul, tasted of blood. When she was a little calmer, Julian said:

'Okay, we've got enough now. We must have enough. We'll go to the police first thing in the morning. It'll be better if we all go, make a joint complaint.'

'Where is the handkerchief?' Jason asked, gathering up the plastic bags.

She stared at them dumbly, realizing too late how stupid she had been. By now the theatre would be locked . . .

'Oh that's great. That's really terrific,' Jason said.

'It was so horrible . . . I couldn't . . .'

'It's all right. Of course not.'

'All we've got is two plastic bags . . .'

'The bracelet, the necklet . . .' Vanessa said, seeing from their faces that it was useless.

'Andy,' Julian said, getting up. 'We've got to get hold of him. If we've both received two parcels, he must have had something by now.'

'And Amanda,' Vanessa said eagerly.

'She's still in hospital . . .'

'That doesn't make any difference,' Jason protested. 'She still gets post.'

'She's ill, for Christ's sake. No, we'd better leave her out.' Seeing that Jason was going to argue, he raised his voice. 'We can tell the police what we know about Amanda and they can check it out for themselves. Now I'm going to ring Andy.'

Jason paced up and down. Vanessa watched him nervously. Now that she had told someone about the handkerchief it was the problem of the almost certain loss of Max that loomed large and miserable in her mind. She could not tell the twins about Max. She looked up when Julian came back into the room, shaking his head.

'I got some bloke out of bed. He yelled for Andy but there was no answer.'

'Shit!' Jason swore.

'It's okay. Keep calm. We can get him in the morning.'

'And what if he hasn't received anything?' Jason wanted to know.

'We'll go anyway. Yes, Vanessa?'

She shook her head. It did not seem such a good idea now that the first enthusiasm had paled.

'Oh come on . . .' Jason shouted.

'We can tell them about the handkerchief, even if it is too late to get it back.'

'When do they clean the theatre?'

'I don't know,' she said weakly.

'You can go there first thing. It might not be too late.'

'I couldn't.'

'We'll come with you. Look, love,' Jason said, sitting beside her and speaking quietly, 'it's important. If they analyse the blood, it might help . . .'

'I just don't know. I . . . I've got other things on my mind.'

'Sleep on it. You'll feel much better in the morning.'

'Can I stay here? Please. I don't want to go back to the flat alone . . .'

'Of course you can.'

'Thanks. I'm sorry to be such a . . .'

'You know, of course, that there is another way?'

They both looked at Jason, startled. He was standing by the fireplace in T-shirt and jeans, barefoot. His hair was tousled into spikes, sticking out around his lean, sickly-looking face.

'How?' Julian almost breathed the word.

'We could fix her ourselves. After all, we did it once before.'

Julian shut his eyes. He realized that he had been dreading that someone would say this ever since the first parcel arrived. He heard Vanessa catch her breath and she clutched his arm tightly. He opened his eyes, covered her gripping hand with his. Their eyes met for a second, but Vanessa looked quickly away.

'We don't know where she is,' Vanessa said in a husky voice.

'We could find her. There must be ways. Anyway, we don't even have to. She knows where we are. She's already approached Amanda. If we have the nerve to wait it out, she'll come to us.'

'And then what?' Julian demanded. He had meant to sound scornful but somehow his words sounded compliant. He had a terrible feeling that he was being sucked into something crazy, and yet it was almost attractive, certainly tempting.

'We could threaten her with the police,' Vanessa said. 'We could warn her off. Yes, that's best. Honestly, Julian.'

'Do you think she'd take any notice?' Jason sneered.

'Yes. She'd have to. If she didn't we really would go.'

'Then you might as well go now,' Julian said, clinging to some straw of reason. Now it was he who could not meet their eyes.

'Because they won't believe us. Or if they do they'll only say wait for her to make another move,' Vanessa said. 'You know that's true. And we'd have to . . . explain.'

Julian said nothing. He was afraid to. If they acted together, emphatically, as they had done before . . .

'Why can't she just go away and leave us alone?' Vanessa asked, her voice breaking.

'Yes. She can't stay forever, surely?' Julian agreed, aware that he was ducking the issue.

'She'll stay long enough,' Jason said with complete certainty. 'Vanessa's right. You know she is. If we wait it out, she'll have to come to us and then . . .'

'All right. If that's what you both want. And if Andy agrees.'

'What about William?' Vanessa said. 'We keep forgetting about William.'

'I suppose you think he'd know best what to do?' Jason said contemptuously.

'No, I meant . . . Julian, your mother would know where he is, surely?'

'I don't think so. Anyway, what does it matter?'

'We're all in this . . .'

'We only assume we're all involved. Maybe William's like Andy. Maybe she's left him out.'

'But William's the most to blame,' Vanessa exclaimed. The twins stared at her. 'Well, you know he is,' she said defensively. 'For God's sake, you can't have forgotten . . .'

'I don't think it matters now, does it?' Julian said, trying to be reasonable.

'It matters to me. If she wants . . . to get back at us, William should get his share . . . more than us . . .'

'Absolutely. I agree,' Jason said.

'Maybe she doesn't know where he is either,' Julian suggested.

'All the more reason for us to find him, then,' Vanessa insisted.

'We should tell her, tell her about William . . .'

'Yes, Jason. That's it. Then perhaps she'd leave us alone.'

'For God's sake,' Julian exploded suddenly. 'Can you hear yourselves? You sound like . . .' He shook his head in disbelief and fear.

'She started it,' Jason said. 'There's only one way to beat her, and that's on her own terms.'

'I don't believe this . . .'

'No, Julian, he's right. We should have thought of it before.'

'And what are you going to do to her?' he asked.

'Right now I could cheerfully kill her with my own hands,' Vanessa said.

'Oh this is ridiculous,' Julian said. 'I'm going to bed.'

'We agreed,' Jason said. 'If you want to change your mind, fine. Just don't tell us what to do.'

Julian walked to the door.

'I'll get a pillow and some blankets,' he told Vanessa.

'And we'll ring Andy in the morning,' Jason insisted.

'I don't know,' Vanessa said miserably. 'I'm so scared and confused . . .'

'It'll be all right,' Jason said coldly, 'if we all stick together. It'll be like before . . .' Vanessa put her hands over her face. 'We'd better get some sleep now. It'll all make sense in the morning. You'll see.'

Andy was furious. For one thing he was barely awake and his downstairs neighbour had given him a hard time about always having to answer the phone for him.

'No,' he repeated. 'I haven't received anything. Even if I had, why should I tell you?'

'Because we must stick together.' Julian's voice took on a note of urgency. 'Look, it's all too complicated to explain on the phone. Can you come over here? Vanessa's with us. We talked last night.'

'I've got a bloody job to go to,' Andy said. 'And you're making me late.'

'Tonight then. Can you . . .?'

'I don't want to get involved. I don't want to know. Can't you understand that?'

'Just because she hasn't contacted you yet, don't think she won't . . .' Julian shouted.

A crooked smile twisted Andy's unshaven face.

'I'll tell you something, Shillingworth. She's already been in touch. I've seen her and spoken to her, and I'll tell you this for nothing. Whoever is sending you nasty presents through the post, it's not Lois. Now just leave me alone.' He slammed the receiver down. His chest was heaving with a mixture of excitement and annoyance. He knocked on his neighbour's door. 'He'll probably ring back. Just let it ring,' he said.

They were starting at ghosts, behaving like a lot of shit-scared kids, and Andy wanted no part of it.

'He's seen her,' Julian said, his voice blanched with surprise. 'He said they'd talked and he says she's not sending the parcels.'

'Oh that's typical,' Vanessa said, pacing up and down. 'Wouldn't you know she'd have to have an accomplice? We should have guessed that.'

'But why Andy?'

'He was always a cowardly bastard,' Jason said. 'But this shows I was right. We ought to have got together sooner. She's probably roped in William as well. She's ahead of us, as usual. If you'd listened to me . . .' He rounded on his brother.

'Oh stop it, you two. For God's sake stop bitching.' Vanessa shouted. In the silence that followed, she felt rude and stupid. She had slept badly and her head hurt. She did not know how she was going to cope with Max and, in the small hours of the long night, the whole idea of forming some sort of association against Lois Carradine made her feel childish and weak. But she had agreed with Jason . . . 'I'm sorry. I didn't sleep well.'

'You're not having second thoughts, are you?' Jason said, a hint of menace in his tone.

Vanessa ran her hand through her tangled hair.

'Yes, Jason, I am. I'm sorry. I shouldn't have come here last night. I got scared, carried away . . . Look, I'd better go.'

'But what are you going to do?' Jason said, taking a step towards her as though to prevent her leaving.

'Nothing,' she said wearily. 'On that point I do agree

with you. If we don't react, maybe she'll get as fed up as I feel now.'

'Some hope,' Jason sneered.

'And if she doesn't?' Julian asked, tense.

'We'll see. I don't know. I just don't want to talk about it any more.' She picked up her bag and coat.

'I'll run you home,' Julian offered.

'No, it's okay. I can pick up a cab. Thanks for the sofa.'

Julian saw her down to the front door.

'I'm sorry,' he said. 'All this is getting to Jason.'

'It's not your fault. Last night, for a minute, it all seemed possible. It was like we had never grown up at all.'

'You have,' he said.

'So have you. And maybe it's important to hang on to that. It's probably the one thing she hasn't thought of.'

He watched her walk away, obviously tired. Upstairs, Jason was waiting for him, brimming with new thoughts, new arguments.

'If she's got Andy on her side . . .'

'Not now, Jason. Give it a rest, for God's sake,' Julian said and went into his room, closing the door firmly behind him.

Jason bit his lip. There were tears in his eyes.

Before setting out for the hospital, Lois telephoned Mr Critchley and asked him, please, in future, to send all information to her direct. He cleared his throat and then politely but firmly explained that he could not do that: Mrs Foss was paying his bills.

'I'll pay,' Lois said. 'You just send your account straight to me . . .'

'Most civil of you, Miss Carradine, but alas . . . You see, Mrs Foss retained my services. Mrs Foss *is* my client. Without instructions to the contrary from her . . .'

'I do not want that woman prying into my affairs any more,' Lois said.

'That, I'm afraid, Miss Carradine, is a matter you must take up with Mrs Foss. Until she informs me otherwise, I am obliged to honour my commitments to her.'

'Okay. I'll speak to her. I'll deal with it. But since we're speaking, did you get any further on William Young?'

'Ah, well, Miss Carradine . . .'

'Mrs Foss told me about that place, Redpaths. All I'm asking is, did you follow up my idea?'

'I think I can tell you without any breach of confidence that Mr Young was enrolled for a short time as a veterinary student in Edinburgh.'

'And?' Lois prompted, excited and impatient.

'He left.'

'Was that before or after Redpaths?'

'Before.'

'And you don't know where he is now?'

'Not yet. And that's all I can say, Miss Carradine. If you'd like to clarify the situation with Mrs Foss and have her instruct me accordingly . . .'

'Sure. I'll do that. Thank you for your time, Mr Critchley.'

'Thank *you*, Miss Carradine.'

So William had pursued his dream . . . only to have it go sour on him or crumble? Where was he now? Where would he go after . . . He'd be around animals somewhere. Of that she was sure. She could check out the likely places, make a few calls . . . But there was no time now. She began to get ready for her hospital appointment. And she still had to do something about Cassandra. Lois knew instinctively that Cassandra would not give up, would not agree to countermand her instructions to Mr Critchley without a struggle. Well, that was fine. Lois was spoiling for a fight. After all, she had something on Cassandra now, something she was more than happy to use.

*

Mr Valentine had a stack of sheets of paper on which a simple, egg-like shape had been drawn in a continuous thick black line. These ovals represented heads. With a felt-tip pen, he sketched lines on the 'face', showing her how the flaps of grafted skin would overlap, how scar tissue would be tightened and drawn back here . . . Lois stared at the sheet of paper. It looked like a patchwork or a pattern, a map remote and removed from her. Her face was round, not oval. Her eyes sockets were not set so, her nose, a mere vertical line drawn by his pen, did not sit so. She was mouthless, dumb.

'Do you see, Miss Carradine? Or may I call you Lois?'

'Please,' she said, touching the sheet of paper with her fingertips, moving it around the desk.

'It looks very crude, I know. In a sense, speaking mechanically it is a crude process, but I promise you the results are excellent.'

He had already shown her a series of before and after, gruesome pictures. It was true, if the photographs had not been touched-up, air brushed, that the results were good, seamless. Yet all those who had received major facial plastic surgery had a frozen look, pale skin stretched too tight . . .

'Perhaps you'd like to think it over? I don't want to pressure you,' he said gently.

'I'm scared,' Lois confessed.

'Understandably. But I give you my word . . .' He came, fatherly, around the desk and laid a hand on her shoulder. 'I don't make mistakes, my dear. I don't promise what I can't do. I can't transform you. Possibly, if you'd come to me at the time of the accident . . . As it is, I can give you a result at least as good as this.' He reached out and picked up one of the photographs. 'Your face will at least be smooth, free of scar tissue, these puckerings . . .'

Just to be able to touch her face and feel smooth skin instead of ridges and whorls . . .

'When?' she asked.

'Ah, now, that is a problem. As it happens, I've had a cancellation, a bed unexpectedly free. If you feel able to take that, we could begin almost at once. If not, six months at the very least.'

'Almost at once?' she said, her voice small with dread.

'We could admit you on Sunday, do the necessary photographs and fine measurements on Monday. We could operate on Thursday.' He paused. 'It would mean spending Christmas in hospital . . .'

Christmas. She had forgotten all about Christmas.

'That's okay,' she said. 'I don't have any plans.'

'Actually, Christmas in hospital is rather jolly. The nurses make such an effort. Of course, you'll be heavily bandaged, probably won't feel much like dancing, but . . . Think of the new year. A new face for the new year. How does that strike you?'

'Wonderful,' she said. 'Yes, I'll do it.'

'I'm delighted.' He held out his hand and Lois shook it. 'I think it's best not to wait, frankly. Your . . . apprehensions won't lessen with time. But you must trust me. You do, don't you, Lois?'

'Yes, Mr Valentine. It's just . . .'

'I know. Now if you'll just come through to the outer office, my secretary will make the necessary arrangements.' He opened the door for her, patted her shoulder reassuringly. 'I'll see you on Monday morning, then. And remember: a new face for the new year.'

A new start, Lois thought. Oh God, a new life.

Seven

Lois kept her finger pressed down hard on the doorbell, listening to its over-long shrill. It had taken a lot of courage to come here but she figured that was better than sitting around, dreading the prospect of going into hospital . . . Besides, there was no other way but a stand-up confrontation.

Luis opened the door, obviously pleased to see her. He invited her in, asked her to wait in the hall. Adrian poked his head out of the sitting room just as Cassandra shouted from upstairs:

'Who is it?'

'Lois,' Adrian called back. 'Thank you, Luis. You'd better come in,' he said to Lois.

Lois followed him into the brightly-lit room.

'Well, this is a surprise,' he said. 'Like a drink?'

'No, thanks.'

'You heard Cass. She'll be down . . . So, how are you?'

'I'm fine.'

'Do sit. Let me take your . . .'

'It's okay. I'm not stopping. I just wanted a few words with . . .'

She turned as Cassandra came into the room, swathed in floor-length black velvet which dramatized her dark colouring and fine complexion. As though rehearsed, obeying a cue, she went to stand beside Adrian.

'Well,' she said, tight-lipped, 'I suppose you've come to apologize?'

'No. On the contrary . . .'

'Look, why don't I make myself scarce?' Adrian offered, moving away from Cassandra.

'No, I'd prefer you to stay, Adrian,' Lois said.

'So would I,' Cassandra agreed. 'If she's going to be offensive . . . Well? What do you want?'

'I want you to tell Critchley to report direct to me from now on. I'll reimburse you for whatever you've paid him.'

'Are you demanding or asking?' Cassandra asked, with a toss of the head.

'Demanding. Telling you. Do it.'

'I say,' said Adrian, looking from Lois to his wife, 'that's a bit thick . . .'

'Will you?' Lois asked Cassandra, ignoring him.

'Why should I?'

'Because it's my business, my life, and I don't want you messing with it.'

'That is gratitude for you,' Cassandra said to Adrian, moving gracefully away from him and sitting down in a smooth swirl of skirts. She folded her arms neatly at the wrist and looked at Lois, her head a little on one side. 'You seem to forget, you asked me to do your dirty work for you. You were glad enough of my help then . . .'

'Yes, I was. But I didn't know then what kind of a person you were.'

'I say, what do you mean?' Adrian asked. Cassandra waved him aside impatiently.

'And what kind of person have you decided I am?'

'I'd rather not go into that. If you'll just tell me what I owe you . . .' Lois opened her bag, looking for her cheque book, 'and promise to call Critchley in the morning . . .'

'I don't want your money,' Cassandra said harshly. 'And I'm certainly not going to tell Mr Critchley anything of the sort. I paid for that information and it's mine.'

'You got it for me. It's not yours. You have no right . . .'

Cassandra and Lois spoke at once, a mêlée of voices that Adrian shouted down.

'What information? What is all this? Hold on a minute . . . *please* . . .'

'He's a private detective,' Lois shouted.

'Detective? But what on earth for?'

'I needed to trace some people . . . Look, Adrian, it really doesn't concern you . . . Will you just tell her to do as I ask?'

'He most certainly will not. Not if he values his life. You get out of here . . .'

'Okay,' Lois said. 'You asked for this . . .'

'Steady on now,' Adrian cautioned.

'These people, Adrian, the ones I asked Cassandra to help me find, they were the ones who scarred my face. I heard the other day that since I got here they've been receiving anonymous packages containing things that remind them of certain things that happened a long time ago. A sort of threat. Naturally, they think it's my doing, but I swear to you that I didn't. When I told Cassandra about it, she thought it was a great idea, very funny . . .'

'It's well known that Americans have absolutely no sense of humour . . .' Cassandra said.

'But I realized that there was one person who knew all about that time, when I lived here as a kid, one person who had all the necessary information to do such a cruel, mean thing . . .'

'That's enough,' Cassandra shouted, 'Adrian, call the police.'

'Sure,' Lois said. 'You do that, Adrian. I was going to lay everything before them myself.'

'But what for? I don't understand.'

'Cassandra's been sending those packages.'

'That is a filthy lie,' Cassandra yelled, jumping to her feet.

'Where's your proof?' Adrian demanded, grasping the seriousness of what was being said.

'All I know is I'm innocent. I didn't do it. I don't believe that any of the recipients would do anything like this. They have every reason not to . . . That leaves Cass . . .'

'You bitch,' Cassandra screamed. 'You're not going to stand there and let her . . .' she continued, swinging towards Adrian.

'Shut up,' Adrian said. 'That's a very serious charge . . .'

'Let her deny it then.'

'Cassie?' He looked at his wife who glared back at him, her face made mean by anger.

'Of course I deny it. She's mental. She's as sick and mad as her friends. Worse . . . Do you know what she got up to when she lived here before?'

'That's scarcely relevant. Tell me, straight out, that you had nothing to do with this.'

'I don't believe this. I am not on trial here . . .' Cassandra protested.

'You can do what the hell you want,' Lois said. 'I'm willing to pay what I owe. I want you to stop whatever you've been doing. And I want you to sack Critchley and tell him to report to me.'

'And I want you out of my house,' Cassandra retaliated.

'Adrian?' Lois appealed to him. 'I want to get out of here, too. But I want assurances . . .'

'Look . . . Cass . . . I mean, we don't want a lot of fuss . . . scandal . . . You shouldn't have got involved in . . .'

'Are you scared of her?' Cassandra faced him.

'He might be,' Lois said, quietly.

There was a long pause, a silence that throbbed with tension and danger.

'What's that supposed to mean?' Cassandra asked.

'Ask Adrian.'

'I don't know what she's talking about.'

'Will you call Critchley?' Lois said. 'That's all I want to know.'

'I will not.'

'Yes, she will,' Adrian said. 'I give you my word.'

'Oh, there speaks a guilty conscience,' Cassandra

shouted into her husband's face. 'Now I see . . . How frightfully naive I've been.'

'You just make sure she does,' Lois said, holding Adrian's gaze. 'Good night.'

As soon as the door had closed behind her, Cassandra strode across the room, away from Adrian.

'You spineless bastard,' she hissed.

'What have you been up to?' he asked in an angry voice.

'You dare ask that of me? What were you up to?'

'I know you, Cass. You can't resist meddling and sometimes . . .'

'And you can't keep your precious cock to yourself, you pig.'

Adrian's face became dark with anger.

'I just don't want any scandal,' he said, trying hard to control his temper. 'Anyway, what do you care about her friends, what she's done? It's none of your business. If you ask me you're well shot of her . . .'

'Is that sour grapes or boredom speaking, sweetest?'

'Leave it.'

'I will not!' She rushed up to him, her fists raised and Adrian, without thinking, drew back his hand and struck her hard across the face. She caught her breath in a scream, stumbled away from him.

'You bastard . . .'

'She's right. You are a bitch. You know how you are . . .'

'I'll take you for every penny you've got,' she said, rubbing her red and stinging cheek. 'I'll drag you through every court in the land.'

'Don't be so stupid,' he said, turning away from her in evident disgust, 'I intend to speak to this Critchley fellow and find out just what you've been up to. And if I find . . .'

'You'll what?' she sneered, drawing herself up and challenging him.

He waited for a moment before turning to face her.

'I'll take a riding crop to you. You've had it coming for a long time.'

Cassandra's stomach curdled with fear. She knew Adrian – he was quite transparent to her – and she knew that he meant what he said.

'Oh for Heaven's sake . . . What are we doing? Why are we rowing about her?'

'No, Cass. I mean it. I don't want any more of your games, your tricks. Just leave it, and remember what I said.'

It was hateful, horrid and she could not believe that this was happening to her. This was not Adrian, darling Ade, who indulged her in everything. But her fear persisted and knotted in her stomach.

'Very well,' she said, mustering what remnants of her dignity she could. 'I'll leave you to come to your senses. And you'd better tell Philomena to make up the spare bed, that is if you haven't got somewhere else to go tonight.'

She would make Lois pay for this, she vowed. If it was the last thing she ever did, she would make her grovel and suffer for this.

Mrs Valerian sat right across the room from Amanda, the back of her chair against the wall. There was something stiff and formal about her, despite the casual clothes and unkempt hair.

'Why should anybody want to make you suffer in this way?'

Wearily, Amanda repeated:

'For revenge . . . I've told you.'

'All right. Let us accept that for a moment. Then what would you think of such a person? How would you describe them? To me for example.'

'Well, that's easy. I'd say they were mad, wicked, cruel.'

'What do you mean by "mad"?'

'I don't know . . . crazy . . . irrational . . . I don't know the right words.'

'Irrational will do. And what else did you say? "Wicked"? "Cruel"?'

'Yes.'

Mrs Valerian turned a pencil in her long fingers.

'And what are your feelings about this person?'

'I hate her.'

'Because she hates you?'

'No. Because she frightens me.'

'What are you afraid of?'

'Of her.'

'Not of what she might do to you?'

'What she *is* doing,' Amanda said.

'Not of her intrinsically?'

'I don't know what you mean.'

'Well, just imagine that you came face to face with her and you weren't afraid. What would you do? What would you say?'

'I don't know.'

'Try.'

'I can't. I can't imagine it. I'd be scared . . .'

'Well, let us look at the alternatives, possible alternatives. Would you run away?'

'Yes.'

'Supposing you couldn't. Would you . . . hit her? Spit in her face? Tell her exactly what you thought of her?'

'No . . . Yes . . . Maybe . . . I don't know . . .'

'Or would you, perhaps, want to say that you were sorry for what you had done to her?'

There was a long pause during which Mrs Valerian continued to twist the pencil in her fingers. She kept it still only when Amanda began to cry.

'Yes,' she said. 'Yes, I'd like to do that . . . I'd like to ask her to forgive me . . . If she would forgive me then all this would stop. Not just for that . . . I *am* sorry. Dreadfully sorry.'

Mrs Valerian waited, let her cry. The interview was almost over and she had got what she wanted. As she waited, she marshalled her thoughts, considering the report she would write. There was a lot of guilt there. It was a pity the girl was not religious. Confession, a sign of forgiveness, would do her a lot of good. She needed to shed some of that guilt, but Mrs Valerian saw nothing unusual in that. She certainly did not believe that Amanda had sent the parcels to herself. Somebody was exploiting that guilt in a peculiarly nasty and effective way. But that wasn't Mrs Valerian's province. Her interest there would lay in the exploiter. If it was this girl Amanda spoke of, then *there* was a suitable case for treatment, and a very interesting one at that. But as far as Amanda Beatty was concerned, a course of psychotherapy would no doubt help, but she did not feel that it was essential. Once the girl was better, she ought to get away from the hospital. In time, given the chance, she would learn to deal with her guilt in her own way. That was always the best way in Mrs Valerian's opinion. Until she had managed that, whether she was a suitable candidate for the nursing profession was something about which Mrs Valerian felt much less sanguine. Nurses needed to be tough, pretty well-balanced and at the moment . . .

'I think that will do,' she said, standing up. 'Unless there's anything else you wish to tell me?'

Amanda shook her head.

'Don't worry about it. What you need is a good, long rest. Try not to go over and over it in your mind. Concentrate on getting better.'

With a brisk nod, Mrs Valerian left the room.

Amanda turned her face to the window, her tears drying tight on her skin.

*

Andy came home early Saturday morning, when the streets were all but empty and the buses seemed to dawdle through the absence of traffic, as though confused by an empty stretch of road. His head ached from the amount of beer he had consumed the night before. He had already forgotten the name and face of the man with whom he had spent the night, out of whose bed and home he had crept at first light. He felt soiled by the night he had spent and welcomed the cold, whipping east wind which buffeted him as he walked. It was cleansing and punishing at the same time. This was the second time he had been with a stranger since his meeting with Lois and the guilt, the sense of self-disgust was stronger than ever. Even the thought of a long soak in a hot bath, liberally dosed with disinfectant, did not make him feel any better. If he loosened for a moment the strict clamp he kept on his thoughts, he imagined Lois laughing about him, despising him for his evident lack of masculinity. So he kept his mind numb, frozen, suspended. He was not worthy of thought.

Body aching, head throbbing, he let himself into the house and stooped automatically to pick up the scattered pile of post. He knew at once that the square manilla envelope which bore his typewritten name and address contained another reminder, was a follow-up to the panties he had already received. He had not been expecting it, but he recognized it. He did so without any marked feeling of shock or dread. It was simply inevitable.

He carried the letter up to the icy room and put it down while he lit the gas fire. He even considered taking his bath before opening it. If he hurried now, before the rest of the household began to stir, he would be sure of plenty of hot water, time to soak before someone came banging on the door. But the envelope was something to be faced, accepted. He could think about it, examine its full implications in the bath.

He lifted the envelope and tore it open.

The picture was obviously clipped from a mail order clothing catalogue. He remembered seeing many such in his home in Scotland when, because of the move, his mother had to economize. For most of their adolescence, he and his brother had worn clothes unimaginative, sensible, cheap, picked from such catalogues.

A photograph of two young boys, arms akimbo, fists bunched on their narrow hips. One standing slightly before the other so that their bodies overlapped. They were dressed in matching singlets and briefs, white and yellow respectively.

At first glance there seemed to be nothing more to the picture. A standard pose offering standard garments at a fixed price.

The boy in the foreground, the one in yellow, who grinned a little shyly into the impersonal lens, was incomplete. He lacked a crotch. The inverted yellow Y between his legs had been snipped out with sharp scissors, leaving a triangular space.

Beside the space, across the boy's thigh, a number was printed. SD155. The order number, which you copied down into the requisite box when ordering . . . The information rattled through Andy's head. A pack of three, matching vests and pants. Suitable for ages 11–13. Best quality cotton. Will wash and wear . . .

The boy had been castrated, cut off, rendered useless.

Andy stared and stared until his hand shook so much that the picture fluttered to the floor. From there the boy grinned shyly up at him, seemed to mock, to claim acquaintance, to issue a dreadful invitation.

Adrian stood over Cassandra who sat, petulant and pouting, at her rosewood writing desk in a corner of the bedroom. Once she had written the letter discharging Mr

Critchley, authorizing him to act for Lois Carradine if he so wished, it would all be over, Adrian thought. She had begged and pleaded with him not to make her telephone. She simply could not do it. It would be such a ghastly loss of face. Adrian had given in, partly because he loved her and partly because a letter was less elusive than a phone call. He could oversee the writing of a letter and post it himself.

He had no idea how culpable Cass was in the business and he was beginning not to care. Working on the rigid principle that there could be no smoke without fire, Adrian simply wanted to make sure that it went no further. He did not want waves, repercussions. His family name and position in the City were too prominent and too precious for him to risk any breath of scandal. Ever since the night Lois had burst in on them, accusing Cassie, he had worked hard to ensure that nothing came out of the incident, no matter how trivial. Adrian was good at putting his own house in order.

Mrs Hamilton-Weir, Cassie's mother, had warned him before their engagement of what she called 'Cassandra's madcap tendencies'. She had mentioned one or two incidents at school, a particularly nasty piece of emotional blackmail in which Cass had been heavily implicated at her finishing school. Adrian had been ready enough to put it down to high spirits. After all, he liked spirit in a girl. Probably, he would have forgotten all about it if it had not been for the unpleasant business of his sister's marriage. It had been going through a bumpy patch: nothing Tina couldn't ride out, in his opinion. But then Cass had got involved. She seemed to be helping at first. As another in-law, she had befriended George, Tina's husband, and provided him with a warm shoulder to cry on. The trouble was, she had not kept what she learned to herself. Adrian and most of the rest of his family believed that the marriage would have trundled on if Tina had not been so graphically informed about George's extra-marital flings. Everyone knew, of course, that he was playing around away from home, including Tina. That had been the cause of the difficulties in the first place. What none of them knew, except Cass, and what Tina certainly did not need to know, was that George's playmates were boys. Tina simply could not stomach that and so there had been a peculiarly messy divorce and an abrupt end to George's career. All quite unnecessary in Adrian's opinion, but that had paled into insignificance alongside the shock of learning that Cassie had penned the vitriolic anonymous letters that informed Tina and ruined George. Letters that had been produced in Court and over which he had spent sweating, sleepless nights. Cass had promised never, ever to do anything like that again and Adrian had truly believed that Sasha would calm her down, put an end to those restless moods when she was liable to stray a bit off the rails. But now he was not so sure. Maybe he was damning her without sufficient evidence, as she claimed, but better that than risk a public disgrace.

'There,' Cassandra said, handing him the single sheet of headed notepaper, covered with her bold, spidery scrawl. 'Does that satisfy my Lord and Master?'

He read the letter through carefully before nodding his agreement.

'Now seal it and address it.'

With a show of meekness, Cassandra did so, handing him the envelope with a little moue of annoyance. Adrian put it in his breast pocket.

'That's all done then. It's a relief, I can tell you.'

'And you won't be beastly to me while we're in the Canaries?' Cassandra asked.

'Of course not. How could I be?'

The Canaries had been Mrs Hamilton-Weir's idea. Nothing pleased Cassie more than a bona-fide distraction. So, without consulting her, Adrian had made all the arrangements and resigned himself to a thoroughly non-traditional Christmas. In addition, he had deposited a lump sum in Cassie's dress account and had told her to get a lot of lovely new things. She was like a pleased child and the bedroom was already littered with expensive dress boxes.

'Oh I'm longing to be there,' she said.

'The time will soon pass. And you've got plenty to keep you occupied,' Adrian reminded her.

'You are good to me, Ade. In your own funny way,' she said, and meant it.

'Just make sure you're the most stunning girl on the island. That's all I ask.'

'And you'll be all bronzed and dishy. Which reminds me, you absolutely must get one of those bikini things. I won't have you flopping around in those ghastly old shorts. I want everyone to see what an absolutely scrummy husband I've got.'

'I'll go naked if it'll keep you happy,' he said.

'Oh, Ade, you wouldn't! I say, it would be rather fun, though, wouldn't it? And I could go topless . . .'

She chatted on but Adrian did not bother to listen. It was all right now. He felt himself beginning to relax. He felt a sense of accomplishment at having contained the situation and made her happy. When she was happy, Cass was a great girl. Maybe she should have another baby. That would cheer the grandparents up, anyway. Adrian patted the letter in his pocket and eyed Cassandra speculatively. Yes, that surely should do the trick.

'Ade,' she said, giggling, 'I can see what you're thinking.'

He just smiled back at her and excused himself for a moment. Downstairs, he locked the letter safely in his desk. Then he ran back to the bedroom and set about the business of making another son and heir, of keeping Cassie occupied.

*

I have a room all to myself on the eleventh floor with a fantastic view right out over the River Thames. There is my own private bathroom en suite, colour TV, three channel radio – I should have stayed here all along! It's more comfortable even than the Foss's. All the nurses I've seen are Australian. They're not regular nurses but what they call Agency nurses. This is all on account of the English not approving of paybeds. It's all very heavy and political but according to Joylene, one of the nurses, it's okay for me to pay because I'm a US citizen.

Lois paused, looked up at the big window. She saw the winking lights of an aircraft crossing the night sky and suddenly felt homesick. She had started to write a long letter to Mr Stryker but her feelings were too complicated to compress into a single letter and when she realized that there was no one else back home to whom she could write, she had crumpled it up and thrown it in the waste bin. Instead she had written a brief note, just informing him that she was going to have plastic surgery in a few days. She signed it formally, with her full name, not really knowing how to address him.

Her lack of friends and family struck her more acutely because of her situation. She frequently heard voices in the corridor, the cheerful voices of visitors and family, bearing gifts. The nurses had described to her the profusion of flowers and fruit and chocolates some patients received and Lois had told them that she would not be having any visitors.

'That's all right, love. You've got us,' Joylene said, with a full smile.

She had left America with only one friend, Cassandra, and now even she was gone. The thought saddened her but she did not regret a word she had said to Cassandra and Adrian. They had never been true friends. She wondered what that phrase meant. She had never had true friends. Oh, perhaps, way back, before Daddy had brought them all to England, to Olton. She had wanted friends so desperately there that she had been prepared to do anything to get them and bind them to her. Andy and William, Vanessa and Amanda, the twins. They had never liked her. Not really, not deep down. Which was why she had been so horrible to them and why they had . . .

She looked down at her journal again, read over what she had written about Cassandra. Lois was convinced now that Cassandra had taken advantage of her life, and manipulated and used it for her own sick amusement. She was prepared to concede, now that she was calmer, that maybe Cassandra had not sent those panties to Andy, but that did not alter the fact that she had regarded Lois, her grief, her pain, her anger as a sort of *divertissement*. What kind of person would do that? No, she felt no regrets about Cassandra. In fact, she felt better for having cleaned her out of her life.

Maybe, after the operation, when the bandages were finally taken off, she would be able to make friends. She still believed that was possible, in spite of everything. If she felt more confident about her appearance, she would be able to make the first move, would be able to stand her ground when people made friendly overtures to her. If she did not look so bad, she wouldn't always smell pity in the air.

When she had said to Andy that she might take some classes when she went back home, she had not really thought about what she was saying. Now it seemed a real possibility. Once Mr Valentine had fixed her up, she could imagine herself on a nice campus somewhere, confident, industrious, applying her mind and willing to be at ease with people. She knew that she was badly under-educated and for the first time in her life she saw that as a disadvantage. After the scarring, she'd never gone back to school. She'd had tutors from time to time, but her parents had always been too sorry for her to insist that she applied herself. She did not really know if she was clever or not.

Mr Stryker said she had a good, quick mind but that it had never been stretched. It had concerned itself with one subject and one only.

She got up and went into the windowless bathroom. She pulled a cord to illuminate the bright neon strip above the mirror and, holding her breath, she combed her hair severely back from her face. She would only have this face she had gotten out of the habit of looking at for a few more days. She wanted to look at it, say goodbye . . .

The skin of her eyeless socket was smooth and paler than the rest. It looked thin and vulnerable. The very centre was puckered and a little inflamed. Scar lines radiated out from it like a child's drawing of the sun. There was scar tissue along her temple, running down in lines like badly finished seams. Her mouth was a little crooked, pulling her smile out of kilter. Her neck looked as if someone had clawed it into ridges that had never healed. All the skin was dry and had a tendency to flake. She touched it with her fingertips, feeling its deadness, its awful pitted texture.

Would Mr Valentine be able to make her pretty enough to lose her virginity?

'Good day. Anyone at home?'

At the sound of the cheery voice, Lois's hands flew instinctively to her hair to pull it forward. She caught sight of herself in the fiercely lit mirror, a look of panic and shame froze on her face. But she was in hospital now, where people were used to looking at horrors. In the next few days her face would be minutely examined, measured, photographed . . . Her hands trembled as she forced them down. Why was she ashamed? She made herself turn away from the mirror and walk out of the bathroom, her heart hammering uncomfortably.

There were two nurses looking at her, Joylene and another, who was holding a vase of delicate, richly scented freesias. The expressions on their faces did not flicker or change and Lois felt her heart steady.

'There you are,' Joylene said. 'This is Nancy. She's on nights this week.'

'I brought these,' Nancy said, putting the vase down on the bed table. 'Got 'em off the old biddy down the hall. She says they pong too much. She can't sleep with 'em in the room.'

'They're lovely,' Lois said, looking gratefully at the flowers.

'Beats me how she can tell,' Joylene said. 'I swear she baths in Chanel No 5. The whole bloody room stinks of it. 'Scuse my French.'

Lois found herself laughing with the two young women.

'Anyway, I'm off,' Joylene said. 'Got to get me kip. Nance'll look after you.'

'Thanks. See you tomorrow.'

'Sure will.'

'Now, what'll it be? Tea, cocoa, Ovaltine? What do you fancy for your beddy-bye drinkie?' Nancy said.

'You know what? I'd like a magnum of champagne,' Lois told her.

'Good on you. Only thing is, we're fresh out. Settle for cocoa. I make a lousy cup of tea, anyway.'

'You've just got yourself a deal,' Lois said.

'Great. I'll be back in a jiffy.'

Lois touched the waxy petals, sniffed up the sweet, thick scent of the flowers. She was not a freak. Those nice, open girls did not think she was a freak. They brought her flowers, chatted to her like she was a normal human being. She sat on the bed, her eye still fixed on the flowers. After the surgery, maybe a man would buy her flowers. She would go out on dates, with her hair brushed back and maybe someone, some man would want to make love to her. She would be able to let him, at last. What was virginity for, if not for losing? It made her dizzy to think what she might gain.

'Here you go,' Nancy said, bustling back into the room. 'One cocoa de-luxe. And don't say I didn't warn you.'

'Thanks.'

'Feeling a bit low? Why don't you put the telly on? Or I'll tell you what, once I've done me pill round, I'll fetch me knitting in and sit with you. We can have a good old chin-wag. What do you say?'

'That would be great, Nancy. Thank you.'

'See you in a tick then.'

Lois touched her face, smoothed back her hair, and she was smiling.

Eight

Shortly before the end of term Jason was carpeted by his head of department. Those dire warnings were underlined firmly but more sympathetically over coffee by his tutor. Jason said that he had not been feeling very well. He said that he would catch up, knuckle down to some hard work next term. By then, he thought, it might all be over and such things as studying would become a possibility again. At the earliest opportunity, the twins packed and loaded up Julian's old car. Together they drove home for the Christmas holidays, not knowing what to expect.

Christmas fever spread by contagion and flourished everywhere. Blue and purple tinsel decorated the dressing room Vanessa shared with three other girls. Bunches of mistletoe appeared in unlikely places backstage. Audiences seemed to be in a specially festive mood and this communicated across the footlights, giving the cast an extra lift. At first Vanessa resisted the prevailing mood of excitement and expectation, but she quickly came to see that by immersing herself in it she was able to distract herself from her problems. She began to perform again with her original zest, tinged now with a touch of almost manic energy. She planned to spend Christmas Day with several other members of the cast and looked forward to the extra Boxing Day matinée. Max Krieger was to be a member of that party and she knew that she would be, outwardly at least, his partner. She had allowed Max to talk her round, pretended to believe his promise that, when the show closed, she would fly straight to New York and be with him. She knew she was a fool, despised herself for not having had the courage to put an end to this uncertain relationship. Unsettled and scared by other events, living in the shadow of fear that further incidents, something worse might occur, she craved affection and security, even though she knew they were ephemeral. She pretended to believe Max, pretended to be happy. It was like crossing her fingers against what the immediate future might bring.

Even Andy could not escape Christmas entirely. Christmas trees, gaudily lit, suddenly blossomed in the sad windows of the street where he lived. Bands of children singing one verse of a carol came banging on the door almost daily. Even the launderette was filled with the muted tinkle of seasonal muzak. His workmates went earlier to the pub and stayed longer, anticipating turkey dinners, days off, the films to be shown on television over the holiday. Andy let them believe that he would return to Scotland and stay through until Hogmanay was past. To his mother he wrote that he had a chance to work on the days between the two bank holidays and that it would not be worth his while to travel so far for so short a time. He would try to come up in the New Year, for a longer stay. When he had finished and sealed the letter, it seemed that he had broken with something, cut himself adrift.

Amanda begged and pleaded to be allowed to go to Durham, to be with her father, but her doctor absolutely forbade it, even if suitable travel arrangements could be made. They promised to let her up, into a wheelchair for the Christmas party and pointed out that, but for the accident, she would probably have been on duty anyway, so she might as well enjoy herself. Everyone was very kind to her for it was fairly common knowledge that the assistant matron, acting on Mrs Valerian's report and in the face of Sister Wilson's opposition, had decided to sack Amanda once she was well. It was felt that she was not suitable for training. She could apply again in a couple of years, when she had sorted herself out, was more mature. If she still wanted to be a nurse, that is. Sister Wilson pointed out that it was the only thing she had ever wanted to be. The assistant matron agreed that that was sad but reminded Sister that Amanda was young and that the young were very resilient. Besides, they had more than Amanda's welfare to consider. They had a responsibility to the hospital, their profession and, above all, to their patients.

Cassandra Foss despatched her son and his Nanny to her mother's house in the country and then, accompanied by several large suitcases of new clothes, flew out to the Canary Islands. Adrian was to join her in three days' time. She amused herself, while waiting, by flirting with a group of German students she met on the beach. Although she did not know it at the time, one of these students made her pregnant hours before Adrian arrived.

Calibrated photographs of Lois's face had been taken, endless X-ray plates made. Her face had been measured with fine instruments and the figures marked down on a chart. Skin samples had been taken from various parts of her body and the most suitable 'donor' areas encircled so that she felt like a living version of those diagrams displayed in butchers' shops, to explain the different cuts of meat. They had clipped and shaved her hair along the hairline and down behind her right ear. Joylene and Nancy said she looked like a trendy punk, setting new styles. Finally, Mr Valentine showed her photographs of herself, the injured side of her face scored with fine pen-lines, to explain exactly how the skin would be grafted. In his funny, fatherly way, seeing her wince of fear and dismay, he told her it was his Blueprint for Beauty. She should think of it that way.

On the morning of the operation she rose early and bathed before putting on the short blue hospital gown which Nancy tied at the back for her, before, yawning healthily, she went off duty. At half-past eight, when the lack of liquid intake was beginning to bother her, the

English sister, Rose, assisted by Joylene, gave her her pre-med and told her to lie very still.

She had not believed that the drug would relax her, but as she lay there staring at the ceiling or at the falling sleet that spattered her window, the awful knots of fear and tension slowly, slowly relaxed and she became sleepy. It was a floating feeling, literally care-free. She closed her eyes, let herself drift pleasantly with the drug. In a detached, quite separate kind of way, she found herself watching the antics of a child, a little girl. She was wearing a man's raincoat, much too long for her, buttoned round her shoulders like a cape. The top half of her face was obscured by an ugly green mask. Moulded warts and pimples coruscated the green skin and a long, curving witch's nose protruded. The girl was capering, dancing, clawing at the air with crooked fingers. Then she was running through a field of snow, Wellington boots on her feet. Lois felt that she was happy, enjoying the space and the bright snowlight. The girl laboured up a hill, her booted feet slipping in the snow, her breath puffing visibly. And William was waiting for her at the top of the hill, handsome, self-contained William. He had a sled and they sat on it together, working it forward with their feet. William's arms were folded chastely but firmly around the girl, holding on to the rope fixed to the front of the sled. They whizzed away down the long hill, laughing into the wind. Only then did Lois realize that the girl still wore her green ugliness and she felt sad for her. It was not a bit sinister, as the girl presumably intended, but simply pitiful. She would be so pretty, Lois thought, without it.

And then Lois herself was in a strange, dark place. Stones, solid walls towered out of the darkness. She was climbing a perilous stairway. Children skittered away in front of her, their laughter hanging on the air. They were visible only as flashes of colour, fair hair dancing on fleeing shoulders. She paused in her climb and looked down into a vast, black pit.

Then she was looking down into her father's coffin, looking at his hastily mended and made-up face. She knew that it was not him but a dummy, an obscene doll they were going to bury in his place. Daddy could not be dead. She could still smell the bourbon on his breath.

Somehow, she had completed her climb and was walking through a large, airy dark space that recalled the barn at Olton. She was wearing a navy blue velvet dress, very formal, with white collar and cuffs. She could hear music, humming voices. As she drew closer to the sound, she saw a girl. A girl all dressed up for a party in her first long dress. She was turning in some private dance.

Happy Birthday to you
Happy Birthday to you
Happy Birthday . . .

Light, treble voices sang sweetly as the girl turned. With a thrill of excitement, Lois recognized the girl by her black glossy hair and elegant carriage. It was Cassandra Hamilton-Weir, dancing romantically and alone. She ran towards her, trying to call her name. The figure, the girl, suddenly turned to face her and it was William, looking grave and serious. William held out his arms to her and she moved smoothly into them. William held her tightly and swept her into the dance, smiling.

As though it had miraculously joined the dance, her bed suddenly rolled away from the wall, swung in a wide arc across the room. Lois's eyes flew open. A thick-set man, dressed in the grey uniform of a hospital porter, was tugging at the foot of her bed, rolling it out into the corridor.

'All right, love?' Joylene leaned over the head of the bed, her face inverted. 'We're taking you up to theatre now.'

'You're coming with me?'

'Dead right I am.'

The bed rolled effortlessly down the corridor. Lois watched the ceiling lights come and go, come and go. They turned a corner, the bed was straightened and, as though from a great distance, she heard the porter and Joylene talking about the elevator. She did not understand what they said. She was rolled into the lift, a big, cold metal box. It rose smoothly. Joylene stood at the side of the bed, a folder of medical notes and a clipboard clutched to her bosom.

'Feeling good and relaxed?'

'Bit sleepy.'

'That's okay. It won't be long now.'

The metal doors of the lift slid soundlessly open and she was wheeled out into a sort of concourse. It felt very cool and she could hear the hum of air-conditioning. The light was cold and yet brightly yellow. The porter, helped by another with a shock of red hair, lifted her as though she weighed nothing and swung her onto a trolley. Joylene rearranged the spread over her.

'It's cold,' she said.

'You'll be all right in a tick.'

'Are you coming with me?'

'No further, love. Got to get back downstairs. I'll see you later.' Joylene gripped her shoulders, hard. 'Good luck, love.'

'Joylene . . .' She tried to sit up.

A figure in dark green grinned at her and said 'hello'. He pushed the trolley through a pair of rubberized swing doors which sighed shut behind them. The man in green said something to her and went away. She lay there feeling cold and very afraid. Then a strong arm grasped the foot of her trolley and tugged it through another doorway into a small room that smelled of disinfectant and ether and other horrible, remembered hospital smells.

'Well, now, what have you been doing to yourself?' Another man smiled down into her spoiled face and lifted her head, pushing her hair into a bag-like surgical cap. 'Feeling a bit drowsy?' He did not seem to expect any answers. He took her right arm and turned it palm upwards. She felt the cold swab on the crook of her elbow. 'Hold steady.' A needle gently pierced her skin.

'Mr Valentine . . .' she said, her voice thick and slurred.

'He's already scrubbing up. Now, I want you to count backwards from ten as soon as I tell you, okay?'

'Ok-ay'.

She felt him fix something to the needle in her arm, turned her head to try and see. He was smiling at her, his eyes very dark and friendly.

'Now,' he said.

'Ten . . . nine . . . eight . . . sev . . .'

His face began to rotate like a Catherine-wheel. It became a sun, beautiful. There was a roaring sound in her ears and she was falling, falling down. The sun-face steadied and came sharply into focus. It was William's face, smiling at her. And then everything went completely black.

It was like floating up through silted water. Just before she broke through the surface, into light and air again, it seemed that she was sucked back down only to rise, rise slowly. She heard a woman moaning, the splash of water. Her eyes flickered open. Low ceiling, grey concrete. It was cold, cold again. A figure in green floated peripherally in her vision. There was something white, fixed at the corner of her eye.

She woke again, startled by a woman's voice, loud and firm.

'Come along now, Yvonne. Come along, Yvonne. Wakey-wakey.'

A woman moaned, screamed out a name, over and over again.

A figure in green leaned over Lois.

'Hello? How are you feeling?'

'Okay.'

Bandages, dressings tugged unfamiliarly at the corner of

her mouth when she spoke. She remembered what had happened to her. Her throat felt very dry and a little sore. She raised her hand, trying to touch the bandages. The figure grabbed her wrist, tucked it firmly under the sheet that covered her.

'I've had surgery . . .' she said.

'Yes.'

The figure bent closer, peering at her. She suddenly recognized the face, or thought she did.

'Will . . . William?' she said, her voice faint. 'William?'

'Hello, Lois.'

Then she was sinking down again, into the silted grey waters of oblivion and rest.

The operation had taken five hours and Lois had a bad reaction to the anaesthetic. When she woke again she was lying in her room. The light was strange and dusky. Her throat felt sore. She felt the harsh grip of bandages about her head. When she tried to lift her arm, to explore the bandages, she discovered that she was on a drip. The stand gleamed beside the bed, a plastic bag of some clear liquid hanging from its top. A series of transparent tubes and valves descended towards her arm where a needle was taped in place. The sight panicked her. What was wrong? What had happened? She needed a blood transfusion? Twisting her head towards the door, she suddenly felt sick. Right down in her belly she felt a dreadful contraction and the irresistible urge to vomit swept upwards through her. Flailing with her free arm she found that the console containing the emergency call button had been swung out from the wall behind her so that she could reach it easily. Frantic, she pressed the red button. Her mouth was too dry to allow her to speak into the intercom. She had to keep swallowing against the upheaval in her stomach.

'Coming,' a voice called through the intercom.

It was Nancy, smiling, familiar, who helped her to sit up, supported her and held a bowl. Lois kept trying to say that she was sorry. She coughed and retched, spat saliva into the bowl but nothing else came away. She was sweating and trembling, feeling that she was going to die when Nancy eased her back onto the pillows.

'All better now,' she said, reassuringly.

'Drink . . . Something to drink . . .'

'Not yet, I'm afraid, lovey. I'll bring you something later.'

'Take this off . . .' She flapped her arm, with the needle in it.

The nurse walked round the bed and checked the valves.

'Can't do. It's only a saline drip, to stop you dehydrating. I'll take it off later. Nothing to worry about. Try to rest.' She bent over Lois, smoothing the bedclothes. 'Still feeling sick?'

'Yes.'

'Hang on. I'll be back in a tick.'

She tried to obey, coughing and swallowing, certain that this time she would really be sick, violently so.

Nancy returned with a newcomer, a pretty blonde girl in a sister's uniform.

'I'm going to give you something to put you to sleep and stop you feeling sick. All right?'

'Oh, please . . .' Lois panted, just before a new wave of nausea swept through her.

Nancy turned her gently onto her side and held her. She did not feel the needle but she became aware for the first time of dressings on other parts of her body, from where they had taken the skin to dress her face.

'There. You'll soon be fast asleep and tomorrow you'll feel as right as rain.'

Lois tried to smile. They eased her onto her back. The sister adjusted the console so that it was within easy reach.

'Rest now,' she said.

'You're going to be fine,' Nancy told her, smiling broadly. 'I'll look in later . . .'

Sleep was already clawing at her mind, claiming her. She gave herself up to it willingly though with the vague, uncomfortable thought that there was something she ought to remember, something very important and strange.

He had two jobs now. That made him smile. Not bad for a man they said was unemployable. He folded his hands around a chipped mug of tea into which he had stirred a dollop of honey. His nails were very short, the skin around them chewed livid. Having two jobs meant that there was very little time for sleeping, but that did not bother him at all. He had got out of the habit of sleeping long ago. On the very rare occasions when he was really tired, he would buy a ticket on the Circle Line and sleep for as long as he wanted. He despised sleep, considered it a waste of time. He preferred to be awake, observing, watchful, planning as befitted a man with a mission.

He sipped the hot, nourishing tea, huddled over the single-bar electric fire. The hut was at the very back of the yard, built up against the towering wall of a warehouse which formed one boundary of Mr Lunn's property. The hut had served a number of nightwatchmen or security guards, as he preferred to be called, though none before him had made it his home. He had done so quietly and unobtrusively, so that when Mr Lunn found out, it was a *fait accompli*, proof of his ingenuity and care. For example, he had not moved one of the cardboard boxes of old and dusty records that were stored there, a fact he drew proudly to Mr Lunn's attention when he came to see what was going on. Mr Lunn was a shark, but a sensible one. He saw the advantages to himself. He did not hang around the yard much during the day – even less so now that he had his second job – but making the hut his own meant that he was never late for the job. And he had taken to grooming the dogs in his own time. They had never looked so good, their kennels never been kept so clean. He had been prepared to take a drop in wages, in lieu of rent, but Mr Lunn had not even suggested it. He knew that he was getting a bargain, a loyal and conscientious employee who, in return for extra services, asked only space to lay a mattress, store a portable radio and a sleeping bag, a few clean and meticulously folded clothes. It was a good arrangement, benefiting both sides.

The money he earned was another source of pride and of surprise. He needed very little, had become used to empty pockets. Now wodges of used notes, pinky-brown, blue, green-white, were pressed into his hand each week by Mr Lunn. Often there was an extra note, a big one, for staying put all weekend when Mr Lunn scented trouble or, more frequently, to leave the gates open for an hour or two, in the small hours. Then he remained in the hut until the delivery had been made, venturing out only at the appointed hour to lock the gates. Sometimes the delivery was a car, sometimes boxes and packages which were stored in the big garage on the other side of the yard. He did not ask questions. He put many of the notes into a recently opened Giro account where, just that day, he had also deposited his first pay cheque from his other job. It gave him pleasure to stare at his bank book, checking the sums. It was amazing how the money mounted up. If he kept on like this, he would soon be quite rich.

He finished his tea, checked his watch and stood up. It was time for his round. Over his warm tracksuit he pulled a thickly quilted anorak. Then he clicked on the switch by the door which turned on the lights in the yard, all but the big floodlights and the spots that illuminated the giant sign: *Lunn's Used Cars*.

It was still snowing. Stepping out of the hut, he pulled up the hood of his anorak and looked up at the nearest light. A cone of sulphurous yellow fell towards the earth, the beam defined and accentuated by the whirling flakes of white. He felt a rush of pleasure. It reminded him of a beautiful object he had found at the back of a cupboard at Redpaths. A heavy glass dome, like a crystal ball, mounted on a red plastic base. The ball was full of liquid. If you held your breath so as not to mist the glass and looked closely, you could see a magical miniature landscape. A background of white hills, dotted with trees. A little house made of wood with a picket fence. A clump of trees no bigger than the parings from a man's fingernails in which two tiny deer stood, sniffing the air. And in the foreground, its white powder puff tail showing, a lolloping rabbit. That rabbit had nearly broken his heart. Then, with a single twist of your wrist, like God, you could cause a snowstorm. One twist set the imaginary sky, the air that was really a colourless liquid, awhirl with snow. So thick it was that the house, the animals disappeared. You could almost hear a wind howl, but only for a moment. The storm was brief and swift and violent, but it passed, and slowly the scene re-emerged, was seen through a veil of snow, falling. It settled on the hills and on the roof of the house, on the trees and on the picket fence. It dusted the coat of the rabbit, which continued to lollop along. And now, his face upturned to the light, the snow, he felt himself inside that glass dome, himself a part of the storm.

He became aware of the sharp cold, stamped his feet, shaking off the dreamy mood of memory. He made a low, almost cooing whistle and at once three large, powerful shapes materialized from various parts of the yard, racing towards him. Major, the largest and most powerful of the German Shepherds, slithered up to him. He reached down and patted his thick coat, which was damp with snow. Solomon, the youngest of the three, whined for attention and affection. He clipped a lead to the heavy choke chain around Major's throat and whistled the others, Solomon and Sergeant, to heel.

On his right were piles of tyres, tall, black towers like some cityscape from the cover of a science fiction paperback. They were already turning white, losing definition. In front of them, stretched forward and across the yard to the big garage, was a packed litter of clapped out old bangers. Some lolled, wheel-less. Many were but the detritus of accidents. Some even bore bloodstains on their battered upholstery. The other cars in this part of the yard were slowly reduced to skeletons as men like vultures picked them clean for spare parts. Eventually, they would be crane-lifted onto lorries and carted off for scrap, only to be replaced by more used, abandoned and broken models. He wove a random path between these cars, Major at his side, the others darting and sniffing from side to side, but always returning to his heels. He checked the doors of the big garage, testing the heavy-duty padlocks that secured massive bolts. Then he proceeded to the front part of the yard where the decent, saleable stuff was set out in rows. Resprayed, retuned, their windscreens decorated with gaudy price stickers, the cars gleamed in the lights, bright colours showing through their dusting of snow. He walked the dogs along the entire length of the front fence: twelve feet of stout chain-link, broken only by heavy steel gates. Again he checked locks. The road beyond was quiet, the wheel tracks of the last passing car clearly etched in the snow. He paused at the gates, watching snow drift round lamp posts, looking for a sign of anything suspicious. There was nothing. He completed his inspection of the street boundary and then turned back down the yard, passing the kennels as he did so. He heard Sheba shift on her palette of straw as he passed, heard her deep, threatening growl which made the other dogs tense and nervous. He stooped a little and slipped the lead from Major's choke.

'Go on, boy. Go on, Major,' he whispered, tugging gently at one of the dog's pricked ears. He took off at once, hunting, partly playing in the snow. The younger dogs scattered behind him. Sheba growled again. Her tail thumped the side of her wooden pen. He heard her nails click on the concrete floor as she padded to the gate at the end of her run, looking for him. He moved on quickly back to the warmth and quiet of his hut.

They had let him keep the snowstorm throughout the rest of his stay at Redpaths and he could have brought it away with him if he had wanted. He had agonized over that: should he, shouldn't he? Finally, he decided against it. He had wanted to make a clean break, put certain things far and resolutely behind him. He had enough money now to buy a replacement . . . many. He considered the prospect, stretching his hands out to the fire. There was a problem. Could he find one that was identical in every detail? He would not want another. Not unless it showed a field in front of the hills, a field where rabbits gazed and gambolled and played. Did such a one exist? If so, he would buy it and treasure it. He was tempted to give himself over to the mental construction of idyllic scenes, all centring on rabbits, that he might find captured under a glass dome, but he pushed the thought away, saved it for a better time. Just now, he had more important things on his mind.

Security at the hospital was pitiful, which was one reason why it had been so easy for him to get a part-time job there. It was the perfect job for him, of course, because a security man could go anywhere. Which, in his opinion, was another error. The trouble was, hospitals were not used to the sort of security they needed nowadays. They lacked expertise, had lagged behind the times. When he left, when his mission was accomplished, he thought he might present them with a report, anonymous, of course, pointing out the gaps and loopholes in their system. He could easily devise an alternative that would be virtually foolproof. He thought he ought to do that. It was only polite, civil. Because there would be a tremendous fuss when he left, heads would roll, which he regretted, and he could save them a lot of time and expense in the ensuing panic, by presenting them with a ready-made watertight plan.

But not yet. Today, for example. Today had been so ridiculously easy it made him want to laugh out loud. He had signed off at the appointed hour, gone to the locker room and removed his uniform. A pair of white jeans was all he had to supply. Wearing them and his white T-shirt, he had strolled casually to one of the service rooms and helped himself to a green gown and cap. No one had even glanced at him as he rode the service lift up to the theatre floor. A uniform hid everything, made you anonymous. The two orderlies working in the recovery room had glanced at him – it had been a stroke of luck, he admitted, that they had been so busy – but that was all. No doubt they had been glad of his help as he moved from trolley to trolley, apparently checking that the comatose patients were all right. He had not wanted to draw attention to himself by making a bee-line for her trolley, even though the extent of her bandages made her immediately identifiable. How ironic, then, that his uniform had not fooled Lois. He had wanted to see what sort of a job they had done, to assess how difficult his task would be. There had always been a possibility, of course, that she would wake up, though he had not banked on it. And if she did, he had thought that she would be too woozy to recognize anyone. It surprised him that she had recognized him so quickly and easily, but it did not alter his plans. On the contrary, it lent spice to them. No one would believe her even if she claimed to have seen him. In any case, he did not exist.

That was another of the advantages of working for Mr Lunn. He was not keen on bureaucracy, slips of paper and red tape. He was not a man who liked questions. But when he had become sure of his new security guard, he had casually offered to fix him up with a National Insurance Card, everything he needed and did not have. Just as long as he did not expect Mr Lunn to stamp it, or anything daft like that. But, as he said, papers were useful, especially when you wanted to move or draw the dole.

Still, it was funny that she had recognized him so easily. In the last few weeks he had passed her many times in the street, had watched her, walked behind her and she had never for a moment noticed him. Nor had any of the others. That surprised him less because he had been much more careful with them. He had drunk shandy in the same pub as Andy, shopped in the same supermarket as Vanessa. He had mingled with the students, trailing Julian and Jason to their lectures, had drunk coffee in their canteen, watching from a safe distance. As for Amanda, well, she was a pushover, the easiest to trace, the least observant. Still, he felt warm towards Amanda for she, unwittingly, had led him to Lois and given him the idea of getting a job at the hospital. He had felt sorry for her when they had carried her into casualty that day, after she had run in front of the van. He had thought that she would be the first to crack as a result of his little presents and then, like a miracle, he had found Lois waiting for her. But he had kept an eye on Amanda, had reassured himself that she was making a good recovery. That was the great advantage of his job: a security man could go anywhere.

And afterwards it had been laughably simple to drop his green cap and gown into one of the hundreds of used linen bags and make his way down to the ground floor. He had walked down, walked down twelve floors, encountering nobody. Then he had gone back to the locker room, adjusting his zip as he entered to suggest, if anyone was there, that he had been to the lavatory. Then he put on his sweater and quilted jacket and left for the day. It was so simple, so easy and with Christmas coming, as many patients as possible being sent home, whole clinics closing down, staff, including the security team, being reduced to skeletal proportions, it would be even easier. So easy, it made him want to laugh.

It was getting light. A pearly light, thickened by the snow. He dressed for the outdoors again and went to the kennels. As usual, he was greeted by Sheba's restless movements and ugly growling. He ignored her and went into the little box-like room beside the kennels to prepare four bowls of food. The dogs came whining to the door, their tails thrashing, but they knew that he always fed Sheba first. He had begun to do so in the hope of winning her round but now he continued the ritual out of a mixture of habit and fear. A light sweat broke out on his face, was clammy on his body as he approached her door. She sat up on her bed, cringed back against the far wall, snarling, teeth bared, the moment she saw him. Swallowing against his fear, he ducked down and raised the little trap door set in the bottom of her kennel door. He pushed the bowl in. At once she leapt forward, snapping and snarling at the bowl, his wrist. He swore under his breath, snatched his hand back, dropping the bowl and let the trap door fall with a clatter. She was getting worse. Normally, she stayed back when he fed her but now, not even that service seemed to be acceptable to her. Shaken, he stood up. She was eating but her wicked eye rolled up at him the moment he looked into the pen. He hated her and she filled him with a terrible dread. His very scent was anathema to her and he had begun to think that this was because she knew. He had never, ever, underestimated the intelligence of animals and these German Shepherds were sharper than many human beings he had known. He had begun to think that she knew, that she could smell, after all this time, that other bitch on him, her blood . . . He backed away from the pen door, from his own terrible thoughts.

Major barked suddenly, demanding his food. With relief, he set off back down the alleyway, opening their kennel doors as he went. The other three smiled at him as they fell upon their bowls of food. He went back to fetch the brush and comb. In an hour it would be time to open the gates and then the rest of the morning would be his. He thought perhaps he would go to Hamley's on his way to the hospital, have a look at their snowstorms. You never knew . . . After all, it was Christmas and he deserved a present.

When Lois awoke properly for the first time, a paperchain was looped along the wall opposite her bed. A tiny plastic Christmas tree stood on her locker, decorated with silver tinsel. She hurt all over. Every muscle in her body protested at the slightest, most natural movement. Joylene told her this was a side-effect of the anaesthetic, resulted from the complete relaxation of the muscles over an unnaturally long period of time. As for the bruises which spread across the good side of her face, making her eye puffy, Joylene joked that that must have been where Mr Valentine had rested his elbow while doing the grafts.

When the surgeon himself came to see her, attended by his Registrar and a flock of students, he was not very cheering.

'The most difficult part, for you, comes now,' he said. 'It will be three weeks at least before we can take the bandages off and even then you won't be a pretty sight . . .'

'I'm used to that,' she said, trying to make a joke that misfired because it gave away how she really felt.

'You'll have to wear a light dressing for some time after that.' To the students he explained about the dangers of septicaemia until the grafts had quite taken. 'But it will be worth it and I know you'll be patient,' he said patting Lois's hand kindly.

For the rest of that day and most of the one that followed, Lois was too preoccupied with her physical discomfort to think about what had happened or to brood about the future. She dozed a lot, dreamed, but the dreams floated away with wakefulness. Time was meaningless, night and day running together in a sleepy cocoon of misery. At night, Nancy gave her pills to make her sleep and their drowsy-inducing effects never seemed to wear off completely.

The first piece of general information she took in properly was that it had snowed, had snowed again and that more was forecast.

'It looks like being a white Chrissie,' Joylene informed her. 'Jesus, me beads, I wish I was back in Sydney. It'll be up in the hundreds. This climate's bad for me skin.'

Both Joylene and Nancy were going to be off-duty over Christmas. Nancy was going to spend the holiday with English cousins while Joylene planned a 'right booze-up with some great fellahs in Earls Court'.

Lois clung to their chatter like a lifeline. Alone, she thought about the snow outside, her few memories of snow – and that led her back to the waking dream she had had before the operation. That must be some powerful drug, she thought, for she and William had never sledded together. That brief spell of January snow, years ago in Olton, had sparked off their rivalry. She had gone down the slope solo, head first. And afterwards she had shamed William into going to look at the barn, had explained to them all how it would be their headquarters. She could fix it for them and all she asked in return was to be leader of the gang. She had looked at William then . . .

William!

She sat up quickly. Pain exploded through her body, making her grunt. Gingerly, biting her lower lip, she eased herself back down on the pillows and lay there panting, waiting for the pain to recede.

She remembered waking up in the recovery room. You weren't supposed to remember that, someone had once told her. They were cold and ugly places. She remembered the cold, sounds, a perspective of grey concrete, with pre-cast beams.

Come along now, Yvonne. Come along, Yvonne. Wakey-wakey.

The sound of slaps, as though the orderly was trying to wake the woman up. Her moans, the sound of running water. William. Her body tensed involuntarily, hurting her. William here, here in the hospital?

No, it was impossible. Poor guy, she thought, whoever he was, he must have thought her crazy, calling him William with such certainty and surprise in her voice. Unless, of course, he actually happened to be called William. But then they would be familiar with the disassociation of patients in the after-grip of anaesthesia. She'd bet they got called a lot worse than William! All part of the job. They probably laughed about it among themselves.

She had been thinking about William immediately before the operation. About sledding with him in the snow and dancing with him. His face, she suddenly recalled, had been the last thing she had seen before the injection knocked her out. So it was not really surprising that his had been the first face she had seen on waking.

It *was* his face. It really was.

Nonsense, Carradine, take a hold of yourself. Some guy, doing his job. Maybe he bore a slight facial resemblance to William. After all, even as a boy William had been a recognizable type. A stranger, a hospital employee onto whose blurred features she had grafted a memory of William.

Hello, Lois. He said, *Hello, Lois.*

Sure, he had. He'd know her name. The woman who was causing all the trouble, moaning, hadn't she been called by her name? Yvonne? For heaven's sake, her name was there for all to see, fastened to her wrist. Besides which they'd have to know who they had in the recovery room, wouldn't they? Come on, Lois. Wake up, Lois. *Hello, Lois.* What the hell were they supposed to say? Excuse me, Ms Carradine, can you wake up? They wanted people to come round, didn't they, respond? So they used a familiar form of address, their Christian names. Sure. Right.

William?

Hello, Lois.

Like they'd just met in the street. Like they'd seen each other only yesterday.

Happy Birthday, Lois.

William stood in the open doorway, his hands cupped beneath a large pumpkin lantern, inside which a candle flickered.

Happy Birthday, Lois.

He walked towards her. She saw her father on the step, smiling.

Daddy?

'This isn't your present, of course,' William had said gravely. *'I've got that in my pocket.'*

Daddy.

Hello, Lois.

Oh God, oh God, it couldn't have been. It had to be a trick, the after-effects of the anaesthetic.

'Here you go, love. A nice hot cup of tea.'

Joylene helped her to sit up.

'You know the recovery rooms?'

'Hm.'

'Do you know who was on duty there when I came round?'

'No. Why? Did you misbehave yourself?'

'No. What makes you say . . .?'

'Anaesthetics, love. You'd be surprised what the most lady-like patients come out with. They're worse than the fellahs. Many a poor theatre orderly's thought he was onto a cracker down there, only to find out the bird in question doesn't remember a thing about it afterwards. Pulse, please.'

Lois lifted her arm, felt Joylene's cool fingers on her wrist.

'Some of the orderlies are men, then?'

'Sure thing. Pulse is a bit up. Are you running a bit of a temperature? Let's check.'

Joylene hummed to herself, tidied the top of the locker while Lois sat with the thermometer in her mouth.

'Did you, though? Make a pass at one of the guys up there? This is okay.' She shook the thermometer expertly and unhooked the chart from the foot of Lois's bed.

'Maybe. Could you find out who was on duty?'

'You mean you remember and you're serious?'

'No, of course not.' Lois wondered if she could blush under the bandages.

'Well, it'll be the same team as yesterday. Okay, I'll check it out for you. But I'll tell you this for nothing. I'm not going to play bloody cupid.'

'Don't be so silly. It's nothing like that.'

'Oh no? You wait till those dressings come off. Then we'll see who's the femme fatale. Drink your tea now.'

She tried not to think any more about it. She turned on the television set and drank her tea. Later, just before she went off duty, Joylene put her head around the door and said:

'I've got bad news for you, Lo. It was two Sheilas on duty that day. You must have been hallucinating or the anaesthetic turned you crook. See you.'

Oh thank God, she thought. It wasn't true. It had all been a dream, imagination.

Mr Valentine had overestimated when he said that Lois would not feel like dancing on Christmas Day. She felt more like dying. The bandages bit tightly into her head and the soreness persisted in her body. Her unwashed hair made her scalp itch and the bruises below her good eye were tender to the lightest touch. She was glad that her room was not constantly thronged with visitors and that she was not on an open ward where, according to the frequent reports brought back by the nurses, a succession of parties were in continuous swing. Raucous voices from the room next door, currently occupied by a young TV actress, frequently frustrated her attempts to doze during the day. She tried to watch television but it made her head ache. The day seemed impossibly long. She tried to appear enthusiastic about the traditional lunch but she had no appetite. Even the glass of tepid champagne, sent by the actress next door as an apology for the noise, tasted sour.

Last Christmas she had taken herself to the beach and sung carols at a cook-out organized by a lot of friendly people she did not know. Come to think of it, that wasn't a whole lot better, only then, at least, she hadn't hurt everywhere. She tried to remember other, happier Christmases but the only one that came to mind with any sharpness was that first and only one at Olton. The Hunters had given a party and she had met all the kids formally for the first time. And they had shut her out on the window-ledge from which she could so easily have fallen to her death. Maybe that would have been for the best, she thought miserably. She tried the TV again, tried to think positively about next Christmas, but her spirits were too low. She could only imagine herself alone, eating fried chicken somewhere and wondering what the hell she was going to do with her life.

She was glad when the nurses finally started throwing the other patients' visitors out, and when they came round with the medication trolley, she asked for something strong to knock her out completely. She wanted to sleep, to escape from the pain and all the waiting that stretched endlessly ahead of her. The nurse brought the pill in a paper cup and remarked that they were giving out a lot of sedation that night. Because of the difficulty of getting nurses to work over the holiday period, there would only be one sister on duty and they wanted her to have as quiet a night as possible.

Lois swallowed the pill gratefully and by the time the

sister, a pale, middle-aged woman called Green, looked in to say good-night, Lois's mind was already muzzy with the tendrils of sleep.

A rapid thaw had set in on Christmas Day but after sunset the temperature plummetted again, freezing the slush to a treacherous, lumpy film of ice. He walked carefully across the yard, hanging onto the cars whenever he could. Mr Lunn had told him there was no need to be on the premises throughout the holiday, just so long as he remembered to leave the dogs out when he was absent. Consequently, he had kept them shut up all day, so that they would be rested and alert during the long night when he planned to be away. Ignoring Sheba's guttural, irritating growls, he opened the other kennels and let the dogs run free. He locked the big gates securely behind him, thrust his shoulder against them several times to check. The gates rattled dully and Major came running, barking at him.

The pavements were slippery and deserted. He decided to take a taxi, if he could find one. Not all the way, of course, for the cabbie just might remember him. But the going was better when he reached the main thoroughfares, where much of the snow had been cleared. Still keeping one eye open for a cruising taxi, he thought that he might be able to walk it, as he had originally planned, if he kept to the major roads. He put his hands in his pockets and set off at a brisk pace, whistling softly.

Another weakness in the hospital security system was the imposition of fixed patrols at night and even those were confined to public areas and main access corridors. On the other hand, this practice enabled him to slip easily into the building unseen and to reach the main stair shaft with minutes to spare before a guard was anywhere near. It was a fact of life, he thought as he began to climb slowly, that if patients and nurses wanted to be secure they would have to get used to men patrolling the wards at night, unannounced. You could not have it both ways. There was no need for him to use the stairs at all. There were plenty of lifts in operation at night where the danger of meeting anyone was minimal. He chose the stairs because the long climb would calm him, give him time to prepare himself mentally. Besides, he enjoyed exercising his body, demonstrating his fitness. When he arrived at the eleventh floor, he would not even be out of breath.

The private patients' wing was L-shaped, running around two sides of the central service core. At the angle of the corridor was a half-glazed fire door which opened onto a wide landing from which the stairs descended and ascended. Standing in the shadows on that landing, he could see the length of the longest corridor. Two-thirds of the way along it was the desk, illuminated now by a single lamp. Its light fell on Sister Green, who had pushed her chair back from the desk and was leaning forward, her head pillowed on her arms. Her cap was a little askew. Gently, gently, he eased the fire door open and slipped through, resting his shoulder against it to control and ease its swing. Moving imperceptibly with the door, he allowed it to close soundlessly. Then, without another glance at Sister Green, he moved into the shorter arm of the corridor, out of sight. He stopped at the third door on his left and, with his gloved hand, quietly turned the handle.

The flush-set central ceiling light, controlled by a remote, common switch, was on dim. Boldly patterned curtains, brown on beige, were drawn across the big window. The light had a greyish, unreal quality which made even the tinsel on the little Christmas tree look dull and leaden. She was lying on her back, sleeping deeply. He barely glanced at her before moving around the bed to stand on her right side. There was a wide shelf fixed to the wall which held a roll of cotton wool, tissues, a thermometer in its phial of disinfectant, a kidney bowl. From the capacious pockets of his coat he took out a plastic bottle and uncapped it to reveal a little pointed nozzle. Carefully, so as to make no noise, he tore a thick pad from the roll of cotton wool and placed it within easy reach beside the bottle. That done, he drew a sharp Stanley knife from his pocket and slid the triangular blade free of its plastic safety covering.

He squatted down then, facing the bed, and studied the conformation and fastening of her bandages. They were held in place by a thick strip of pink surgical tape which passed around the back of her head. He saw that he need make only one cut, from temple to jaw. It was going to be easier than he thought.

He stood up again and moved to the foot of the bed. From another pocket he drew a long, slim white box which he placed on the bed table, nudging it with his finger so that its edge aligned with that of the table, neatly. He liked things to be neat.

It had begun already, the throbbing in his groin. When he squatted again beside her, the posture, the tightness of his clothes increased the pressure, sending a tingling spasm of pleasure through him. So it had been on that other, fateful occasion when he had squatted beside her prostrate form, a long, lighted purple candle in his hand. The explosion that had occurred in his boy's body shortly afterwards had taken him by surprise, had been momentous, had fixed every detail of that earlier scene in his mind forever. He looked wistfully around the room. It lacked candles. He wished it was possible to fill the room with candlelight, the smell of wax. His hand trembled a little as he held out the knife, advanced it towards her sleeping head. He pressed the razor-sharp point down into the pink tape at her temple. Pierced, it pulled apart, shrinking under its own stretched elasticity. He had to be quick now, strong and deadly accurate. Holding his breath, his lips pursed, he bore on the knife hard and pulled it in one flowing cut down towards her neck. The tape, the bandage, the cotton wadding and the surgical lint severed and parted as he stood up, pocketing the knife.

She moaned, turned her head away from him. With his left hand he squirted chloroform onto the cotton wool, smelling its sharp reek.

'What?' Her voice was thick, drugged. She rolled her head instinctively towards him.

He reached down and seized the ragged edge of the bandage. With all his strength he tore it across her face, away from him, exposing Mr Valentine's livid work. He dropped the bandage across the good side of her face. She was struggling now, making incoherent, whimpering noises of surprise and fear. He picked up the prepared pad and clamped it down over her mouth and nose. He held it tightly in place, leaning all his weight down through his palm onto her head. She twisted and turned. Her arms flapped like the wings of an injured fledgling and, with a long, gurgling sigh, she grew still. It was almost done and his excitement was boundless. He attacked the bandage again, tearing it across and away from him. The tape came away from her hairline with a rough ripping noise.

He looked down at her exposed face, at the bright pink and dead white patched skin. One graft had peeled completely away, was stuck to the bandage, he supposed. The others, he felt sure, must wither and die now.

He could not stay and feast his eyes, much as he longed to, could not linger until his body reached its ecstatic conclusion. Hands shaking badly, he got the top back on the plastic bottle, patted the heavy shape of the knife in his pocket and dropped the bottle on top of it. He checked the placement of the white box and took one last, lingering, hungry look at her face.

It reminded him of the bitch in Edinburgh, her pink

flesh laid open – and the memory forced him to move. Like a shadow, he was across the room, his hand on the door knob. It turned silently. He opened the door a crack. Nothing moved in the corridor, no sounds or lights. He slipped out and shut the door, turned left and walked down the corridor. At the end was a heavy sliding door which divided the ward from a wide concourse, opposite a bank of six passenger lifts. The door, as he had thought it would, stood open. He ran across the carpeted concourse and into a narrower corridor at the side of the lift shaft. At the bottom was a smaller, unmarked lift, reserved for staff. He saw that it was at theatre level. He pressed the call button, heard a distant hum and, at once, saw the green lights flash on . . . 12 . . . 11 . . . He slid into the lift and pressed for the first floor. From there he would use the stairs, slip out through a side entrance, just in case she had managed to raise the alarm. And as the lift slid steadily down, he pressed his hand into his crotch and swiftly finished what some perverted accident of nature had begun.

He was sweating, breathing heavily as he stepped out of the lift and hurried to the fire doors, down the stairs. On the ground floor, beneath the stairs was a narrow little door. Outside, the cold air struck him like a douche of icy water. He stuck his hands in his pockets and moved quickly towards the back of the building, his mission accomplished.

Nine

Sister Green was an experienced and excellent nurse, with the admirable ability to stay calm in stress situations. She woke the moment the buzzer sounded. Almost at once the screams began. She paused only for a second, knocked back by the reek of chloroform in the room. Then she snapped on the light switch and hurried to the bed. Her repugnance and sorrow at what she saw was fleeting. Her first coherent thought was that the patient must have torn the bandage off herself, but the smell of chloroform made her suspicious. As she bore down on Lois's bucking shoulders to restrain her, speaking rapidly in a precise and calm voice, she saw the soaked wad of cotton wool where it had fallen beside the patient. She retrieved it, placed it on the locker top and pressed the red alarm button that connected her with the central communications desk.

'Emergency. Get a doctor up here at once,' she said, flipping the partly severed dressing back over Lois's wounds. 'And Security. Get them up here as well. It's urgent.'

Part of Lois's panic had been caused by the inability to see at all. The turned-back bandage had covered her good eye. She became quieter at once and was able to make some sense of what sister was saying. She tried to obey her when she insisted that she must keep still, wait just a minute for the doctor to come.

Sister Green met the running, half-asleep young houseman in the corridor and rapidly told him what had happened and how she thought it must have happened. He went in to see Lois and sister talked to her, soothed her while he lifted the dressing pad and winced. Lois would always remember his tone as he said:

'God, what a mess.'

Sister frowned at him fiercely. For a moment his mind was a blank. First, he realized that he had no expertise, was not sure how or if the grafts could be saved. Then he realized there were three priorities: to calm the patient, take precautions against infection, re-dress the wound. He sent Sister Green to prepare the necessary trolley.

'How did this happen?' he asked Lois. 'Why is there a smell of chloroform?'

She began to babble. She didn't know. Oh she knew. She knew all right.

She was not going to be beautiful. It had all been for nothing.

Outside, in the corridor, Sister Green bellowed at several patients who, woken by the noise, were anxiously asking to know what was going on, to get back into their rooms and stay there. She enlisted the aid of the overweight security guard and then told him, as she deftly prepared a trolley, that she suspected an intruder. If ever she had needed a junior to help her it was now. If only it had happened at any other time of year . . .

'I'm going to put you to sleep,' the houseman said. 'You've had a terrible shock. We're doing everything we can. It'll be all right, you know.' He did not sound sure. Before turning his attention to her wounds, the houseman spoke to the central desk and told them to get hold of Mr Valentine, immediately.

The snow had been particularly heavy in the south-east. Ten minutes later the switchboard reported that the lines were down in Kent where Mr Valentine had his country home.

By then the patient was calmer, growing drowsy. Sister Green competently removed the sliced bandages and prepared a temporary, light dressing.

'Then get hold of his registrar. Tell him to get over here at once.' The houseman shook his head at Sister Green. 'Wouldn't you know? I don't want anyone coming in here. No one at all until the registrar arrives.'

Outside, in the corridor, the security guard told him the police were on their way. His men were searching the building.

'Okay, okay. But nobody sees her.'

He made a number of calls, succeeded in borrowing two nurses from quiet wards and persuaded a doctor on duty in Casualty to come up and give a second opinion. He deputed Sister Green to deal with the police.

She had seen nothing, could tell them nothing. However, she showed them the cut and torn dressing and the pad of cotton wool, in separate plastic bags. They agreed that it looked fishy. Until they could speak to the patient, though . . . They said they would have a talk with Security and a good look around. They would return in the morning.

By now the hospital was stirring. There seemed to be people everywhere. Assistant matron was on the ward, barking orders, organizing. The registrar arrived and, attended by the houseman and Sister Green, made a thorough examination of Lois's injuries. He shook his head. They had done everything they could, he assured them. Mr Valentine might have been prepared to try remedial surgery, perhaps even a new graft, but with nothing prepared, the patient in shock, he would not take the risk. Not without speaking to Mr Valentine, anyway. And since only one theatre was operative . . .

'If only it had happened at some other time . . .' he said, fixing the dressings back in place. 'Keep her quiet, Sister. And let's see if we can get a telegram or something through to Mr Valentine.'

As dawn crept across the sky, the bustle subsided. A nurse made some tea and they gathered morosely at the desk to drink it.

'How could this happen? You seriously expect me to believe that some maniac could walk in off the street and do this?'

'What else can we think, Matron?' the registrar said. 'There's no doubt the dressings were cut . . . And then the chloroform. She couldn't have done it herself.'

'Were you asleep, Sister?'

'No, Matron. Anyone could get to her room without my seeing. I was here, at the desk . . .'

'Oh well, we'll go into all that later. There will have to be a stringent internal enquiry, independent of anything the police may decide to do. What a terrible nuisance.'

'Who could do such a thing?' the houseman asked. 'That's what bothers me. No matter how . . . Who would think of such a thing?'

'He must have been in the know,' the registrar said. 'That's for sure.'

'Don't,' Sister Green said, looking paler than ever. She shivered.

They looked at each other with dread in their eyes.

'Heads will roll,' assistant matron said. 'Well, I'd better set the wheels in motion. I shall want to see the police but, remember, there is no question of anyone seeing the girl until Mr Valentine has examined her. Understand?'

They nodded.

'What a bloody awful Christmas,' the houseman said.

'Cheers.'

They kept Lois sedated. The police, forbidden by Mr Valentine, who had finally been contacted in the small hours of the day after Boxing Day, to speak to her until he had prepared her, posted a man on the door. His presence made patients and staff alike uneasy and drew the attention of newspaper reporters who were swiftly and firmly dealt with by assistant matron. Emergency committee meetings were called to discuss security.

Lois was oblivious to all this. Occasionally she heard voices discussing her, saw shadowy figures moving in and out of the pervading gloom. Nurses changed her dressings. She had no desire to ask them questions. Once she had recognized Mr Valentine and had tried to question him through dry, puffed lips. He had answered her in his soothing, fatherly voice, telling her to rest, rest. They would talk soon. Her arms and rear were sore from the many injections they gave her. There was a drip again, sealed to her arm. She existed in a half-world, not waking, not sleeping and often it occurred to her that she was dead or dying. Then, gradually, without reason or coherence, she began to be awake for longer periods. She would find herself sitting up, drinking from a cup or glass, swallowing pills. She became aware that the heavy, constricting bandages had gone, were replaced by lighter, more flexible coverings, beneath which her skin felt sore and hot. One day, she asked a nurse who seemed to be sitting with her what day it was.

'Friday,' the girl said.

She looked at the window. The light was indeterminate.

'What time?'

'Half-past four, almost.'

Morning or afternoon? Which Friday? The questions seemed irrelevant, not worth the effort of asking.

'Can you bring me a mirror?'

The girl nodded, went through into the bathroom and came back with a hand mirror. She put on the lamp beside Lois's bed and adjusted it. It seemed to Lois that she waited tensely, her body poised for action.

She stared at her face, at the familiar side of her face, which looked gaunt. The skin was yellow where the bruises had begun to fade. There was a purple mark of tiredness under her eye. The rest of her face was covered by a gauze-like bandage, held in place by narrow strips of sticky tape at several points. There was nothing to see. She laid the mirror aside.

'Would you like a cup of tea, something to eat?'

Suddenly she realized she was ravenous.

'Yes. I'm hungry.'

'There's a good girl.'

To her surprise, the nurses did not leave her but used the intercom to order the food and drink.

'Are you guarding me?' she asked, suspicious.

'No. Mr Valentine just wants you to have . . .'

'Someone should be. I'm in danger.'

'No. You're perfectly safe.'

'I want to see Mr Valentine. I must see someone.'

'It's all right. There's a policeman outside. Now don't distress yourself. I'm not even sure I should have told you.'

'A policeman?'

'They want to talk to you.'

'Good. Fine. Bring them in.'

'No, I can't. Mr Valentine wants to see you first. They've got to wait until he says so. He'll see you in the morning.'

Lois felt too tired to argue, insist any further. When another nurse brought in a tray of tea, bread and butter, a slice of fruit cake, she asked again if there really was a policeman out there.

'Good,' she said when they assured her there was.

The food lay hard and uncomfortable on her stomach, but she drank three cups of tea and a lot of orange juice. When another nurse came on duty, she removed the drip and brought Lois a small white pill.

'I don't want any more sleeping pills,' she said, pushing the nurse's hand away.

'That's okay. This isn't a sleeping pill. Just something to calm you down.'

'I am calm.'

'Come along now . . .'

She took the pill, too weary to protest.

Weary though she felt, bone weary, she slept little that night, aware of the nurse in the corner of the room who checked her pulse and temperature every few hours, filled up the glass of orange juice from time to time. The pill made her feel detached, as though screened off from something. She tried to think, but her thoughts would not connect properly in a sequence. The pill seemed to foil connections in the brain, leaving her with fragments which she seized upon eagerly, only to find that they grew repetitious, became an ugly chant in her head, leading nowhere. At last she fell into a light sleep which brought neither dreams nor rest.

It was as though the sedatives combined with the suppressants and the antibiotics to create a mental garden in which black thoughts took root and flowered into hatred, a lust for harm. When she awoke again it was with a sense of deadly purpose. Her path had never been more clear and straight: a vicious swathe cutting straight through into her bleak and bitter future.

The nurse suggested that she might like a bath, offered to help her. Lois accepted gratefully. The girl combed Lois's hair as best she could and drew it back from her face. Dressed in one of her own nightgowns she lay flat on the bed, eyes closed, while sister changed her dressing. She did not ask how her face looked. She never would ask, she vowed. Again, she found she was hungry and ate a full breakfast, followed by another of the little white pills.

'Mr Valentine will be in to see you directly,' the nurse said, plumping her pillows.

'Good,' said Lois. 'I want to see him.'

The pill helped her to wait patiently. She sat, her hands folded in her lap, not listening to the radio's quiet drone. Bright sunlight fell through the window, dazzling her unaccustomed eye. The nurse said the snow had melted.

There was a heavy frost but it was a lovely day. Lois replied:

'There's no such thing. What the hell do days matter, wet or fine?'

'Oh, you mustn't be depressed. You'll soon feel much better. Wait till you see Mr Valentine . . .'

'I am waiting,' Lois told her and turned her face away from the window.

Mr Valentine came in a few moments later. He was casually dressed, a sand-coloured roll neck under a brown tweed jacket. He motioned the nurse away and came to the bed with a warm smile.

'How nice to see you sitting up. You look so much better. How are you feeling?' He took her hand which resisted his.

'I'm fine, thank you. Really terrific.'

He could not overlook the harshness of her tone, the barely contained anger in her voice. He sat down, withdrawing his hand discreetly.

'I'm so sorry,' he said. 'In all my years as a doctor, nothing like this has ever happened to one of my patients. I know it can be scant comfort to you, Lois, but this has been a blow to me, too. I take a pride in my work . . .'

'I bet,' she said drily.

'You're still upset, of course. I can understand that . . .'

'The nurse said the police wanted to talk with me. I want you to authorize that . . .'

'Of course . . . Just as soon as we've . . . Do you think you can throw any light on . . . what happened?'

'Yes,' Lois said, and clamped her lips shut.

'You wouldn't like to tell me?'

'You can sit in, if you want. I don't want to go over it time after time . . .'

'No, of course. Quite right. Well, you'll be wanting to know the medical position . . .'

'Will I?' She turned her face towards him, her single eye blazing.

'You're upset, naturally . . .'

'I don't want a lot of crap,' Lois told him, her voice shaking. 'Just come right out and tell me if it's going to be worse than before . . . The whole damn thing was a waste of time, wasn't it?'

'If things had been allowed to take their course, I'm confident . . .'

'But they weren't, were they? He came in and he ripped those bandages off. What's the damage?'

He sighed. Her manner, her barbed approach cut across all his training, his years of experience. It hurt him to tell her:

'Bad, I'm afraid. Two of the grafts haven't taken at all. The third . . . I'm certainly optimistic. There are some lesions, of course . . . A lot depends on how well it all heals now.'

'Okay. I get the picture. How soon can I go?'

'Oh my dear, it's too soon to . . .'

'I won't stay here, Mr Valentine. Apart from anything else I can't afford to.'

He cleared his throat awkwardly.

'Yes, well, under the circumstances . . . I would not feel justified in presenting my full account . . .'

'I don't want hand-outs.'

'It's not like that, my dear. What we ought to be talking about now is further surgery . . . in six months or a year . . .'

'No,' she said. 'No. I want to go home, back to the States. I'm grateful . . . Look, I really am . . . but I know now I've got to live with this. No amount of patching up is going to . . .'

'You feel like that now because you're depressed. You've had a terrible experience . . .'

'Don't tell me. I know,' she said. 'I'm sorry. I've just had too many terrible experiences . . .'

'We'll have another talk in a few days . . .'

'No. Mr Valentine, I'm leaving here just as soon as I can. Now, if you won't tell me what's best to do, whether I have to come back or anything, then I shall just discharge myself . . .'

He took a deep breath.

'Very well. I'll make a full examination on Monday morning, then I'll give you my considered opinion. But you will definitely need medication and I shall have to see you again. The dressings will be a problem . . . still,' he said, standing up, trying to sound cheerful, 'I've no doubt we can sort something out, if you're adamant . . .'

'I am,' Lois told him.

He cleared his throat again. He was worried about her. He thought that she was probably clinically depressed, while her anger was frightening.

'I expect you'd like to see the police now,' he said.

Her face averted, she nodded her head.

'Please.'

She remained looking at the window while he went to the door and spoke to someone in a low voice. It was bad. He said it was bad. She knew what doctors really meant when they admitted something was bad. She would kill for this. She would kill them all.

'This is Miss Carradine,' she heard Mr Valentine saying and turned her head to look at the two plainclothesmen who stood at the foot of the bed. 'Detective-Sergeant Burgess and Detective-Constable Mazarok,' he went on. The men nodded. The constable took out a notebook and flipped it open. 'Miss Carradine has no objections to my staying, if that's all right with you, Sergeant?'

'That'll be all right, sir. Now, Miss Carradine . . .' Burgess walked to the side of the bed, took the chair Mr

Valentine had recently vacated. 'I'm sorry to trouble you, but if you feel up to making a statement . . .'

'Fine. I'm good and ready.'

'Good. Well, the best thing would be if you told us all you can remember about what happened on the morning of 26 December.'

Lois took a deep breath, visibly marshalled her thoughts. 'I had a sleeping pill, quite early. I guess around ten, ten-thirty. The nurse will be able to tell you. I was very tired. The pill worked, I guess, because I don't remember anything else until I felt the air on my face, on this side of my face,' she explained, indicating the dressing. 'Sounds weird, doesn't it? But the pain came later. I just felt that it was . . . wrong, you know? I remember thinking that maybe I was dreaming but I knew I wasn't. He was standing by that side of the bed, the right. I turned my head. All I saw was some sort of shape . . . Somebody in the room, definitely. And then the smell, like ether. Very strong. My face began to hurt then, but I thought he was trying to suffocate me. He just pressed down on my face. Then everything went black. It was a lot like the anaesthetic, you know, upstairs? Like that only slower . . .'

'And then?' Burgess prompted quietly.

'I guess I must have come round. I couldn't see at all. I thought I was totally blind. I am blind on this side . . .' Again she touched the dressing. 'It's always been one of my fears that one day I'd lose the sight of this eye . . . Anyway, that's what I thought. I tried to sit up, feel for the console, there, to call the sister. I felt the pad fall away from my face. I still didn't realize that why I couldn't see was because the bandage was lying across this side of my face. I began to scream and shout, I guess. I can't remember whether I found the console, managed to press the button or what. But the nurse came, sister, I mean. They started to fix me up . . . It's all so confused . . .'

'But you are definite that there was someone in your room. A man?'

'Absolutely. But, okay, it might have been a woman . . .'

The constable stood up and handed a plastic bag across the bed to Burgess. From it the Sergeant drew a sealed, transparent bag and held it out on the flat of his palm.

'Is this the pad you felt fall from your face?'

Lois looked at it. She shook her head.

'I don't know. It could have been . . . I couldn't see . . .'

'No. I understand that. It's a pad of cotton wool. Sister Green found it on the bed beside you, soaked in chloroform.'

'Then that's the one.'

'And this? Does this mean anything to you?'

He took out a slim white box, about a foot long, slightly shiny.

'No. What is it?'

'Open it, Miss Carradine.'

He pushed the box across the bedclothes towards her. Some premonition warned her, made her shrink back against the pillows. She snatched her hands up, away from the box, and held them pressed against her breast. Such little colour as she had drained from the visible side of her face. Mr Valentine watched anxiously, ready to intervene if she became further disturbed.

'No.' She shook her head. 'You open it, please. Or tell me . . .'

'It's nothing so very dreadful, Miss Carradine,' Burgess said, picking up the box in his square, rather fleshy fingers. 'You see?' He slipped the lid off, tilted the box towards her. 'It's only a candle, a purple one.'

'Oh, God, no . . .' She covered her face with her hands, cried out as she pressed too hard on the raw part.

'Please . . .' Mr Valentine said to the policeman, starting forward. Burgess nodded, reboxed the candle and put it away.

'When you're ready, Miss Carradine . . .'

'Yes. Sorry.'

'What did the candle mean to you?'

'Where did you get it?' she asked.

'It was found here, in your room, after the attack.'

'That's it, then,' she said. 'It must have been William. William or one of them . . .'

'I think you'd better tell us all about it, Miss Carradine.'

'Okay, but it's a long story . . .'

When she had finished, Burgess took her through it all again in detail. Mr Valentine arranged for some tea to be brought in. Burgess asked a lot of questions, trying to pick holes in her story, but it held together remarkably well. Only her insistence that she had seen William in the hospital, in the recovery room, struck Burgess as unlikely. But then, the whole story was decidedly odd. So odd, in fact, he was inclined to believe it.

'And you don't know where this William Young is?'

'No. I told you. But I can give you the addresses of all the others.' She took the rather dog-eared folder out of her locker. 'Look, see, Vanessa Hunter, the twins . . .'

'Make a note of those addresses,' Burgess told Mazarok. 'But you're inclined to think William Young's our man?' he asked Lois again.

'I'm sure of it. But I doubt that he acted alone. Look, I told you, the others thought I was persecuting them . . .' Suddenly, a new thought struck her. 'Oh, but if William . . . I hadn't thought of that. If he left the candle here . . .'

'Yes, Miss. I'd begun to think along the same lines. Well . . .' he stood up. 'You've been very helpful, Miss Carradine. We shall look into all this straight away. I think, unless you've any objections, we'll keep an officer on your door . . .'

'Oh yes, please. I'm scared.'

'You, sir?' Burgess turned to Mr Valentine.

'Certainly, officer. By all means.' He was staring at Lois as though he could not believe that he could ever have met a person to whom such terrible things had happened.

'Contact the others,' Lois said. 'Contact Andy. They'll bear out what I've told you.'

'We'll do that, don't worry, Miss Carradine. And we'd better have a look at the register of staff here at the hospital, too, Mr Valentine, if you can help us to that?'

'I'll speak to matron,' he promised.

'Well, thanks again, Miss Carradine, I'll be in touch. And . . . er . . . I hope you make a speedy recovery,' Burgess said, nodding.

Lois did not bother to reply. What recovery? Her face was ruined, would be worse than when she had entered the hospital. William had torn her dreams to shreds when he had torn off that bandage. But that didn't matter. All she wanted was for them to find William and punish him. All for a rabbit, she thought. Oh God, William, how could you? For a rabbit?

It takes time to find and question five people and so Detective-Sergeant Burgess was delighted when it seemed they had a couple of lucky breaks. What he did not know was that the junior police constable, who had been set to check the list of more than five thousand names on the hospital staff roll, was so excited at spotting Amanda Beatty's name there, that he failed to see the significance of one other name: Billy Younger. The name had been added to the printed list in ink, denoting that he was a new employee. His address and other personal details had not yet been inscribed.

Amanda Beatty's presence in the hospital cut down on the leg work and she was interviewed that same afternoon. Without an accomplice, Burgess could not see how she could have done it, weighing as she did a little under eight stone and being mobile only in a wheelchair. Still, she was on the premises and if a total stranger could walk into the hospital at dead of night, Burgess was prepared to believe that a patient might be able to travel unnoticed from one ward to another. And if Carradine really had seen William Young in the recovery room . . . Burgess left a question mark dangling over Beatty's name.

His second stroke of luck was finding Vanessa Hunter at home. Everything she told him bore out Carradine's bizarre tale. He did not like the look of the deliberately crippled photograph she showed him, while her story of having blood thrown at her and being sent a bloodied handkerchief made him distinctly uneasy. As he said to Mazarok as they drove away:

'I'm beginning to think we've got a maniac on our hands.'

'Let's hope you're wrong. Still, for sure it wasn't her. Smashing girl, wasn't she? Did you cop her legs?'

'Keep your mind on your work. Maybe. But we'll have to check out her alibi. We can do that later. Let's pay the twins a visit.'

But the Shillingworths weren't at home. A faded woman, who had lived for twenty years in the ground floor flat, said she thought that they had gone home for the Christmas holidays. They were students, she assumed Burgess knew. They seemed quiet, nice enough lads, but you could never tell these days, could you? You read such things! She supposed it was political? She did hope they had not done anything very bad. No, she had no idea of their home address. She kept herself very much to herself. This had once been such a nice house, such a nice class of people had lived there. Now there were Arabs, students, all sorts . . .

'That leaves Mercer and Young,' Mazarok said.

'Yeah.' Burgess was thinking, a frown creasing his forehead. 'They can wait. You leg it over to the college –

there must be someone on duty – and get the Shillingworths' home address.'

'Then what?'

'Come back to the station. I want to start putting this lot together.'

'Okay, but what about Mercer?'

'The local lads can handle that, and the Shillingworths if you get something. There's no point in us trailing all the way over there only to find he's on bleeding holiday as well.'

And so it happened that a young constable, fresh out of Hendon Training College, knocked on the door of the house in which Andy lived shortly after six that evening. After a long wait, a young man answered the door and denied that he was Mercer.

'Haven't seen him for over a week,' he said. 'You can go up if you like.'

The constable went up to the first floor and knocked on the door to his left. He knocked again, called Andrew Mercer's name. It was an uninquisitive household, he thought, as he stood there, waiting. Nobody peered around the other doors to watch him. The young man who had let him in had shut himself away in his own room. He knocked again and, convinced now that Mercer must be out or away for the holidays, he tried the door handle as a matter of routine, in case someone should ask him later. To his surprise, it was not locked. The door opened inwards. It was dark in the room and there was a smell, a stale smell he had never encountered before and which he did not like. Calling again, he groped for the light switch, found it and turned it on. It did not help much, though. The constable advanced slowly into the room, feeling ahead of him for obstacles. The smell got stronger. He saw that the curtains were drawn closed, shutting out the street lamps' glow. And he saw the shape on the bed, the bulk. He went towards it as though drawn. He pulled a handkerchief out of his pocket and clapped it over his mouth and nose as he reached to put on the bedside lamp. When it came on, he wished he had not.

Andy was propped, with the aid of pillows, against the ancient headboard. His head was thrown back, his mouth open. His right hand dangled to the floor, close to the constable's feet. Still looped on his stiff fingers was a pair of scissors like the constable's mother used for dress-making. Their blades were stained brown with a crust of dried blood. The same ugly brown colour had saturated the bed and the sheets which were bunched between Andy's splayed legs. It looked as though, after he had castrated himself, he had tried to staunch the flow of blood. Before he turned away the sickened constable saw not only what Mercer had cut off, but a pair of innocent looking kid's panties and a photograph of two little boys in their underwear.

The constable blundered across the room, knocking over a chair, and deposited the contents of his stomach in the tiny kitchen sink. Only when he had stopped retching and swilled the sink clean did he unclip the short-wave radio from his belt and tremulously give the call sign.

Burgess and Mazarok, the latter eating Kentucky Fried Chicken as he did so, reviewed the situation prior to making a routine report to the inspector in the morning.

'Vanessa Hunter,' Mazarok said, reading from a list and waving a chicken leg in the air.

'Alibi pretty good. Five other people in the house, one of whom, Max Krieger, spent the night with her.'

'And she doesn't drive, so she couldn't have got to the hospital and back without an accomplice.'

'You've got a note of the threats, though?'

'Yes. All down here.'

'Which could also be a motive, if Carradine sent them.'

'Right. Next?' Burgess nodded. 'The Shillingworths, Jason and Julian.'

'Submit report from Hampshire. At home, with parents and sister and elderly aunt. Typical family Christmas.'

'They'd've been hard pressed to make it to the hospital and back too,' Mazarok mumbled with his mouth full of food. Burgess leaned over the desk and helped himself to a chip. 'So, Amanda Beatty?'

'On the premises, which argues opportunity. Is in a private room off the ward, which argues ditto. But the staff say she never left her room and its highly unlikely that she's strong enough to commit the assault or mobile enough without help.'

'Right. But then she has the strongest motivation – worms, dead spiders and bloody near kills herself running away from Carradine.'

'Except that the psychiatrist who saw her says there's nothing wrong with her but a bad dose of guilt and nervous exhaustion brought on by these taunts, or whatever they were supposed to be. Anyway, when you consider the result, you could say that Mercer was more upset by what he received than Beatty.'

Mazarok craned his neck, reading from the list beside his box of food.

'A pair of knickers and – we assume – a mutilated picture. Doesn't seem much to me.'

'Enough to make him top himself in a peculiarly nasty way.'

'Remorse after the attack?' Mazarok suggested.

'You haven't seen this,' Burgess answered, waving a typewritten report at him. 'The result of the PM. Pathologist puts death at between four and seven p.m., Christmas Day.'

'Hours before Carradine was attacked. That rules out Mercer then.'

'Looks like it,' Burgess agreed. 'Poor sod.'

'So, that leaves William Young . . .'

'About whom we know sweet Fanny Adams.'

'All right then. Where do we go now?' Mazarok wiped his fingers on a paper handkerchief.'

'Let's go through the hospital roll again. *You* go through it . . .'

'But why? It's been checked . . .'

'I'll tell you why. First, because it's the only thing we've got and second, because everything Carradine told us so far had checked out, spot on. And she swears Young was in the recovery room when she came round. I don't believe he just walked in off the street. It's a hell of a big place, that hospital, like a rabbit warren. There's two ways to get to know the lay-out of a place that big: architect's plans or by working there. I'll check the architect . . .'

'Hang on, Chief,' Mazarok said. 'There's another way. The easiest way, really . . . Being a patient.'

'Good thinking. Right. Check the admissions' list for the last year, all departments.'

'Oh no!'

'If you're going to be bright, you must accept the consequences. Right. That'll do us for tonight. See you nine sharp tomorrow.'

'Yes, Chief. Night, Chief.'

'Unless you want to make a start now?' Burgess laughed.

Mazarok shook his head miserably.

Julian was not at all sure why he had come. He hoped his motives were not morbid. Maybe it would help Jason if he could report back himself, and no doubt his mother was right that it was a mark of respect. He looked around the court, expecting to see Mr and Mrs Mercer, perhaps some other familiar faces. He was quietly relieved when he recognized no one at all.

The inquest on Andrew Charles MacFadden Mercer

took only a few minutes. Counsel acting for the police asked for an adjournment. With the coroner's permission he read a prepared statement. While there was no reason to believe that Andrew Charles MacFadden Mercer had not taken his own life, certain evidence connected with that case was the subject of separate and ongoing enquiries by the police. They requested an adjournment on the grounds that a public hearing of all the evidence concerning Mercer's death would be detrimental to these other investigations. The coroner agreed to an adjournment of three weeks.

Julian felt let down and relieved at the same time. It was taken out of his hands for another three weeks and, in that time, things might change for the better. As he left the courtroom, he was startled by someone calling his name. He turned around and saw Vanessa hurrying towards him. He smiled with genuine pleasure.

'What are you doing here?'

'I don't know really. I decided I ought to come. Then, when I got here, I just couldn't face it. What happened?'

'It's been adjourned. Hey, look, you're shaking . . .'

'It's nothing.'

'Come and have a drink . . . Oh, the pubs won't be open yet. A cup of coffee? I saw a cafe . . .'

'Yes, yes that would be great. I can't stand these places.'

He hung on to her arm and she did not seem to mind. They crossed the street, Julian feeling proud to be seen with her, and entered a small cafe.

'Jason didn't come?' Vanessa asked, nervously lighting a cigarette.

'No. He's . . . Well, the truth of the matter is, he broke down when they told us about Andy.'

'God, wasn't it awful?' she said, shivering.

'Terrible. Anyway, Jason just went to pieces. He couldn't stop crying. Ma got the doctor and they decided he should go into hospital . . . a mental hospital . . .'

'Oh, Julian . . .' Impulsively, she reached across the narrow table and touched his hand.

'They don't think it will be for long. They think he's just been under so much pressure . . . That's why I came today. Ma thought it would help him to hear about it from me.'

'You were always so close,' she said sadly.

'That's the worst part. He hates being separated from me. When we were kids, I was ill once. I had to go to hospital. He never really got over that. He always said it was worse for him than for me. And now . . .'

'But you can't live in each other's pockets all your life, can you?' she said.

'No. But just now . . .'

A tired-looking young man brought their coffees and left a crumpled bill. Vanessa changed the subject deliberately.

'Have you heard about Amanda?'

'No. So much has been happening . . .'

'They've sacked her. They say she's not suitable for training.'

'Because of all this? But that's not fair.'

Vanessa shrugged.

'Do you ever think . . . I keep thinking that, in a way, we've all been punished for what we did.' She looked at him, her eyes very wide.

'I keep thinking how she's been punished . . . Lois. From what the police said . . .'

'Andy's dead,' Vanessa insisted. 'Jason . . . Amanda really wanted to be a nurse, you know. She cared about it.'

'Lois . . .' he repeated.

'Yes, all right, her too,' Vanessa agreed, but her voice was quiet and without warmth.

'Which leaves us,' Julian said. 'We haven't . . .'

'I don't know about you, but I feel as though . . . Well, I've had as much as I can take.'

'Yes. Sorry. I wasn't thinking.'

Julian drank his coffee, embarrassed by his thoughtlessness and by what seemed to him his own immense good fortune.

'Do you think something else might happen? I'm still scared, Julian. I keep thinking . . .' She turned her hand over, gripped his, invited him to hold hers.

'No, of course not. Not now the police are involved.'

'You sound so sure.'

'I am.' He squeezed her hand.

'I wish I could believe you. I want to . . .'

'Has it ever occurred to you that perhaps we're . . . Oh, I don't know how to say it without sounding patronizing . . . More balanced than the others?'

'Sometimes I don't feel it.'

'No, but it is true, isn't it?'

'But why? We hated her so much. We were there . . .'

'No. I didn't hate her.' She looked disbelieving, tried to pull her hand away. Julian held on to it, tight. 'No, I really didn't. I was just very, very scared of her.'

'And now?'

'I'm ashamed.'

'Me, too.'

It was a relief to say it. It was like a cloud moving away from the face of the sun. Suddenly, she could see more clearly and the prospect was not entirely bleak.

'Thanks,' Vanessa said. 'You've cheered me up.'

'I'd like to . . . Can I see you again?'

'Me?' She looked surprised.

'Like I said before, we're grown up. When all this is over . . . Okay, you can call me sentimental, romantic . . . but I'd like something good to come out of all this. I like you, very much.'

Vanessa was silent, looking into his eyes, a puzzled expression on her face. At last, Julian looked away, began to colour up.

'That sounds like a good start,' she said, smiling.

'You mean it?'

'Yes. Like to drive me back to town? I've got a class this afternoon.'

'Love to,' he said, and they smiled at each other, tentatively but happily.

It was time to move on. He had known it for days but kept putting it off. He had not reported back to the hospital after Christmas and the time hung heavy. He debated with himself whether to tell Mr Lunn he was leaving or not and decided that a note would suffice. He was afraid Mr Lunn might want him to hang on a bit longer, show a new man the ropes and that would mean having to explain about Sheba. For several days now he had not fed her at all. She was skinny, her coat matted, and she paced endlessly around her pen, lacking exercise. His fear of her had become all-consuming. He had to get out before Mr Lunn discovered about Sheba or something worse happened.

His sleeping bag was already rolled up and strapped to his backpack. An old leather attache case stood beside it, ready for leaving. It contained his tattered paperback copy of *Watership Down*, several postcards of rabbits, his bank book, other papers and a healthy cache of money drawn from his Giro account, to see him through. Now the note was written and it was time to let the dogs out for the night. There was nothing left to keep him except a longing to know.

He carried the note across the yard to the office, which was really a part of the big garage, and let himself in with his key. He propped the note on the cluttered desk, where it would easily be seen. As he did so, he saw the telephone sitting there, silent, inviting. He tried to resist, but in the end he had to give way to temptation.

★

Lois was packing. Her street clothes felt bulky, rough and uncomfortable after weeks of wearing nightdresses and the occasional robe. Mr Valentine had fought her every inch of the way, had argued and put every obstacle he could devise in her path. Even with a policeman on duty at her door, she did not feel safe in the hospital. And it was true that she could not afford to go on staying there indefinitely. In the end, she had forced Mr Valentine's hand by ringing the hotel in Pimlico and arranging to take her room back. He had capitulated then, as long as she promised to take the medication and return to the hospital every other day to have her dressings changed. She promised. Maybe she would. She could not think straight as long as she remained in the hospital. Every night her nerves remained on edge, alert for his return. And she could not bear to think what he might do next.

Suddenly, the telephone rang. Lois jumped. For a second she could not think what the ringing meant. She had not received a single call since she had been admitted to the hospital. She picked up the receiver.

'Yes?'

'Call for you, Miss Carradine. Go ahead, caller.'

There was a click and then silence.

'Hello?'

The line was not dead and she listened to the silence that was a faint, electronic hum. She knew that someone was at the other end of the line, listening to her, and a terrible dread rose in her.

'Hello? This is Lois Carradine. Who is that?'

Still nothing. The silence stretched and she felt something like excitement. She had to stay cool, say something, make him talk to her. She began to pray that he would not hang up.

'William?' she said, her mouth suddenly dry. 'Is that you, William?'

She heard him catch his breath in reply and her heart began to beat very fast.

'I can hear you, William. Won't you please speak to me?'

Oh, please, God, let him speak. Please, please.

'How . . . how is your face?' It was a whisper, barely audible.

'Speak up, William. I can't hear you . . .'

'I said, how is your face?'

'Oh that's better. I can hear you real good now. Is that why you called, William?'

'Yes. I want to know. Also to say I'm moving on.'

'Moving on? For where, William?'

'Oh no . . .' He laughed a little.

'Then where are you now?'

'Doesn't matter.'

'William . . . William . . . Don't hang up, please.'

'I've got to go now.'

'You want to know about my face? You do, don't you, William. Well, listen . . .'

'Tell me . . .'

'William, I can do better than that. William, I want to show you my face . . .'

'Show me?'

'I want to see you, William. I want to talk with you . . .'

'No. You'll bring . . .'

'No. I promise. No one. This is between us, William . . . Isn't it? Don't you feel that? It always has been, just between us.'

'Yes . . . Your face . . .'

'William, listen. I'm going home soon. I'm leaving here tonight. I'm going back to the States. And you're leaving . . . William, there is one last chance . . . You owe me, William.'

'No.'

'Listen, William, we won't have another chance. You know that: And we should meet. Besides, William, I want you to see my face. Please, William? Let me show you my face.'

He was breathing in a funny, rasping kind of way. On a sigh, almost ecstatic, he said:

'Yes.'

'Then I'll tell you what, William. You tell me where you are and I'll come straight over. I'm all ready. It won't take me . . .'

'You'll come alone?'

'I swear it, William. What do you want me to swear on? Anything . . .'

'And you'll let me look at your face?'

'Yes, William. Just as long as you like.' She waited, her toes curling in her shoes. She thought he was going to hang up and she had run out of things to say, words . . . Suddenly, he was giving her an address, the words separated, broken up by his laboured breathing. 'Say that again. William. Wait, I have to write it down. Go on, William.' He repeated it, slowly and clearly. 'Okay, William, I've got that. I'll be right over. You'll wait for me? Promise?'

'I promise.'

There was a click and the line went dead.

'Have you finished?' The operator's voice sounded loud in her ear.

'Yes. Yes, thanks, I'm all through.'

Lois put the receiver down and sank, slowly, onto the bed.

'Anything?' Burgess looked up, his eyes red and sore with tiredness. It had been a long day.

'I don't know, Chief. Might be. Look here.' Mazarok placed a single sheet from the hospital roll before the detective-sergeant.

'Billy Younger,' he read and then he made a soft whistling sound.

'There was no address on the previous sheet. He was new, part-time . . . This is the clincher, though. He never turned up after the Christmas break. Not a word.'

'This has got to be our lad,' Burgess said, sounding triumphant. He was already getting up, reaching for his jacket. 'Get a car, quick. We're going to pay Billy Younger a surprise visit.'

Nancy carried Lois's bag down and saw her into the waiting cab. The police had insisted that she give her address to no one, so she told the driver to turn left and drive straight up the road. She thanked Nancy, pressed her hand and promised to see her soon. When they were out of sight of the hospital, she leaned forward and instructed the cabbie to take her to the address William had dictated to her.

Now that she did not have to keep up a front with the staff, she began to shake again: her teeth chattered. She had no idea what she was going to do. She had responded intuitively to William's silence and that had set her on this course. She did want to see him. It was the only thing left to her, all that she could salvage from the whole trip. Though whether to kill him or to understand too late why he hated her so much, she truly did not know. To find out was the important thing, to put an end to it, draw the lines and close the books.

The taxi crossed the river and carried her south-east, followed a main road for a long time, pausing at frequent traffic lights, flanked on either side by night-lit shops. Then it turned into side streets, a maze of narrow, mean-looking roads that made Lois feel she was penetrating the heart of some undiscovered country. At last, the taxi slowed.

'What number did you say, love?'

'Is this it?' She pulled down the window and looked at a street nameplate. 'Okay, fine. Drop me here.' She got out quickly, tipping the driver with the last of her cash.

'Are you sure you haven't got far to go?'

'No, no, it's right here. Thank you.'

She picked up her bag and walked quickly away. The sound of the cab leaving was the loneliest she had ever heard. The street was an odd, unfamiliar mixture. One side was bounded by terraced houses, small and shabby. They faced onto yards and warehouses, even a small factory. She read the signs tensely, watching for Lunn's yard. That was what William had said: Lunn's yard.

The big red-on-white sign was not illuminated but she could read it by the light of a streetlamp. This had to be it. Her heart was skipping and hammering, out of control. She peered through the chain-link fence, moved on to the big gates. There were a few, well-spaced lights on but they only showed her the gleam of parked cars. She set her case by the gates and stepped back, looking for some kind of bell-push or other means of attracting attention. She could see none. She went back to the gates, pressed close.

'William?'

She did not want to shout for fear of attracting attention from the houses across the street.

'William, are you there?'

She put her hand up, gripped one of the vertical bars of the gate and it gave easily under her touch, swinging inwards, smoothly. Lois picked up her case and stepped into the yard.

'William? It's me, Lois. Where are you, William?'

As though to answer her question a whole bank of floodlights came on, dazzling her. She turned away, only to face more. Gradually, she adjusted to the lights. After a while, she was able to see beyond them and there, she was sure, half-concealed by a litter of broken-down cars, was a shadow. A man's shadow, which moved. Lois straightened up, faced full into the lights, knowing that was what he wanted.

'William? Where are you? You can see me but I can't . . .' She saw the shadow move again, come closer. 'William? Is that you?' She looked around. The nearest bank of lights, set on the ground, were to her left. Behind them she could make out the dark shape of a small building of some kind. William was ahead of her and a little to the right. She began to walk steadily to her left.

'No,' he called, his voice carrying easily in the silence. 'This way, over here.'

Lois stopped but did not look in his direction.

'Switch the lights off, William. I can't see.'

'You don't need to see.'

'Oh but I do.'

'You said you'd show me . . . Your face is bandaged.'

'Well of course it is, William. But I'll take them off for you. I swear it. If that's what you want . . .' She paused, sensing him close, just behind the lights now. 'I'm going over here, William. If you want to see my face, you come too.'

'No, this way.'

She ignored him. Instinct told her that to assert some measure of control was essential, might make all the difference. She stepped between two floodlights and found herself close to the wall of a shed-like structure: two sheds, facing each other, connected by a roofed and concreted alleyway. She heard rustling, thought for a moment that she had walked into a trap, then recognized the snuffling of a dog. She turned around, looked across the brightly illuminated area and saw his silhouette quite clearly, moving slowly, just behind the lights, towards her.

'I want to see you, too, William. That's only fair. It's been a long time . . .'

At the sound of her voice, the dogs began to bark and

jump up at the walls of their pens. The upper parts of the walls were covered in wire mesh and she saw the flash of white teeth, the gold of a hungry eye. William shouted at the dogs.

'Come away from there. They're dangerous.'

Lois stood her ground.

'They're penned up, William. They can't hurt me.'

'Quiet, Major. Solomon, quiet.'

He was hurrying now, loping along the line of lights, towards her. Without thinking, Lois stepped back, into the narrow alleyway between the kennels. William appeared just a few feet from her. He spoke to the dogs, soothing them. He was good with them. They quietened down almost at once. All except one who whined and growled, paced back and forth as though in distress.

'Come away from there,' William said. 'Where are you? You'll set the dogs off. They'll attract attention.'

'And we want to be alone, don't we, William? So that we can have a good talk.'

He moved closer. She watched his body blot out the light at the end of the little alleyway. She put out her hand, felt the wire of one pen, the rough wood of the door. The dog behind it began to snarl, a low, continuous, threatening note. Then the alleyway was flooded with light. He stood at the far end, his hand on an outdoor, metal light switch. Lois looked up, saw a single, dusty bulb covered by a metal cage, fastened to the corrugated sheeting that roofed the alley.

'They're dangerous, I tell you. Come away from there.'

'Surely you're not scared of dogs, William? You were always so good with animals. Look how quiet they've become. All except this one . . .' She turned towards the kennel which contained the restless dog. 'Tell it to be quiet, William.'

He swallowed. She could see his throat working.

'Quiet, Sheba,' he said, his voice shaking.

The bitch hurled herself at the door, making it shake. She barked and whined and clawed at the door in a fury.

'She's the worst. Come away, get away from there.'

Lois looked at his face, sickly white, lightly filmed with the sweat of fear. He had not grown as handsome as he had promised. Odd, she thought, that Andy should have turned out . . . Lois pushed the thought away.

'Oh I don't think she'll hurt me.' She moved closer to the door. 'Hey, baby. Hi, Sheba. Hi, lady.' The bitch backed off, looking at her. Lois saw that she was in terrible condition, that her pen was filthy. Slowly, the bitch came forward, raised herself weakly on her back legs and laid her sharply pointed muzzle against the wire. Lois saw the mute, dreadful appeal in her dulled eyes and thought she understood. 'Okay, baby. All right, Sheba,' she whispered. 'There, you see? She's quiet now. She seems to have taken to me.'

'She's dangerous,' William repeated. 'I've told Mr Lunn she'll have to be put down.'

At the sound of his voice, Sheba began to growl again, threateningly. Lois saw William back away a little.

'Well, I didn't come here to talk about dogs, William, though it seems a shame . . .' Slowly, she put her bag down between them. As she did so, she felt behind her, her hand concealed by her body, and felt for the bolt on Sheba's door. She straightened up again, her hand resting on the bolt. 'So . . . this is hello and goodbye, William.'

'Yes, you'd better go . . .'

'Go? But you haven't seen my face yet . . . Changed your mind, William?'

He swallowed again, shook his head like an embarrassed boy offered some intensely imagined intimacy.

'Okay, but first, William, won't you tell me why you did it?'

'Did what?'

'All of it. Those things you sent to Andy, the twins . . . Why you tore my bandages off.'

'I'm not saying anything.'

'Why not? I know you did it. Was it to put me in bad with them? Is that what you wanted?'

'No.' He shook his head. 'I wanted to remind them. They shouldn't get off scot-free. It's not fair . . .' His voice rose, quavered petulantly. Sheba responded at once, scraping at the door, growling. Quietly, Lois shushed her. William did not seem to notice. 'They were responsible too. It wasn't fair just to punish me.'

'What were you punished for, William?'

'You know . . . what we did to you.'

'But they were punished, too, William. I'm sure they were. If not quite so much as you, well then . . . After all, you planned it, William. You stayed on alone with me.'

'They're walking around. They haven't been locked up,' he burst out.

'Oh, you mean Redpaths.'

'How do you know about that?' His fists clenched, his whole body became rigid.

'You're not the only one who can find things out, William. You see, I was looking for you. I'm sorry they put you in an asylum just for what you did to me.'

'It had nothing to do with you,' he said, his head snapping back on his neck as though she had insulted him. 'That was because of something quite different.'

'Even so, you felt you were taking all the blame for me, isn't that so, William? So you decided to get back at the others . . . Vanessa, Jason and Julian . . .'

'Yes, if you like . . . All right,' he said, angrily.

'Well, I can understand that, William. What I don't understand is why you had to do this to me.' Holding his eyes, she raised her left hand and lightly touched the dressing on her face.

'Oh don't you?' His voice was contemptuous, sneering.

'No, I don't. Not unless you enjoyed it.'

'What if I did?'

'I'd hate to believe that.'

'You can believe what you like, only don't pretend. Don't pretend you know nothing.'

'Was it because of the rabbit, William? Was it?'

His eyes flickered away from her. They were large and luminous in his pale face. His face frightened her. It was mad, the face of someone completely out of control and yet there was a great sadness in it, an irreparable loss.

'Oliver,' he breathed, pronouncing the forgotten name with a lover's tenderness, a kind of bleak warmth that almost moved Lois.

'Yes, that's right, Oliver. You couldn't make up your mind whether to call him Oliver or Henry. I remember now. But then you settled for Oliver.'

'Oliver . . .' he said again and his eyes took on a dark sparkle, as though they were full of tears.

'I didn't kill him, William. I only let him out. I want you to understand that. He ran off. I didn't know he would.'

He shook his head, put his hand up, over his eyes.

'It doesn't matter. It was all the same. You knew I loved him. He was the only . . . thing . . . ever . . . that was mine . . . that I loved . . . You knew that.'

'Not as much as I should have done, William,' Lois said and meant it. 'I'm sorry.'

'Oh it wasn't that. Not just that. It was everything. We were all right until you came.' He dropped his hand. His eyes were angry now. 'You ruined everything. You made all of us . . . vicious . . . sick. Take Andy. Andy was all right, till you came. Then he was always . . . touching . . . dirty . . . touching girls . . . even me . . .'

'You?' She was genuinely surprised.

'It never happened,' he said suddenly. 'I don't know

what he said but I never . . . I never let him. I never did anything.'

'It doesn't matter anyhow, not now,' Lois said and heard her own voice sad for Andy. 'So you hated me that much . . .'

'You ruined everything. You made everyone bad. Someone had to stop you . . . I was always stronger than you. I was the leader, till you came. You asked for it. Someone had to stop you . . . It had to be me . . . I had to be the leader again. It was right. Right and proper.'

'You always were a very proper little boy, William, very English . . .'

'Don't you sneer at me!'

'And you enjoyed it. You enjoyed blinding me and making me ugly. What did it do for you, William?' Her voice suddenly became harsh, cold and ugly. 'Did it turn you on, making a mess of my face?'

He stared at her, his mouth hanging open as though he meant to speak but could not. His lips were very moist and pink in the harsh light. She saw his tongue move in his mouth, over his lips . . .

'You said you'd show me . . .'

'Sure, William. Come closer. Would you like to take the bandages off again?'

His tongue swept his lips compulsively. He moved forward, very slowly, his eyes fixed on the dressing which covered half her face. He swallowed and slowly nodded his head.

'Here I am, William. You come close and take the dressing off and then you can have a good, long look . . . You can see . . .'

She wanted to scream, to run. What she saw in his face was lust, a cruel and dreadful, sickeningly sexual thirst for pleasure. But she had to stand her ground, had to keep still, let him come closer. In a minute, she thought, he is going to start salivating . . . She could not bear it and yet she had to bear it. She had to let him close enough, close enough to lift up his hand, reach towards her face. His hand close, closer, fingers reaching towards the dressing, the tapes that held it in place . . . Close enough to let his fingertips just brush against her hair . . .

She jumped back, dragged the bolt of Sheba's kennel door free of its hasps and yelled at the dog.

'Get him, Sheba. Go get him, Sheba.'

The door flew open under the bitch's hurled, ferocious weight. It swung back violently, catching William a blow in the chest. He cried out, staggered back, his hands flailing at the air. Lois, cringing against the wall at the end of the alleyway, saw a single streak of matted fur and muscle leap. She saw William go down, screaming, the German Shepherd on top of him. She thought she heard his head crack on the concrete. Then his cries and Sheba's terrible snarling mingled, became one great, continuous scream of agony and retribution. She saw the dog shake her big head from side to side, worrying at him. She remembered that her father had told her once, long ago, that German Shepherds always went straight for the throat. She felt quite detached about it, watching the dog and the man grappling together. She saw his fists beat against her pitifully thin rib cage and he somehow managed to draw his legs up and heave Sheba off. Her hind legs slewed weakly under her. She seemed exhausted, half-lay, half-sat against the kennel doors, behind which the other dogs were barking furiously and jumping up, demanding to be let out.

Lois looked at William. He was kneeling, his hands on the concrete floor to support him. There was a small pool of blood, red even in the shadow he threw, and she saw more drops splashing into it. A red puddle, red rain. She took a step towards him. Sheba swivelled her head, her mute eyes imploring. William straightened up, shuffled back. He put both hands to his throat so that he looked like a child again, pantomiming strangling himself. Blood oozed through his clasped fingers steadily. His eyes rolled. It would be so easy, she thought, to think that he was just fooling around. She could not help smiling at him. He saw her smile. It showed in a new rictus of fear on his face and he pulled one hand away from his bleeding neck and slapped the wall beside him, seeking purchase. Red handprints, finger smudges bloomed on the wall. Then he got a hold on a ledge and hauled himself upright, his body crashing into the wall. His eyes rolled towards her again, wildly, and he said something but she only heard a gurgle and saw the flow of blood increase, staining his sweater all down the front. He clapped his free hand back to his throat and tottered down the alley, swaying like a drunk but gaining speed. Lois stopped, touched the panting, exhausted bitch who whimpered, not looking at her but pursuing William with her eyes.

'Go on, baby,' Lois whispered. 'Go on, Sheba. You can do it.'

All the dog's muscles seemed to clench and quiver under her touch. She whined again and, like a coiled spring, gathered her energy, her unclipped back claws scrabbling against the concrete. She stood up, took just a moment to balance herself and then she trotted after him. Lois saw him, silhouetted against the lights, and he must have sensed or heard the dog for he glanced back once, over his shoulder and forced his feet into a stumbling run. Lois ran too, ran to the end of the alley and out into the cold night. Sheba leapt silently, a streak of dreadful movement, and fastened somehow to his back. William staggered, lashed out with his hands, tried to shake her free. She was snapping at his head, slipping from him. Her claws tore his clothing, shredded it. As she hit the ground, weals appeared on his pale skin and magically bled. He kept moving, swaying and shuffling one foot in front of the other. Sheba leapt again and her strange cry sounded almost triumphant. The impact of her jump, her weight, pitched him forward onto the ground and she straddled him, snapping and snarling, wool from his sweater tangling in her teeth, infuriating her and making her shake her head.

Lois could have left then. She knew that. There was a split second of inaction when she could have walked to the gate, walked away. But she did not. She followed after the dog and stood looking down. She was using her claws now, raking at him savagely. It seemed to Lois that she wanted him to turn over and that he wanted it too, since only then could he fight back. The dog danced away from him, yelping, and he managed it, he rolled over. Even in the semi-darkness, the blood showed darker. Sheba smelled it. With the last of her strength she went in for the kill.

Though Lois would never, ever tell anyone, she was always sure that she heard his flesh tear, ligaments snap, just before she heard the squeal of brakes and turned towards the fence to see men leaping from a car parked crazily half-on, half-off the pavement, its headlights blazing. She ran towards them, screaming and shouting for help.

'Miss Carradine . . . What the hell are you . . .?'

Mazarok caught her arm while Burgess ran ahead, his hand up to shield his eyes from the lights. She saw a third man, a uniformed policeman coming through the gate.

'It's a dog,' she said. 'I think she's . . .'

'Jesus Christ,' Burgess yelled. 'Get an ambulance, quick.' He held a heavy flashlight. Its beam cut through the deep darkness beyond the lights. She saw Sheba's eyes, red in its beam, saw her turn and snarl at Burgess like a lioness protecting her cubs or prey. 'Got to get this bloody dog off . . .'

Mazarok pushed Lois behind him.

'No,' she said, suddenly afraid for Sheba. She caught

hold of his arm and clung to it. 'Let me. I think I can do it.'

'Get back.'

'No, listen to me. I can get the dog, okay?' She ran forward, dazzled by the lights. 'Back off, Mr Burgess,' she yelled. 'I can handle her.'

He looked at her, opened his mouth to order her back, but he saw the animal's big head swivel towards Lois and its straggly tail wagged.

'Okay, Sheba. Good girl. All right now. Leave. Leave. Come here, okay? Come to Momma, lady. Come to Momma.'

Burgess watched, appalled, as the big, shaggy dog stepped almost daintily over the prostrate and bloody body of the man and slunk towards Lois Carradine. Almost on her belly, whimpering, her tail thrashing, Sheba went to her.

'There's a good girl. That's my girl.' Lois dropped down onto one knee. The bitch sat up, whining.

Mazarok ran forward, giving Sheba a wide berth, to assist Burgess, who was kneeling beside William. The flashlight showed his face and the bloodied mess that was his throat. The skin hung in ragged fronds and there were slippery, grey-looking tubes hanging loose and useless. Lois even thought she saw the white of bone, splintered, before Burgess yelled at her not to look and switched off the light, making William seem to vanish into the shadows.

Lois put her arms around the bitch's neck, feeling the awful state of her thick coat. Her mouth and parts of her neck were sticky with his blood. Lois put her head down, let it rest against Sheba and began to weep.

Epilogue

'How did the dog get out, Lois?'

'I don't know, Mr Stryker. I guess he must have . . . William could have knocked the bolt free as he was coming at me. They said it must have worked loose . . .'

'He could have?'

'Well, maybe I could have, too. They said the bolt was loose on account of how she had been worrying at the door. You see, he hadn't let her out or cleaned her pen or fed her for days. And that just shows what a monster William had become, doesn't it? I mean because William always loved animals. Really loved them. Why, almost the last word he said to me was "Oliver" . . .'

Stryker leaned forward, handed back to her the cutting she had given him.

HOSPITAL ATTACKER SAVAGED BY GUARD DOG the bold, black headline screamed. Lois took it, looked at it and then put it into her bag.

'I would throw that away, Lois, if I were you.'

'Oh? Why?'

'You don't need it. You're not going to forget something like that.'

She was silent, her fingers drumming on the arm of her chair. Stryker studied her: he was impressed and intrigued by her new, sophisticated appearance. She wore the brim of a big, startlingly red straw hat pulled over a royal blue scarf which served as the hat's crown. The scarf was drawn tightly down her face, obscuring most of it, to pass like a choker around her throat and was tied at the back somewhere, he supposed. In addition, she wore enormous sunglasses and her lips, which were really all he could see of her face, were very well made-up in a red that exactly matched the hat. If you did not know Lois Carradine, he thought, the weird headgear looked simply exotic, something a model or starlet might wear to draw attention to her anonymity. With it, Lois wore a red and blue spotted blouse, knotted below her breasts to display her tanned midriff. Red pants, ending at the knee, completed the outfit which, he had to admit, she carried off with style.

'I can see sometimes,' Lois said at last, referring back to the cutting, 'that people don't believe me when I tell them about it. The cuttings help to convince them I'm not a liar.'

Stryker noted the plural.

'You tell people about it?'

'Why, sure. Why not? I've nothing to be ashamed of. You see, William was a very sick person. I found out afterwards why he was put in Redpaths, this mental asylum.'

'Do you want to tell me about it?'

'Why not? It might help you to understand. He was a veterinary student and he went berserk one day. He killed a dog, a bitch. He slit her stomach open . . . He savaged her. For no reason. Oh, he was supposed to have said afterwards that she had caught and killed a rabbit but I don't know if I believe that. Anyway, what if she did? That's part of a dog's nature, isn't it? Still, it proves William was sick, really sick, long before I met up with him.'

'He met you years ago, Lois.'

'Sure, but I meant this time. Anyway, he's dead. It's better that he's dead.'

'Do you really think that?'

'Don't you? Who knows what else he might have done? All those things he sent to the others . . . My God! The only thing they don't think he did was to throw red paint at Vanessa Hunter on Hallowe'en. They think that was some kind of practical joke. But there was no doubt, not a shadow of a doubt that William attacked me, ripped off my dressings . . .'

'I don't doubt it. It's just that I find it difficult to be so detached about a death.'

For a moment her mouth puckered in the old, child-like way, but when she responded it was not in the expected, sulky tone.

'I'm not detached about it, just glad that no one else is going to suffer because of him as I've suffered.'

'Well . . .' Stryker let it hang. He saw no point in arguing with her yet, perhaps ever. Her image was well projected, the façade pretty secure, he guessed. But he did not know how deep it went. 'So, you're pretty satisfied with your trip, all in all?'

'Oh come on, Mr Stryker. You know better than that.' She paused, gave him a chance to say something. When he remained silent, his expression bland, she went on: 'There was one good thing came out of it. It made me grow up. That's what you always wanted and it's happened. I've changed . . .'

'So I can see.'

'And you know what, Mr Stryker? I think you don't like it because I did it on my own, my way. Not through sitting here with you.'

'You mean I didn't help at all?'

'Of course I don't. You helped. You helped a lot. All the time I was away, I wrote to you, in my diary. I kept on thinking how you would react, what you would say. That helped me a lot. But eventually I had to cut free, free of you. I don't keep a diary any more. Isn't that what growing up is all about?'

'It's part of it, certainly . . . Well, I guess I won't be seeing you any more.'

'I don't need it. I can stand on my own feet.'

'Well then . . .' He spread his hands in a gesture that could have been an acknowledgement of defeat or of willingness to let her go.

'Wait a minute,' Lois said. 'I want to show you something. Just a minute, okay?'

He nodded. She bore herself well, straight-backed, head high. She opened the door and went into his reception room. Seconds later he heard the click-click of nails on the parquet. Lois came back grinning with a beautiful German Shepherd on a short leash, in magnificent condition. At the slightest of pulls on her choke-chain, the bitch sat, her glossy flank pressed companionably against Lois's leg. Stryker regarded the dog sadly.

'That is . . .?'

'Sheba,' she said. The dog responded by whisking her tail across the floor. 'You wouldn't recognize her, would you, from how I described her?'

'No. Indeed not.' He raised his eyes from the dog's muzzle to Lois's dark glasses. 'Why, Lois?'

'Oh not what you think, not at all.' She chuckled and shook her head from side to side. 'For companionship and protection. Nobody wanted her. She saved my life. I loved her on sight. She's what I've always wanted: a friend, a companion, someone to love, who loves me. I guess I understand William a whole lot better now. I guess I understand how he felt about Oliver. Anyway . . . That's it. I'd better go now. I know you're busy.' Sheba trotted beside her as she came towards him, held out her hand confidently.

'There's just one other thing, Lois. Your face . . .'

'Oh. Yes. You know I keep forgetting about that? I bet you find that hard to believe.'

She turned away, easily, looped the dog's leash over the arm of her chair. Her back turned to Stryker, she pulled off the straw brim, dropped her glasses on top of it on the chair seat. He watched her hands, competently unknotting the scarf at the nape of her neck. She shook her hair out, fluffed it with her fingers, then turned to face him.

'Oh, Lois,' he said. 'Oh, my dear . . .'

THE BIRTHDAY TREAT

Robert Rush

Her name is Lois. She is twelve years old. And she will make their lives a tortured nightmare.

They were ordinary schoolchildren living in an ordinary street. Like kids everywhere, they each had a birthday party.

Birthday parties had been fun. But then along came Lois. And what started as a party game turned into a terrifying ordeal.

And then into something much, much worse.

Futura Publications
Fiction/Horror
0 7088 2104 9